"Kathryn Springer's refreshing writing style and sense of humor make this story sing!"
—Neta Jackson, bestselling author of
The Yada Yada Prayer Group

"A tender, insightful read and a great debut—
I want more from Kathryn Springer!"
—Judy Baer, bestselling author of
The Whitney Chronicles

"A delightful package of humor and gentle truths,
Front Porch Princess is poignant and honest, a compelling, well-written story that will find the nooks and crannies of your heart and linger long after the book is done. Highly recommended!"
—Susan May Warren, bestselling author
of *In Sheep's Clothing*

D1550449

This book is dedicated to God, who patiently and gently teaches me to smile at the future. There is no other way to express it—I stand in awe.

And to Lindsey and Norah, my beautiful, adventurous daughters, who have small-town roots and big-city hearts. When the time comes, I promise I'll let go—but if you want to move next door, that's okay, too!

KATHRYN SPRINGER

TM
Steeple
Hill
Café

Published by Steeple Hill Books™

*IF
Springer*

STEEPLE HILL BOOKS

ISBN 0-373-78558-5

FRONT PORCH PRINCESS

Copyright © 2006 by Kathryn Springer

www.SteepleHill.com

Printed in U.S.A.

And she smiles at the future.
—*Proverbs* 31:25

chapter 1

After twenty years, Prichett is as familiar to me as my own reflection in the mirror. Most of the time I am indifferent to it, used to it even, but never completely comfortable with it. Prichett is the town my mother, a schoolteacher, dragged me to when I was a sophomore in high school—a small farming community with a mind-set as narrow as its main street. I hadn't wanted to move there and throughout the rest of high school, Prichett and I had been locked in silent combat—Prichett trying to hold on to me while I struggled to break free. I had the days counted until graduation. Then I planned to wave a merry goodbye, so long, see you later to Prichett and only come back during the holidays to gloat over my victory. Just visiting, you know. See you next year.

But wouldn't you know that small town and I became bound together. Forever. By a simple gold band given to me by a twenty-year-old farmer with sky-blue eyes and a crooked smile. My husband, Sam. Prichett and I were forced, like two sisters with nothing in common, to live together in tight-lipped civility because my husband's first love was one hundred acres of fertile topsoil, although I like to flatter myself that I came in at a close second.

Even though the farm is three miles outside it, there is no pretending that I'd escaped the town's grasp. The grocery store, the post office, the school and our church are all tucked like hankies inside Prichett's small-town bosom. And the beauty salon. Which happened to be the place I was heading when I noticed that the playground equipment in the park was in terrible condition. It was like suddenly noticing a mole on my face that I was sure hadn't been there before.

Now, in the world that exists beyond the city limits of Prichett, I'm absolutely sure those tall metal slides, the ones with an incline so steep they rip out your stomach on the way down, have been the cause of countless lawsuits, which have led to them being dismantled lug nut by lug nut and thrown into a scrap pile somewhere. But not in Prichett. Prichett is still searching for the elusive *thing* that will catapult it into celebrity status. Or at least will be the excuse for a really nice community barbecue in the summer. I could just imagine it—Welcome to Prichett, Home of the Nation's Most Dangerous Playground Equipment—printed on a billboard stationed proudly next to the city limits sign. A billboard which, by the way, proclaims an absolute lie. There is no denying that Prichett's population is shrinking, but still the town stubbornly refuses to change the sign that announces Prichett's population is 1,532. It's kind of like continuing to put your pre-baby weight down on your driver's license, even though you *know* you are never going to weigh that again.

I slowed down and studied the merry-go-round. My daughter, Bree, had always loved to lie on the bench, kick her shoes off and trail her toes in the sand while I pushed it in lazy circles. Any kid that tried to stretch out on the bench now would most likely end up with a stomach full of splinters. I shook my head.

As parks go, the one on Main Street sure wasn't keeping up with the twenty-first century. But that didn't surprise me. Neither was Prichett. At some point, the town had choked, sputtered and gotten stuck in some sort of Nick at Nite time warp. And I knew that my friend, Bernice, had to be partially responsible.

Bernice owns the beauty shop and she is her best, and only, employee. When she'd moved to town and opened the Cut and Curl, she'd somehow managed to find those ancient hair dryers that look like something you'd find in a mad scientist's lab. The chairs lined up against the window, in an array of ice cream pastels, are the squishy plastic kind that stick to bare skin like chewing gum on warm asphalt. There are stacks of celebrity hairstyle magazines everywhere and a pot of coffee so strong you can get a caffeine buzz that lasts all day just by smelling it. By the looks of the place, you almost expect Bernice to tease your hair into an enormous beehive and turn you out into the streets of Prichett a half hour later looking like a bewildered June Cleaver.

I get away without making an appointment because I give her free eggs and satisfy her addiction to salsa, which I can in the fall.

"I don't have time for you this morning." Bernice's voice rose above the bell that trilled whenever a customer walked in. She was coloring Mabel Marvin's hair. Mabel looked like she'd been attacked by a roll of tin foil. So far, I'd been spared the Star Wars extra look. There was not a strand of gray hair on my head, even though I could see forty on the horizon. I confess that I'm vain about my hair. Part of the reason is because that's what Sam told me he first fell in love with— my hair. He said it reminded him of corn silk. Now that may sound hokey and sentimental, but in nineteen years of marriage, I can count the times on one hand that he's gone poetic on me. The others aren't open for discussion.

I sat down and Bernice rolled her eyes at me. Mabel's fingers searched under the voluminous plastic cape for her glasses.

"Elise? Is that you?" Mabel squinted in my direction.

"Yes, it's me." I picked up a magazine and ignored Bernice's meaningful cough. She might say she didn't have time for me, but somehow she always manages to squeeze me in between a perm and a set. I know exactly how fast my hair grows and that I need to get it trimmed every six weeks, but Bernice has the you-need-an-appointment lecture down word for word and I hate to disappoint her. That's what friends are for.

"Here you go, Mabel," Bernice crooned in the elderly woman's ear. "Under the dryer for a few minutes. Do you want a cup of coffee? A magazine?"

Mabel reached up and touched her hair, smiling when the foil crinkled in her fingers. "Is it finished?"

Bernice shook her head and put her hand on Mabel's arm, as if she was afraid the woman was going to jump down and head outside, scrambling radio stations across the county. "You have to go under the dryer for a few minutes." Her voice rose slightly.

Mabel nodded agreeably. I watched as Bernice fussed over her, settling her under the dryer as lovingly as she'd tuck a newborn into a bassinet.

"My next customer will be here in ten minutes." Bernice turned from Mabel, the favored child, and glared at me, the prodigal. I grinned.

"Just this much off." I pinched my thumb and finger together. "It'll only take you ten minutes. You know you're good." Bernice didn't scare me. She has a soft spot for the very young and the very old, but everyone else is lumped into the pain-in-the-neck category. Myself included.

Not many people moved to Prichett by choice, so she'd

been the source of a lot of gossip when she'd first moved to town. There was a rumor that she was Tammy Holowitz's cousin, but as far as I knew, she and Tammy never spoke and Tammy drove half an hour to Munroe to get her hair cut at the strip mall. That kind of blew a hole in the cousin theory as far as I was concerned. The only explanation Bernice ever gave me for moving to Prichett was that she liked small towns. End of discussion. I sensed there was more, but something in Bernice's eyes had told me not to push. There was an old injury there and I try not to stare at people's scars.

We'd met for the first time when I walked into the Cut and Curl (without an appointment), took one look at the place and almost bolted right back outside. Bernice, feeling the pinch of being new in Prichett and on display like the prototype for next year's tractor, was obviously prepared for that possibility. She'd stationed herself between me and the door. With a curling iron in her hand. Plugged in. I admit, I'd come mostly out of curiosity. But now I was stuck. I should have just stared at her through the window like everyone else.

"I'm Elise Penny," I'd finally said. "Like the coin."

"I'm Bernice Strum." She'd paused. "Like the guitar."

We stared at each other, both of our faces reflecting the same did-I-really-just-say-that-and-why-am-I-such-an-idiot expression and then we burst out laughing. I didn't think we'd become friends. I call her a townie. She calls me farm girl. She lives alone above the Cut and Curl in an apartment decorated with black-and-white posters of movie stars. She says she isn't sure she can warm up to a God who makes some girls popular and some girls wallflowers. As someone who had fallen into the first category, I was of the opinion that both kinds had their problems—and I wasn't sure how much God had to do with that kind of thing to begin with.

As cynical as Bernice was about men, she loved Sam and he didn't mind when she showed up at the farm and swished back and forth for hours on our big porch swing. And even though she's lived in Prichett for ten years now, I still have the uneasy feeling that one day I'll come into town and there will be a For Sale sign in the window of the Cut and Curl and Bernice Strum will be gone.

"Get in the chair." Bernice jerked her head toward the metal perch by the mirror. "I won't have time to wash it."

"That's okay, I already did."

Under the dryer, Mabel was humming "Amazing Grace."

"Running errands today?" Bernice clipped a bright yellow plastic cape around my neck.

I closed my eyes and let myself get swept away in the music of Bernice's scissors as they snipped at my split ends. "I've got to pick up a few groceries and go to the bank. Have you noticed that the park equipment is in bad shape?"

Bernice chuckled. "Did you park way over there again?"

That's the trouble with friends. They know every chink in your armor. Prichett was tiny but I still hate to parallel park on Main Street. Put it down to a traumatic experience with the DMV the day I tried to get my first driver's license.

"You can't find a place to park," I said in my defense. "Not when every retired farmer in the county shows up for the ninety-nine-cent breakfast special on Wednesdays. They keep their own chickens, why do they need to go to the café?"

"Like I haven't heard that one before." Bernice's scissors clicked lightly. Then paused. "My, my. What have we here," she murmured.

"What? *Ouch!*" I jumped six inches off the chair.

Bernice grinned at me and dangled something in front of my eyes. A hair. A *gray* hair. It couldn't be. Maybe it was just one of the lighter blond strands. My hair always bleaches out in the summer.

"Don't look so tortured." Bernice dropped the hair on the floor and it disappeared against the ceramic tile. "It happens to the best of us, El. Time goes forward, not backward, you know."

"I'll be sure to cross-stitch that on a dish towel for you this Christmas," I said sarcastically, even though I knew I was being silly. What was one gray hair? It didn't mean I was ready to be wrapped in tin foil like a baked potato on the grill. Like Mabel.

Face it, Elise Penny. You're like that playground equipment. Showing your age. Starting to splinter. You've got a daughter leaving for college in the fall. But you're still here. Growing old right alongside Prichett.

chapter **2**

One thing I learned about small towns is that you have to give yourself an extra hour when running errands, in order to stop and chat with everyone you just know is going to want to talk to you. Because everyone knows each other. Too well. That was one of the things I hated about Prichett when Mom and I moved there. Having come from Chicago, I felt as if I was constantly under surveillance. Mom loved it. She settled into small-town life like a mama duck on a down-filled nest. And being sixteen and selfish, I didn't realize at the time that mama ducks sacrifice a lot of their own feathers to make those nests.

Main Street is the backbone of Prichett. A three-block-long, don't-blink-or-you'll-miss-it assortment of practically identical brick buildings. Somewhere in Prichett's history there is a smooth-talking brick seller who no doubt retired to an estate on his own private island.

I try to do my errands as quickly as possible without looking as though I'm practicing for a marathon. I do this for two reasons. The first one is that in the past few years, half the businesses have gone under, leaving hollow-eyed windows staring forlornly at me. The second is because the rest of the businesses are gasping for breath and looking for oxygen. Translation: they need customers with cash in their pockets. The owners of these businesses occasionally hang out in the doorway, looking for victims.

I skirted past Sally's Café, the hardware store and Ed's Garage and Salvage and, with a sigh of relief, sought refuge in the bank. No problem, I'd be home by noon.

"Hi, Elise."

The bank. And friendly townsperson number one— Josephine Cleary, the teller. I'm not sure why I was so cranky. Maybe it was the playground equipment. Or the gray hair.

"Hi, Jo."

"Elise, I'm sure you've already met Annie Carpenter, haven't you?"

Carpenter. Our new youth pastor at Faith Community Church was named Carpenter. I'd heard they were coming but with spring planting and Bree's graduation, I had lost track of exactly when they were arriving.

I glanced to my right and saw a girl. I smiled and looked past her. Then to my left. There was no one else there. Okay…this had to be her! Even though she didn't look much older than Bree.

"We haven't officially met yet," I said and looked at Annie Carpenter. "I'm Elise Penny."

."It's nice to meet you, Mrs. Penny."

Suddenly I felt sixty years old. I half expected to see that Sam's mom had materialized beside me. I smiled. "Welcome to Prichett." *I hope you aren't too disappointed, you poor thing. Maybe another job will come along.*

"I love it here already," Annie Carpenter said, smiling widely. She was cute in a fresh-faced tomboy way. Tall and slim, with no hips and a nonexistent bustline that no doubt had had her crying into her pillow when she was thirteen. Her hair was the only thing that kept her from looking like someone's younger brother. It was long and heavy, in that mix of auburn and gold that can't be copied from a bottle. I'd have to tell Bernice. She was forever searching for new victims at the Cut and Curl. She attended style shows twice a year and couldn't convince anyone to be her guinea pig. Not even me.

"Elise and Sam have a farm just outside of town. It keeps them pretty busy in the summer," Jo sang out helpfully. Then she smiled at the person who had come into the bank and sneaked around Annie and me. I edged closer to the counter, just in case someone else tried to cut in.

"A farm." Annie repeated the word and if possible, her eyes got a little wider. "That must be a lot of work." She glanced down at my feet and I wondered if she was looking for cow manure on my shoes.

"It is." I turned my body slightly toward Jo, hoping Annie would get the hint.

She did. "Well…I hope we see you Sunday." Her smile had faded ever so slightly and I felt immediately like I'd kicked a puppy.

"It was nice to meet you, Annie." I still had to get to the grocery store. "Um, stop out at the farm sometime."

"I'd love to." Annie nodded enthusiastically.

Jo shot me a skeptical look. Which I ignored.

On to the next errand. I was just crossing the street when I saw Bree talking to someone on the corner by the drugstore. A boy someone. I slowed down and tried to place him. Tall and lanky, he had dark hair and…oh, no. It couldn't be. He looked just like a Cabott. There weren't any Cabotts that were Bree's age that I knew of, but there were a few who hovered around the age of twenty. Jill Cabott was one of those women who'd turned out children in batches like sugar cookies when she was young.

"Bree!"

Her body jolted as if my voice had touched her with an electrical current. "Mom."

We stared at each other.

"I would have given you a ride into town if I'd known you were coming in."

"Dad sent me to the feed store," she said quickly. She glanced at the boy, who was studying me. Most teenage boys twist into an uncomfortable, crunched-up pose when faced with a parent, but this one looked me straight in the eye. He had Dan Cabott's nose and his mother's dark, baby-fine hair. And it was so long it touched his collar. I moved closer to Bree. That mother-duck thing reared its head.

"Mom, this is Riley Cabott."

Riley. Who names their son Riley? Probably someone addicted to soap operas. Oops, daytime dramas. "Hello."

"Mrs. Penny."

If anyone else called me Mrs. Penny I was going to scream. Honestly. People have called me that before, but never on the same day that God blessed me with my first gray hair.

"What are you doing in town?" Bree's face was pink. She had my fair skin and therefore was unable to hide her emotions, although I'd gotten pretty good at it over the years. She took a casual step away from Riley Cabott. That step was *so* casual that the "mother alarm," which is standard issue at conception, suddenly began to shriek and my internal hard drive instantly downloaded everything I knew about the Cabotts.

They'd lived in the county all their lives and their offspring never venture any farther from Prichett than you can throw a rock. They raise quarter horses and one of the boys was a state champion in team penning who had been mentioned in the newspaper several times. If I had to guess, it was probably this one. There is nothing that Bree loves more than horses. I'm sure if there was a way, she'd be taking her horse, Buckshot, to college in the fall.

"I have a few errands," I told her. "Want to tag along?"

Bree shot a quick glance at Riley, who was looking at her with an expression on his face that suddenly had my heart in a clamp. I'd seen that look before. On another young man's face when he wanted a girl to melt like a puddle at his feet. Sam Penny. My husband. On the day he'd shown up at my door with a handful of wild daisies and asked me out.

chapter 3

"I don't think you've mentioned Riley Cabott before," I said casually as Bree fell into step with me.

"He's just a friend, Mom."

Then why do you sound so defensive? "Nice-looking boy."

I'd discovered while navigating the river of teenage angst with Bree over the past four years that I got a lot farther if I remained cheerful and upbeat. Any hint of nagging, judgment or displeasure immediately took me into a swirling vortex of whitewater rapids that ended when I found myself all alone, having been pushed overboard.

She shrugged.

Oh, this wasn't good. Whenever Bree had been interested in a boy, her eyes would light up when she'd talk about him and she'd get that lovesick look on her face. Now her eyes were guarded. This was serious. She was keeping something from me.

I had the overwhelming urge to take her to an abandoned warehouse, tie her to a chair and shine a bright light in her face until she spilled everything. When had she met Riley Cabott? Was she involved with him? *How* involved with him was she?

"Mom, I know what you're thinking."

I certainly hoped that wasn't true.

"We're just friends. Really."

I remembered the look on his face. Be positive. Be upbeat. "I believe you."

Bree smiled and I saw Sam in her smile. Bree was a patchwork of both our features that had matured into a beautiful work of art. She had my platinum-blond hair and high cheekbones, partnered with Sam's deep-set blue eyes and appealing smile. She had inherited his height and my curves. "Let's get some M&M's at the store, Mom."

M&M's. Bree's weakness. That one I could live with. A handsome young man with serious eyes I wasn't so sure about.

The thing about being a farmer's wife is that you have to be willing to kiss your husband goodbye before the sun rises and not see him again until it sets. At least during three out of the four seasons. Most people complained about Wisconsin winters. Not me. I had quickly learned to love winter because it generously gave me back my husband.

Sam would stop in at the house occasionally during the day, but the lines of division had been clearly drawn after we got married. I may have become a farmer's wife but I *wasn't* a farmer's daughter. I took care of the house and vegetable garden and Sam farmed. As a newlywed, I had sat on the tractor with him, snuggled against his chest, but I didn't drive it and I certainly didn't know how to fix it if it was broken.

Concerned about Bree, I didn't want to wait until he slipped in at eight or nine o'clock. Experience had taught me that by late afternoon, some piece of equipment had broken down or was being temperamental. I checked the machine shed first and found him bent over an engine.

"Hi, honey."

Sam glanced up from the engine he was tinkering with. He was stripped to the waist and his hands were covered with black grease. Sweat beaded his forehead. "Hi, El."

"I brought you a glass of lemonade."

He grinned and used his wrist to push back a swatch of brown hair that was stuck to his forehead. "Thanks. I think it's over eighty degrees today."

We were talking about the weather. I felt a surge of frustration.

"I went into town earlier and saw Bree. She was talking to that Cabott boy."

"Riley Cabott?"

"You know him?" I blinked in surprise.

"Not really."

He was keeping something from me, too. I could see it in his eyes.

"Is there something going on between them?"

Sam shrugged. "Nothing that I know of. He came over last week and asked Bree about Buckshot. He's thinking about buying a horse from the same breeder. He hung around for a few hours and watched her practice barrels."

"I never saw him."

"He seemed level-headed enough."

Level-headed went a long way with Sam. In fact, I think that was his highest compliment. It wrapped up common sense and good manners into one tidy package.

"Are you coming in for supper soon?"

Sam shook his head. "Not unless God shows up with a wrench. Just keep it warm for me tonight. I've got to get this fixed before dark."

I wasn't sure why I'd asked, having already known the answer.

"You can keep me company for awhile," Sam said.

"I've got things to do inside."

Sam leaned toward me and brushed a kiss against the side of my mouth. His lips were cold from the lemonade.

"See you later."

I heard the phone ringing when my foot touched the top step of the porch. I hurried inside, pulling a muscle in my ankle that I didn't even know was there. Gasping, I grabbed the phone and collapsed onto one of the kitchen chairs at the same time.

"Hhh…hello."

"Hi, Mrs. Penny. This is Annie Carpenter."

I winced. Pain ricocheted around my foot and channeled into all five toes. "Oh, hello."

"I hope I didn't catch you at a bad time," Annie said. "When I got back to the church this morning, I ran into some of the ladies from the hospitality committee."

And even through the fog of pain, I knew what was coming. Those women had alternately tried to cajole or guilt me into serving on their committee before the rice had hit the sidewalk on my wedding day. And now they'd found a new avenue—the perky youth pastor's wife.

"They mentioned the church rummage sale coming up next month and suggested I call you."

I'll bet they did. "I'd be happy to donate a few things." The pain had subsided to a manageable ache now and I could think a little more clearly. "Um, I'll drop a box by the church before Sunday."

Silence.

"How does that sound?" I dropped the question into the silence and heard an echo. The echo of my doom.

"They said that since the rummage sale benefits the youth mission trip next summer, I should be in charge of it," Annie finally said. "I don't know many people in the congregation yet and I was hoping you could help me."

A dozen excuses poured into my brain and I couldn't grab hold of a single one. "I'm sure they don't expect you to be in charge of the rummage sale." I took a quick detour while trying to find the excuse that was most believable. The one guaranteed to free me from committees for the rest of my life. "The hospitality committee has been organizing that since the Civil War." Okay, a *slight* exaggeration.

"I think that's why they wanted me to take over," Annie said seriously. "But if you don't have time, I understand. I was just hoping…"

"Hoping what?"

"That we could get to know each other better."

Why? That was the first question that popped into my head. I was distracted when Bree walked into the kitchen. She was dressed to go riding. Black tank top, patched blue jeans and scuffed cowboy boots. Hair in a long braid down her back. She paused to grab a muffin off a plate on the table.

"Just a sec, Annie." I covered the mouthpiece of the phone. "How long are you going to be gone?"

"A couple of hours."

"Going alone?" Normally, I would have taken that for granted, but the memory of seeing her with Riley Cabott was too fresh in my mind.

"Yup." The screen door snapped behind her.

"Annie? I'm sorry about that. I had to talk to my daughter. I'll be sure to get a box ready for the rummage sale tonight."

"I appreciate that, Mrs. Penny."

"Please." I shuddered. "Call me Elise, all right?"

I told myself that I'd imagined the disappointment I'd heard in her voice when I'd turned her down. The women on the hospitality committee had been bluffing. They wouldn't put a raw recruit like Annie Carpenter at the head of Operation Church Rummage Sale.

But my guilty conscience prodded me to limp up to the attic after I'd hung up the phone.

The house we lived in had been in Sam's family since forever. It is a typical farmhouse. Two-story, in the shape of a wedding cake, white with green shutters on the windows. A covered porch that wraps around the front. On the outside, it could have been on a postcard. Inside, it's a maze of small rooms connected by narrow doorways with zero closet space. I'd insisted on a dishwasher when Sam and I moved in, but that, along with some updated electrical and plumbing, are the only major changes the house has seen in fifty years.

The attic is exactly like the kind you'd see in a scary movie. Dusty gray globs of cobwebs strung together, connecting old furniture to towers of cardboard boxes. Most of the boxes were filled with Sam's parents' possessions. Two years after Sam and I were married they'd sold the farm to us and moved to Arizona. Mary had promised me that she'd "get the rest of their things later" but so far, *later* hadn't come and I doubted she even remembered what they'd left behind in the attic. I was beginning to think that maybe if a person couldn't remember what was in their attic boxes, they shouldn't even look. Just tape them shut and put them on the curb.

Some of the stuff was ours—Bree's old toys that I couldn't part with yet—and broken things that Sam had promised me he'd fix but had never got around to.

I sneezed. Three or four things that I'd *rather* be doing started to clamor for my attention. I glanced around and grabbed a box close to the door, giving it a few good shakes to loosen any spiders that may have been waiting for an opportunity to get out of Dodge.

I carried the box down to the sewing room and put it on the floor. Let me just make one thing clear—I don't sew. The only reason that it's called the sewing room is because someone in Sam's family tree *did* sew, and I'm sure there's a box of calico aprons somewhere in the attic to prove it.

I blew a layer of dust off the top of the box and saw some words written in permanent marker. *Elise Collins.* My maiden name. There were girlish scribblings around my name. Some hearts. Curlicues. For the life of me, I couldn't remember what I'd put in this particular box.

If you don't remember, how important is it? Just seal it up with some tape and get rid of it!

I chased the mocking voice in my head away with logic. Maybe my teenage diary was inside. I didn't want that to end up in the hands of the hospitality committee, now did I? With that ammunition, they'd have me single-handedly coordinating every rummage sale, children's Christmas program and pancake supper until the trumpet blew.

Peeling back the top of the box, I saw a cloud of cotton balls. Obviously, whatever was inside was fragile. Oh, oh. I remembered the hard shake I'd given it and frantically started digging. My fingers snagged against metal and I drew it out of the box. Cotton balls clung stubbornly to it and I shook them off, but more gently this time.

My tiara. I'd actually kept it.

chapter 4

The "diamonds" still held their cheerfully brazen shine, even after being crammed into a box for almost twenty years. When I was eighteen, they'd looked real. Now, glancing at the hedge of tiny diamonds on my wedding band, I knew the difference. The tiara practically shouted for attention. Whoever had picked it out had either had a motto—more is better—or a hidden agenda—let's make this thing as cheesy as possible.

I ran my thumb across the "diamonds" and felt one wobble in its setting like a loose front tooth. Shaped like an antique iron headboard, it was at least six inches high and probably had the capability to blind someone under strong lighting. There was a bobby pin still dangling from the wire and I plucked it off.

The tiara was from the county fair's Miss Sweetheart contest. I'd won the title. And met Sam.

I confess that the only reason I'd entered the contest in the first place was because Susan Richman had entered. Susan and I had been rivals since I'd moved to Prichett. We were the perfect foils for one another—our English teacher had even humorously dubbed us Snow White and Rose Red.

I was the tall Nordic blonde, Susan was a petite brunette. Before I'd moved to Prichett, Susan's popularity had rested on two things—she was the prettiest girl in the school and she was the head cheerleader for the Prichett Falcons, probably because she was small enough to do all the stunts that involved being lifted, launched and twirled.

A year after I'd moved to Prichett, I was picked to be the fall festival queen. The day after the vote, I could see the light of battle in Susan's eyes and I rose to the challenge. We made an unspoken pact to use each other—and each other's failures—to rappel our way to the top of the Prichett High School hierarchy. Not that I really cared, but it gave me something to do.

The county fair's Miss Sweetheart contest was to be my final coup. Susan tried to keep the fact that she was entering a secret, but I heard about it. And immediately began to plot my strategy. What did one have to do to be the county's sweetheart?

One had to write an essay about the future of agriculture, that's what one had to do. The fair board was practically asking for a thesis. I knew that Prichett was surrounded by a patchwork of farms, all attempting to walk the tightrope of changing milk and produce prices. I knew that our high school even had a drive-your-tractor-to-school day in the spring and that half the boys wore stained baseball caps that advertised pesticides or a favorite brand of machinery.

Future in agriculture? There probably wasn't one, but I had to bluff. Someone suggested I talk to the Penny family. They'd been farming in the Prichett area since the turn of the century and were mildly successful.

I drove out to the Penny farm, armed with a yellow legal pad tucked under my arm and an attitude of condescension. I hadn't thought to call first, but Mrs. Penny was home and she listened to my well-rehearsed opening speech and then pointed to a dilapidated building near the barn.

"Will is out in the field today, but I think my son is working in the shop. You can go talk to him."

"Oh, but I…"

She nudged me down the front steps with a gentle hand on my back and a smile. "Go ahead. Sam doesn't bite."

I reluctantly followed a horrible grating noise to the building she'd pointed to. My steps slowed when I got closer to the door and I decided to go with plan B—hang out at the feed store and take a general survey of the future of agriculture from the men who stood around the sludgy coffeepot at the counter. I pivoted slightly and saw Mrs. Penny on the porch, watching me with a big smile on her face. Scrap plan B. Escape was not an option. Back to plan A.

I took a tentative step inside just as the noise stopped. I hadn't had time to form any expectations of Sam Penny. It was probably a good thing, because even in my wildest imagination, I wouldn't have gotten them right.

He was standing in a beam of dusty sunlight staring at the floor, his hands planted on lean, quarterback hips. A dab of a kitten was perched on his shoulder. Even from the distance separating us, I could hear it purring.

"Ah, hello."

His head lifted and his gaze swung toward the door. He grinned. "It's you."

It's you. What did that mean? I didn't recognize him. He didn't look that much older than me, but we definitely hadn't gone to school together. I would have remembered. Sam Penny had a face that a girl wouldn't forget. I pulled my unruly thoughts in line. *You will forget his face, Elise, because Sam is probably president of Future Farmers of America. And farms aren't in your future!*

The only reason I needed to know anything about farming was to beat Susan Richman for the title of the county's Miss Sweetheart.

Holding the legal pad in front of me like a shield, I told him why I was there. With a casual motion, he snagged the kitten off his shoulder and deposited her on a tool bench.

She squawked faintly in protest, looked at me accusingly and then sneezed.

"Come on." He sauntered outside into the sunlight and I followed him. "How much time do you have?"

"An hour." There was no way I was going to spend more than that in Sam Penny's company. His eyes were the blue stones that hypnotists used to wipe out a person's past and future.

I stayed two hours and by the time Sam walked me to the car, my thoughts were muddled. Somehow, he'd made farming sound like the most exciting ride at Disney World. A ride filled with unexpected twists and turns that built character, deepened a person's faith and probably helped prevent tooth decay.

On the ride back home, though, my thoughts gradually cleared again. I had one single purpose in mind before leaving for Chicago in August: to be the new Miss Sweetheart.

And I was. In addition to the essay, I'd had to answer a few questions for a panel of fair board members and it was obvious they were impressed with my insight. After my interview, I'd silently thanked Sam. It had been his words I repeated, his enthusiasm I reflected. But it worked. My mother and I shopped for a new dress and my victory was made complete on a Friday night on a rickety stage by the cow barn, where the previous Miss Sweetheart carefully pushed the tiara into my updo.

I'd looked at the cluster of people gathered around, hoping to catch a glimpse of Susan. Instead, I saw Sam. At the farm that day, he'd been wearing patched blue jeans and a filthy white T-shirt with the sleeves hacked off. For the fair, he'd upgraded to a denim jacket over what looked to be a clean T-shirt and the same pair of blue jeans only minus the grease stains.

I made a speech I can no longer remember and hugged the bouquet of drooping red roses against my new dress. When I stepped down from the stage, Sam was waiting for me.

"Congratulations."

"Thank you."

Sam slipped his denim jacket off and put it across my shoulders. The warmth that lingered from his body seeped into every exposed pore. He stepped back and studied me.

"You are so pretty."

I'd heard it before (had even said it to myself on occasion) but the way Sam said it was different. I made the mistake of looking into his eyes, to see what was there. And I forgot everything else.

"Ellie?"

The scrape of the screen door yanked me out of the time warp I'd fallen into. Quickly, I pushed the tiara back into the box and raked cotton balls over the top of it.

"In the sewing room." I stood up and brushed at a cobweb that had glued itself to my pants.

Sam tiptoed in, as if walking slowly and carefully would prevent the gunk stuck to the bottom of his boots from falling out onto the carpet. "I…" His gaze was drawn to the box at my feet. "What's that?"

"Nothing much. I told Annie Carpenter that I'd donate a few things to the church rummage sale."

"Nice young couple," Sam commented, again making me feel like Grandma Moses. When was this general feeling of crankiness going to go away?

"I met her today. She isn't much older than Bree."

"I think she's twenty-five."

Leave it to Sam to know how old she was. I had totally forgotten the Carpenters were even moving to town but Sam's ear had always been pressed against the heartbeat of Faith Community Church.

"She looks younger than that."

"She's going to be like you," Sam said. "You still look exactly like you did on our wedding day."

I forced a smile because I knew he expected it. Maybe I should tell him that Bernice had found a gray hair. And pretty soon he'd have to take out a second mortgage on the house so Bernice could keep up with changing those strands back to the color that he had fallen in love with.

"I just came in to tell you that Gordon stopped by and asked me to help him move some hay into the barn this evening," Sam said.

I tried to squelch the flash of irritation I felt at hearing Gordon's name. Maybe I'm perimenopausal but instead of hot flashes, I am getting *cranky* flashes. That would certainly explain the way I'd been feeling all day.

Gordon relied on Sam for just about everything. It wasn't enough that Sam put in his own twelve-, sometimes fourteen-hour days, but Gordon made sure that Sam put in one or two extra for him. Gordon was a fellow farmer, though, so Sam's loyalty ran as deep as our well.

"Let me make a sandwich for you." I headed toward the kitchen, read Sam's mind and executed a neat little dodge before he could pull me into his arms.

"Are you all right? You aren't still worried about Bree, are you?" Sam caught me by the kitchen sink and pinned me there.

"A little." I couldn't lie, so I told him a half-truth. *Now tell me,* I begged silently. *Do I have anything to worry about?*

"Elise, she's eighteen years old."

Not what I wanted to hear. "And she's leaving for college in the fall. The last thing she needs is to get involved with some local boy…" I realized what I was saying and swallowed the rest of the sentence.

A shadow passed through Sam's eyes. "Just skip the sandwich. I'll eat later."

He walked out. I closed my eyes, angry with myself for my careless words but frustrated with Sam that he'd so easily misinterpreted them. There was no way he could compare the two situations. Sam had been the beginning of my future. But Riley Cabott? I was worried that all he could be was an obstacle in Bree's path.

chapter **5**

It was nine o'clock the next morning when I heard a car door slam. I pushed aside the kitchen curtains and saw an unfamiliar vehicle parked in the driveway. And then saw a familiar figure get out.

Annie Carpenter. Had I missed something? Had she mentioned she'd be coming over to pick up the items for the rummage sale? Hadn't I said I'd bring them to church by Sunday? I didn't trust my memory anymore. It was starting to fail me on a regular basis. Memory was probably linked to the same circuit board as rogue gray hairs and cranky flashes.

Clancy, my golden retriever, ambled up to her, bowing and scraping and quivering with excitement at the sight of unexpected company. Sam refers to him as a porch decoration and since he doesn't use him to hunt, the only purpose

Clancy serves is to keep me company throughout the day. He takes his job very seriously.

Sam and I have his-and-her dogs. He bought Clancy for me after Shadow, my black Lab, died a few years ago. Lady is Sam's dog, an Australian blue heeler built like a military vehicle, solid and low to the ground. Her mottled coloring blends like camouflage into her surroundings. Unlike Clancy, she isn't the kind of dog whose soft fur invites cuddling. Strictly functional, that's Lady. She loves Sam but won't acknowledge that I exist. Bree is a cat person. She has a mammoth tomcat named Diesel who keeps a summer home in the hayloft but winters in the wingback chair in the living room.

Sighing, I wiped my wet hands on a towel and headed toward the door. Clancy could be a bit overwhelming in his unending quest for affection. I decided I'd better rescue Annie.

"Good morning."

Annie looked over at me and gave a little wave. Clancy followed her to the porch, brushing against her legs in a not-so-subtle attempt to get another scratch behind his ears.

"Hi, Elise. I hope you don't mind that I'm here. I was just down the road and thought I'd take you up on your offer to stop by some time."

Had I really offered that? Yes, I had. At the bank when we'd met. Yesterday. And I remembered why I had offered, too. Pure, undiluted guilt.

"I don't mind. Come in." I felt the starch in my smile. I

had planned to spend the morning mentally untangling the knots that had formed in my life the evening before. Bree had retreated to her bedroom right after she'd come back from riding. Her closed door demanded privacy with the invisible No Questions Allowed sign firmly in place. Sam had snuck into the house after I was in bed and I wondered if I should apologize out loud or just curl around him and kiss his shoulder instead, the silent apology. He hadn't given me the chance to do either. After brushing his teeth, he had gone back downstairs to watch the news. I fell into a restless sleep long before he came back upstairs.

Now it looked like I was going to have to untangle those knots later. I had a suspicion that Annie would be here for awhile.

"I love dogs," Annie said, finding the button behind Clancy's ear that controlled groveling and blissful eye-closing. "We can't have any pets in the duplex, so I'll have to get my animal fix at other people's houses."

I nodded in understanding. The duplex was close to the church and was owned by Fred Thomas, one of the deacons.

"Would you like something to drink? Tea or coffee?" On the way to the kitchen, I grabbed the damp bath towel Bree had slung over the banister. She spent her summers working for the local large animal vet and they'd gone on an early call. She'd left at five while Sam was still in the shower.

"What are you having?"

"Coffee."

"That sounds great!"

I was beginning to figure out that Annie talked in exclamation points. I poured her a cup of coffee and topped mine up, wondering what was going to happen next. I put the cups down but Annie didn't join me at the table. She was prowling around the kitchen and dining area, eyes wide.

"I love country decor," she said.

Country decor. I looked around and saw Sam's Great Aunt Ina's china cabinet filled with the teacups and saucers she'd collected over the years and then left to Mary when she died. Mary had decided china wouldn't travel well to Arizona so they became mine. I think she simply got tired of dusting it all. Sam had rescued the pie safe from the old chicken-coop-turned-potting-shed. The valances on the windows had been sewn from vintage tablecloths by some unknown Penny relative. Everything I could see was over fifty years old but if old stuff had suddenly become "country decor," that was fine with me.

"Most of the things here are pretty old," I told her. "They were passed down from Sam's grandparents and aunts and uncles. Do you want cream or sugar in your coffee?"

Annie wasn't done yet. She touched the armless rocking chair in the corner and set it in motion, smiling at the flannel teddy bear who sat on it. The fireplace in the dining room drew her attention and I fought against the rush of stress that I felt, similar to the feeling I'd had when airline security had gone through my underwear on our trip to Arizona the year before.

She looked at the framed pictures on the mantel. "Is this your daughter?"

I gave up on the coffee. "Breanna, only we call her Bree."

"I saw her yesterday in town. She looks a lot like you." Annie studied the picture as though she was memorizing it.

"She just graduated in May."

"I'm sorry that Stephen won't have her in his youth group," Annie said. "What are her plans?"

"She's going to UW-Madison for pre-vet," I said casually. I'd learned to brush a thin veneer of casualness over that answer, to cover my pride.

Annie moved on to the next picture. "Your mom?"

How had she known that? My mother and I looked nothing alike and she was alone in the picture. Cat eyeglasses, Hollywood starlet waves created from rollers resembling prickly metal pot scrubbers. I remembered those rollers. They hid in the drawer in her bathroom and bit little fingers searching for lipstick to play with.

"Mmmhhh."

"I'm sorry." Annie took my arm, reeling me into an unexpected hug. "You were close."

I wiggled away. What had she seen in my expression? It was an unsettling thought. The bright, inquisitive light in Annie's eyes had softened to a warm glow. She reached out to touch my hand and I had to make a conscious effort not to yank it away.

"Breast cancer," I heard myself say. "Right after Sam and I were engaged."

Annie nodded. And moved to the next picture. By the time we reached the last one, she knew what my wedding dress looked like, that Bree had been bald until she was three and the first and last names of half the Penny clan, now deceased. She knew that Bree's horse had won best of show three years in a row and that she'd gone to the prom with Dave Morgan, the Falcon's star quarterback. *Future dentist. Nice haircut.* I put him next to Riley Cabott in my mind and you-know-who definitely came up lacking.

By the time Annie wandered back to the kitchen table and sat down, I felt exposed—as though I'd walked down Main Street in the nightgown Sam had bought me for Valentine's Day.

"I was wondering if you'd thought any more about helping me coordinate the rummage sale," Annie said.

I thought that I'd already thought about it. And said no. "I don't think so, but I've got a box put together that you can take with you." *When you leave.*

"I appreciate it." Annie's smile didn't fade. "We'll take anything your husband would be willing to donate, too. It's a plus if there are some things guys can pick through."

"I'm sure there are a few old tractors he could push to church."

I was only half joking. Sam is careful not to let our yard become a graveyard for rusty farm equipment, but there *was* that old tractor someone had asked Sam to take a look at. Sam had pronounced it dead but the man hadn't returned yet to give it a decent burial. Now it was hiding behind the machine shed, housing a nest of sparrows for the summer. When they moved on, Sam promised me the tractor would, too.

"I always thought that farming would be a lot like missionary work," Annie mused. "You really have to rely on God every day for a lot of things other people take for granted. And trust that He's going to take care of you."

I didn't know what to say. I wanted to open my mouth and have something wise and wonderful come out. I knew that Sam would have. When we'd started dating, I had been both drawn to and intimidated by his unquestioning faith.

I see God's reflection every morning when I go outside, he'd told me simply one summer evening when we'd taken a walk together. *It would be kind of stupid not to believe, wouldn't it?*

Pastor Charles talked a lot about God being our Heavenly Father, and I'd grown up without one, so it was harder for me to imagine that He'd notice Elise Penny, a farmer's wife in a town so small you'd miss it if you blinked. Watching the way Sam was with Bree helped me understand a little more, but even though I talked to God, I tried not to draw too much attention to myself. If He paid too close attention to me, I was half afraid of what He'd see—like I was under a spiritual magnifying glass and He'd be able to read the things that were in my heart.

Annie got up and retrieved the coffeepot, refilling mine

first. "Stephen's mother was a teacher at a mission school in Brazil. She broke pencils in half so everyone could have one and then they'd fight over who got the end with the eraser. He told me a story about a time when they were almost out of paper and she had them pray every day for two weeks. One day a truck went through the village and a box fell out and broke open. Paper. It blew everywhere. His mom sent everyone outside to chase it down. The driver told them he didn't have time to wait, so they could keep it."

It was a nice story but I couldn't help but wonder why God hadn't made it a little easier for those children. A nice airmail delivery from a church in the States maybe?

"I'll bet things like that happen all the time on a farm, don't they, Elise?"

I don't know, I was tempted to say. What I said was, "Yes, they do." After all, Sam always gave God the credit for every plant that sprouted out of Penny soil.

From the smile on Annie's face, I felt as if I'd just passed a pop quiz.

"I'll get that box for the rummage sale." I jumped up and made a dash for the sewing room but discovered Annie at my heels, as close as Clancy would have been if I hadn't banished him to the porch.

I'd thrown a few vases, some old hardcover books and two sweaters Bree didn't like into the box but suddenly the contents looked pathetically meager. "I didn't have a lot of time after you called yesterday, but I'm sure I'll come up with some more by Sunday," I assured both Annie and my guilty conscience.

"There haven't been a lot of donations yet."

I could see it in her eyes as clearly as if someone had pulled back a curtain and exposed her thoughts. She was nervous. And I knew why. This was a test. And as brave and upbeat as Annie was trying to be, she *knew* this was a test. I remembered hearing some grumbling from people in the congregation that the Carpenters were young and hardly "green broke."

"If you have an hour or so, we could go up in the attic and find some more things." Did I really say that out loud? Judging by the expression on Annie's face, I guess I had.

By the time Annie was ready to leave it was almost noon. The back seat of her car was filled with boxes. The Penny attic had yielded enough bounty to carry the entire rummage sale on its own. If no one else donated a thing, the junk we'd unearthed would fill the fellowship hall and two Sunday-school rooms.

"Don't forget the box that started this whole thing," I called as Annie sprinted up the front steps for the last load. "It's in the sewing room."

"Okay." Annie disappeared inside, with Clancy permanently attached to her shadow.

Across the field, I could see the tractor moving with slow precision and the tiny figure of Sam at the wheel. I felt a stab of regret at my careless words the night before. I just wanted *more* for Bree. Was that such a bad thing? I wanted her to experience college. To meet people who weren't constantly complaining about the weather and how it was going to affect this year's crops. To realize that there were a lot of beautiful places in the world beyond Prichett and to be able to see them through her own eyes, not through someone else's.

She was so close to stepping out into the future and discovering life beyond Prichett...

"Was this box supposed to go, too?" Annie was at my side, with the box marked Elise Collins balanced on top of the other one.

"No!" I snatched it out of her arms.

"It was sitting right next to the other one, so I thought maybe..." Annie's voice trailed off. "Is that your tiara? Or Bree's?"

She'd looked in the box.

"Mine."

The word came out of a cranky two-year-old. Me. I repeated it in my thirty-seven-year-old voice. "It's mine." Better. Calmer. Not so protective.

In the few hours we'd spent sifting through dusty old boxes, I'd learned that Annie was the kind of person who said out loud what she was thinking inside. Those kinds of people terrify me. They don't play emotional hide-and-seek. Because they let you see the buttons and switches in their hearts they expect that you'll let them see *yours*. That was the scary part.

"Did you win some kind of pageant?" Annie asked.

"Just the county fair's Miss Sweetheart contest when I was eighteen," I said. "Nothing that got me more than my picture in the paper with the Olsens' prize-winning heifer."

And a dozen wilted roses.

And a warm denim jacket on a cool August night.

And my first kiss.

And Sam.

I stepped away from the car and closed the door with my hip. "Well, I still have some errands to run today."

Annie suddenly reached over and hugged both me and the cardboard box. "Bye, Elise, and thank you again."

She slid into the driver's seat and rolled down the window. "Let me know when you have some free time, all right? I'd love to get together again for coffee."

My life was full. Sam. Bree. The house. My flower gardens. A standing lunch date with Bernice once a week. There were a lot of women who would reach out to Annie. She was so friendly, I could see a line forming to get to know her better.

She didn't need me.

chapter **6**

Clancy followed Annie's car halfway down the driveway. When he finally turned and ran back to me, there was a dejected look in his eyes.

"I'll bet you liked her," I murmured. "Someone your age to play with." I glanced at my watch and sighed. My morning was gone but at least the attic boxes were lighter. I made a quick tuna sandwich for myself and an extra for Sam in case he came in to grab a bite to eat while I was gone. I eased past Clancy, who was taking his early-afternoon nap in the sun, and drove into town.

Even I had to admit that Prichett was pretty in the summer. From a distance, it rested snugly in the center of lush green farmland like a pearl on emerald velvet. It was only upon close inspection that you could see the flaws. The tiny cracks and spots rubbed thin from the rough years, when many of the farms in the area went under.

I stopped in to see Bernice. She had one customer but all I could see was a headless torso leaning back in the shampoo chair while Bernice worked her magic.

"Don't tell me you found another one?" Bernice asked, laughter in her eyes.

I'm not sure why Bernice was still single, but maybe it was because none of the bachelors in Prichett could get past her ever-changing hair color (this month it was a brassy magenta), her unusual clothing (today it was turquoise cowboy boots, a yellow broomstick skirt and rhinestone-studded tank top) or her rather formidable personality. She just looks like the type of person who won't take garbage from anyone. Taking all that into consideration, it meant that the men in Prichett were either shallow or wimpy. In which case she was better off alone anyway. When she'd first come to town, one of the farmers did take an interest in her. She never did tell me the whole story, but when I caught a glimpse of green hair peeking out from under his John Deere cap, I figured somehow he must have offended her. It certainly made the rest of the bachelor population think twice about asking Bernice Strum out. Or at least going to her for a haircut.

"I'm not here for a refund," I told her. "Just for a whiff of coffee."

The headless torso sat upright and I saw Jill Cabott.

"Elise!"

She greeted me so enthusiastically that warning bells began to go off in my head. Jill and I were wave-across-the-street acquaintances at best.

"I can come by later," I said, looking at Bernice. "It's nothing important." I started to inch my way to the door. The last person I wanted to make small talk with was Jill Cabott.

"Your daughter is the sweetest girl I've ever met," Jill gushed. "And pretty, too. But look at her mama. No surprise there! Riley can't stop talking about her. Honestly, that boy is completely twitter-pated."

My feet were stuck to the floor now. Jill was talking about Bree like she *knew* her.

"When she was over the other night, she was playing cribbage with Old Dan and Riley couldn't take his eyes off her." She gave a dramatic sigh. "Young love."

Young love.

Nooo! a voice in my head screamed. *There is no young love here. It can't happen that fast!* My brain began to sort through her words. *Over the other night. Cribbage. Couldn't take his eyes off her.*

"When was this?" I asked, surprised that my voice sounded normal.

Bernice knew better. She walked Jill to the chair and her gaze slid cautiously to her scissors drawer. Discreetly, she closed it. I was tempted to stick my tongue out at her.

"A night or two ago, I think," Jill said. "She rode over on Buckshot. They have so much in common."

"Bree and Buckshot?"

Jill laughed. "You're so funny, Elise. I meant Bree and Riley."

Bree must have gone to their house the same day I'd spotted them together. The same day Bree had told me she was going riding. Alone.

"Is, ah, Riley home from college for the summer?" Somehow I knew he wasn't, was only desperately fishing for information to put my mind at ease.

"Riley and school never got along very well." Jill chuckled. "He's working for the Sawyers right now."

The Sawyers. That meant he was milking cows. Low pay. Long hours. No insurance.

Bernice cleared her throat. "Ah, Jill, did you want me to do anything special this time or just trim it like always?"

"Same as always," Jill chirped. "I'm not much for change. Thirty years. Same haircut. Same husband." She laughed at her joke as though she was working an audience at the Blue Light Lounge, which held amateur stand-up comedy twice a month.

"You know that Bree is planning to go to Madison in August," I said casually. "Pre-vet."

Jill frowned. "Riley didn't mention that."

"She was valedictorian, you know." I helped myself to a cup of coffee and sat down on one of the chairs by the dryers.

"That's a lot of school."

"Seven years."

To the casual observer (exception—Bernice), we were two women having an ordinary conversation. Here's how it looked in translation:

"Riley didn't mention that." *She can't seriously be considering leaving for college or my boy would have told me.*

"She was valedictorian, you know." *My daughter is a brilliant young woman. She has plans for her life and your son better not mess them up.*

"That's a lot of school." *She's going to meet someone else and break my little boy's heart.*

"Seven years." *You better believe it. He should start looking for someone else. Right away.*

We stared at each other until Bernice rattled the comb tray and started asking Jill questions about the rest of her children. Her questions flew faster than her scissors and then, in what had to be a record, she'd trimmed, blow-dried, curled and fluffed Jill's hair and ushered her out the door.

"Now what on earth was all that about?" Bernice asked as soon as the door closed behind Jill.

I sank against the back of the chair. "I think it was about Bree and Riley. Who, according to my daughter, are just friends."

Bernice shook her head. "Maybe they are."

"Did you hear Jill?" I straightened in the chair. "Bree has been spending time at their house. Playing cribbage with Old Dan. While Riley gets more…*twitter-pated!*"

"Bree's dated boys before," Bernice pointed out. She took out a broom and began to sweep up the floor.

"She lied to me about this one."

"That doesn't sound like Bree."

"I know." That's what had left a bitter taste in my mouth.

"Just because Riley might want something more serious doesn't mean that Bree does," Bernice pointed out. "She's got a good head on her shoulders, Ellie." She winked at me. "And a pretty one, too." Her voice was an exact imitation of Jill's singsong tone.

"Why didn't she tell me about him?"

Bernice sighed. "Maybe because there is nothing to tell. If they're just friends, why would she mention him?"

That made sense. Still, I remembered the way Riley had looked at her. But Bernice was right. Over the last four years, I'd seen an awful lot of longing gazes following Bree around town. She had been sweetly oblivious. She was never without a date for a movie on the weekend but she seemed to enjoy spending more time with Buckshot than a boy. I silently thanked God for putting horses on this earth for teenage girls to love.

"You're right." I forced a smile. "She's leaving for school in August. She's not going to get involved with someone local at this point. Bernice?"

Bernice was ignoring me. Her gaze was fixed on something outside. "Or maybe not," she murmured.

I twisted around in the chair and tried to see what had caught Bernice's attention.

Across the street was the black pickup that the vet used to go from call to call. I recognized it by the logo on the door. My mind registered this at the same time I realized that Bree was sitting in the driver's seat. The lower half of Riley Cabott's body was on the street, the upper part was leaning through the open window of the truck. He was kissing her. And from where I sat, it was more than just a friendly peck on the cheek.

"Hold on, El." Bernice had to practically sit on me to keep me from dashing out the door and across the street, where I would have provided Prichett's rumor mill with enough grist to keep it running for the next six months.

When she trusted me to stay put, she poured me another cup of coffee and disappeared into the back room. She emerged again seconds later, holding a pan of brownies. She didn't even bother to cut one. Just handed me the pan and a fork.

"Here. It's all yours."

"Did that look like *just friends* to you?" I asked between sips of coffee, bites of brownie and huffs of frustration.

Bernice dared to smile. "In my dreams."

"Bernice!"

"Sorry, El. You'll have to talk to her. Tell her you saw them today and go from there. But Elise, if there is anything going on…"

I choked on a crumb that took a detour into my windpipe. Bernice calmly thumped me on the back. "If?" I croaked.

"*If* there is something between the two of them, this might be exactly why she hasn't told you about it."

"What might be exactly why?"

"The way you're reacting."

"I'm reacting this way because she didn't tell me the truth," I argued.

"You're reacting this way because you're afraid she's going to do what you did. Skip college and marry a local boy."

Was that what I was afraid of?

No. I was terrified.

chapter 7

Bree was born ten months after Sam and I got married. Technically, we were still honeymooners when we became parents.

We were living in a mobile home on the farm, a stone's throw away from Sam's parents. It wasn't unusual at all for Sam's dad, Will, to wander past our living-room window in the evening. I started keeping the curtains closed and the shades pulled. Selfishly, I wanted to pretend that it was just Sam and me. But a little over a month after our wedding day, I pulled a package of bacon out of the fridge to fry for Sam's breakfast and then dropped it on the floor as I raced to the bathroom, my stomach churning. It was the first clue that *we* were going to be *three*.

Sam was ecstatic when we found out I was expecting. Before when he'd hug me, it was always face-to-face. His arms would wrap around me, tight as insulation on a pipe, and he'd lift me off the floor while he spun me in circles around the room. But after we discovered I was expecting, he'd turn me in his arms so we were both facing the same way and bury his face against my neck. His arms would slide around my waist as soft as a whisper and his hands would rest low on my stomach, including the baby in his embrace.

As the word spread about my pregnancy, there were jokes about boys from family and friends. Sam's two older brothers had drifted away from the farm, causing calluses to form on their parents' hearts. One was in construction, the other had gone into the military. Sam was the last hope to keep the farm in the Penny family and I knew that Will and Mary were thrilled that he wanted to be a farmer. After we made the announcement, Will constantly teased me about starting early on the next generation of Penny farmers. I wondered if Sam wanted a son for the same reason.

When Bree was born and the doctor told us we had a daughter, I immediately searched Sam's face for disappointment. What I saw were tears. And awe.

"She's beautiful," he said. "She looks just like you, Elise." Then, he smiled at me. The crooked smile that I'd fallen in love with. He whispered in my ear, "I didn't tell you this before, but I was praying for a little girl who looked just like you."

As a preschooler, Bree followed Sam around the farm like

a puppy. As much freedom as I'd give her, she took. But I knew how dangerous the farm equipment was, how quickly accidents could happen. I kept her with me as much as possible. As she got older, she chafed more and more against the boundaries I set. I could see her love for the farm quickly catching up to Sam's and it worried me. She had no interest in dolls or playing with friends. Instead, she spent hours in the barn, playing with the endless supply of kittens that a stray calico provided.

By the time she was ten, she had her own flock of fancy chickens and a palomino pony named Sunny. I sighed with relief. Her passion was animals and they kept her busy and close to the house. In eighth grade, she'd decided she was going to incorporate them into her future. She wanted to be a veterinarian.

We weren't able to have any more children. I don't know why. I heard a woman speak at a church luncheon once and she said that God was the one who opened and closed a woman's womb. For reasons I couldn't understand, He'd opened my womb for one child and when it had closed again, somehow He must have misplaced the key. There would be no Penny sons. No sisters for Bree to share secrets with. I tuned into Sam's heart, listening for regret or resentment. There weren't any. Not for either of us. Bree was enough. She filled the house with giggles and model horses and running footsteps. Later with damp bath towels, muddy boots and the occasional tantrum and slammed doors.

When I heard conversations about the "empty nest," I didn't join in on the woe-is-me side. I couldn't. I knew I would gladly sacrifice Bree's presence in the house if it meant she would leave Prichett. I wasn't so sure about Sam. He didn't talk much about her leaving. He listened patiently as she pored over the fall course catalog, trying to decide what classes to sign up for. He spent quiet hours in the evening with our financial papers fanned out on the table, figuring out how much we could afford to help out. He promised he'd take care of Buckshot and pet Diesel whenever he was in the barn. Promises I knew he'd keep.

I had to assume that he was as excited about her going to college as I was. I needed him on my side.

I went home after assuring Bernice that I wasn't going to do anything stupid—although the two rows of brownies I'd just eaten definitely qualified. Now I'd have to walk three miles the next morning instead of my usual two.

When I pulled down our road, I saw a car parked next to the house and an elderly couple standing in the driveway. The woman was aiming a camera at the house. I couldn't place the car or the people and I felt a stab of irritation.

"Hello."

They turned toward me and the woman waved her camera.

"I hope you don't mind, dear," she said. "Gladys Watson mentioned that you have the most beautiful flower gardens. We just had to take a peek. I'm going to send some pictures to my niece in Virginia. She buys those gardening magazines all the time. These are lovely, just lovely."

"Thank you." I had never quite gotten used to the fact that my flowers drew people from all over the county. It was a hobby I'd started when Bree was small. Mary hadn't had time for flowers but did valiantly try to keep a small rosebush next to the porch alive. Sam had given it to her one year for Mother's Day. When Mary and Will moved to Arizona, it became my responsibility. Unfortunately, I knew as much about growing roses as I did about raising children, so I checked out books from the library and spent the winter reading while Bree napped in the afternoons. By spring, I'd decided that I could copy some of the gardens I'd seen in the books.

"Must take a lot of time," the woman's husband said suddenly. "Don't you work?"

I blinked.

His wife shot him *the look*. "Of course she works," she scolded, jumping to my defense before I could open my mouth. "You don't think being a farmer's wife is work? Don't you remember your cousin Cicely…?"

I swallowed an impatient sigh. "Feel free to walk around. I'm sorry I can't take time to chat, but I have fifty cows to milk."

The husband's neck got red above the collar of his polo. Apparently brownies weren't a cure for cranky flashes. Suddenly ashamed of myself, I mumbled a generic "Have a nice day" and escaped into the house.

Sam must have come in for lunch. Dirty dishes were stacked in the sink and the mail was on the table. I glanced through the slim stack of envelopes until I got to the thick manila one at the bottom.

Mrs. Elise Penny.

I glanced at the return address. A Cupful of Blessings Productions. Probably address labels. Or next year's landscape calendar.

Dear Mrs. Penny,
It is our pleasure to inform you that you have been selected, after careful consideration, to take part in the preliminary round of the Proverbs 31 Pageant. Please be advised…

I stopped reading and dumped out the rest of the envelope's contents. There was a glossy newsletter and a photo of a woman, smiling and waving at…at someone. Wearing an evening dress. And a tiara.

This had to be someone's idea of a joke. A new scam or something. I hadn't sent in an application to be in the Proverbs 31 Pageant. I'd never even heard of the Proverbs 31 Pageant. In fact, I wasn't exactly sure what Proverbs 31 said.

I scanned the letter again, searching for the part where they wanted me to call an 800 number and give them my name and my credit card number.

Only one woman from the state of Wisconsin will be chosen to go on to compete at the national level. This year's competition will be in Madison....

I riffled through the papers again. Probably every woman in the county had received this mailing. I stuffed everything back in the envelope and went to the next envelope, feeling a tingle of excitement when I saw the return address was the University of Wisconsin-Madison. To the parents of Breanna Penny. It was an itinerary for freshman orientation. The timing was perfect.

Bernice had warned me not to jump all over Bree when she came home. Assume that nothing has changed, she'd told me. Even if she was kissing him, a little summer romance before she leaves isn't the end of the world.

Get a grip, Elise. She hadn't said the words but the implication was clear.

The telephone rang and I picked it up.

"Hello."

"May I speak with Elise Penny please?"

A telemarketer. *Lord,* I directed my gaze toward the ceiling. *Is anything about this day going to turn out to be normal?* "This is she."

"Mrs. Penny, this is Shelby Hannah from Cupful of Blessings Productions. I'm calling to find out if you have any questions concerning the packet of information we sent to you last week regarding the pageant."

You have got to be kidding. I'd just opened that packet of information. Did they have someone sitting in a tree, watching the house? How was I supposed to deal with this particular scam when I'd never heard about it on the news?

"I didn't send in an application for the pageant," I said. "There must be a mistake."

"I have your application right in front of me," Shelby said in a musical voice.

"That isn't possible," I said patiently. "Because I didn't fill one out."

"Elise Penny. W5412 Lilac Road, Prichett, Wisconsin."

Did I even dare verify my address? Who knew what she'd do with that information?

"Tell me the truth, you sent that packet to half the women in the state, didn't you?"

Silence. Then, "Mrs. Penny, the Proverbs 31 Pageant is not only legitimate but highly respected. Only five women in each state make the preliminary round. A woman must be recommended for the pageant. Someone filled out the application on your behalf."

Her musical voice had a slight edge now, like a kindergarten teacher correcting an unruly student. I felt like sliding under the table.

"I'll look it over." I was still trying to process the fact that some anonymous person had entered me in a pageant.

"Great." The edge was gone. "It was so nice to talk to you. I'll call back tomorrow. What's better, morning or afternoon?"

I couldn't believe I actually answered her. "Afternoon."

chapter **8**

As I made supper, I found myself watching out the window for Bree's car. My movements around the kitchen were too fast and erratic, resulting in a jar of bread-and-butter pickles shattered on the floor and me standing in the center of a pool of pickle juice and shards of glass, smelling like vinegar and crying hot tears.

Into this chaos wandered my unsuspecting husband.

"Ellie, are you hurt? Did you cut yourself?" He bounded across the kitchen in three steps and grabbed my hands, looking for blood. Since all the bleeding was internal, I was sure he wouldn't notice.

"I'm all right. I just broke a jar of pickles."

"You did a good job." Sam's gentle teasing, meant to lighten the moment, did just the opposite.

"It was an accident." The anger in my voice surprised me.

"Elise, I *know* that." Sam studied me for a few seconds.

For some reason, his calm demeanor was like a light shining into the shadows of my soul, illuminating all the cobwebs and dust. Instead of basking in the warm glow of being cared for, I wanted to burrow deeper into the darkness and lick my wounds in private. But there is something about light that sweeps out all the gunk caught in the corners. I ended up spilling it all.

"Annie Carpenter showed up this morning out of the blue and I went into town to see Bernice and I saw Bree and that Cabott boy, *kissing.* She's supposed to be at work today and they were on Main Street *kissing*—in front of everyone. Two *strangers* were traipsing through the yard, taking pictures of my gardens and then I got this weird phone call from someone telling me that I was in the preliminary round of some *pageant...*" I had to pause to take a breath, the eye in the middle of my verbal hurricane, and noticed that Sam's eyes had glazed over.

"I think we should get this cleaned up."

That was my practical husband. I knew he wanted to listen, but it was hard when he was standing in a puddle of wet glass and beginning to smell like a deli. He picked me up and moved me into a safe zone by the refrigerator where the pickle juice wasn't able to reach because our floor wasn't quite level. Then he grabbed a paper sack and started to pitch the larger chunks of glass into it.

Bree came in, humming. *Humming.*

"Wow, what happened?"

This is all your fault, I wanted to vent. *For kissing Riley Cabott on Main Street.*

"Mom just dropped a jar of pickles," Sam said casually, as if it were an everyday occurrence.

I scowled. Bree glanced at me, then tiptoed around the kitchen table and grabbed the roll of paper towel that I keep by the sink. Within five seconds, she was down on her knees, mopping up pickle juice.

"There we go. No big deal," Sam announced, opening the kitchen window a bit wider after he had finished with the glass.

Bree sent a soggy wad of paper towel sailing toward the wastebasket and then whooped in delight when it found its mark. She high-fived Sam, who smiled indulgently. "Three points. Yes! I'm going to take a shower now." Like a shooting star, she was gone.

I found myself wishing that all messes were cleaned up so easily.

"El, can we talk later tonight?" Sam asked.

His expression was so wary that I felt a ripple of guilt. It wasn't his fault that his normally unflappable wife had turned into a stranger who cried when she broke a jar of pickles.

I nodded.

"Bree…"

"I won't say anything." *Yet.*

Sam looked relieved as he left. He wasn't the kind of man who enjoyed conflict, especially on the peaceful isle of hearth and home. Not that I blamed him. I could already predict that Sam would think I was overreacting. I needed someone to talk to who would be on my side.

It occurred to me that I didn't have many choices.

Over the years, I hadn't cast out a large net for friends. Sam, although my best friend, couldn't help that he saw life through testosterone-tinted glasses. He tackled problems in much the same way he handled stubborn pieces of machinery—first patiently tinkering and then, if they were still uncooperative, hammering or sanding them into line. The result was something that worked. It might not look like the original, but it worked. He could live with that.

Bernice. She was the one with whom I could safely be *me,* but as easily stirred as she was, *she* had even cautioned me not to jump to conclusions about Bree and Riley. She was my confidante, but in this case, I wasn't sure she could give me sound advice. She'd never been a mother. She didn't know what it was like to have your offspring teetering on the edge of the nest and you suddenly in a panic, wondering if you'd taught them enough. If they were strong enough to fly. If the wind would catch them on that first free fall and bear up those fragile wings.

You can talk to Me.

The thought suddenly swept in and cut a glittering path through the center of my thoughts. A whisper. So loud that it momentarily drowned out all the echoes of anger and fear inside me.

For a moment I clung to it, then reluctantly let it slip away.

It couldn't have been God, I told myself. *I'm sure He has much more important things to do than listen to you complain.*

Annie's story about the paper edged into my thoughts.

If He delivers a box of paper to a bunch of missionary kids in Brazil, what makes you think He doesn't care about what goes on in your life, Elise Penny?

Several answers to that question immediately raised their irreverent heads, clamoring to be heard and I squashed them all down. I believed in God. Believed that He had created everything…even me. Believed that He sent Jesus to die on the cross in my place. I knew He loved the generic multitude, but wasn't sure He really hung on every word I said or had my picture in His spiritual wallet. We exchanged words on occasion, saw each other Sunday mornings at church.

It had always been enough. I knew I had made it enough.

Then, less than an hour later, a rumpled blanket of dark clouds unfolded in the sky, making me wonder whether God was smiling at my stubborn skepticism. The fact that I wondered at all made me wonder even more. For some odd reason, I blamed Annie Carpenter. That first stroke of lightning seemed like an exclamation point at the end of a sentence, *"See, Elise, if you really want to know if I care about your life…!"*

Then the rain started to fall.

It brought Sam in from the field and held Bree captive for

the evening. And brought us all to the supper table at the same time, a rare occurrence in the summer.

"With the pickle disaster, I forgot to mention that your schedule for freshman orientation came in the mail today," I said to Bree, carefully watching her expression for a) signs of excitement or b) College? Oh, that's right. Sorry, decided not to go.

I didn't see anything. Bree had the proverbial poker face. There was not a flicker of anything in her eyes and I felt a stab of unease. When had she gotten so skillful at hiding her feelings? And *why* did she feel like she had to?

"When is it?"

That's when I noticed she was dissecting her chicken breast into tiny pieces. She might have been able to keep her thoughts from reflecting in her eyes, but she hadn't figured out that the hands are just as important.

"I didn't open it yet. I thought you'd want to have the honor."

"Maybe I can take a day off and go along," Sam said.

"In August?" Bree shook her head. "The farm needs you, Dad. That's your busiest time."

"I'm sure that you're more important to Dad than the farm," I said. "But if he can't come with us, maybe we'll take a few days and get acquainted with Madison. Do some shopping."

Bree looked less than enthusiastic. I should have known better. Unlike many girls her age, shopping was not the way to Bree's heart. The fact that she could fit four seasons' worth of clothing into her narrow closet was testimony to the fact that Bree loved other things more.

"Sure, Mom. Maybe." She glanced at Sam and then smiled at me.

Translation: Not a chance.

A mixture of worry and resentment began to brew inside me. If I were her, I would have been ecstatic to be so close to leaving Prichett. I would have jumped up from the table and ripped into the envelope before taking another bite. The letter about freshman orientation would have been another exciting marker on the road to my future. And all Bree could do was ask a halfhearted question. *When is it?* Although I tried to convince myself that this wasn't a good time, the worry turned into words.

"I saw Jill Cabott at Bernice's today."

Sam's fork hit the side of his plate and out of the corner of my eye I could see him staring at me.

"Really?" The slightest flicker in Bree's eyes. She shoved a piece of dinner roll into her mouth.

"She mentioned you were over the other night."

"Mmmhhh."

"That would have been the same day you told me you and Riley Cabott are just friends."

"Ellie…" Sam, always the voice of reason, murmured my name.

"We *are* friends, Mom."

"And that would be why you were passionately kissing him on Main Street this afternoon."

"You were spying on me?" Now there was some emotion in Bree's eyes and she half rose out of her chair.

"I didn't have to spy," I said in exasperation. "I was talking to Bernice and there you were. It wasn't like the two of you were being discreet."

"I like Riley, Mom. There. Are you satisfied? Yes, we're friends, but I really like him. So sue me."

Sam growled a warning. As much as he indulged Bree, he never allowed her to be disrespectful.

Bree's chair scraped away from the table. "Please excuse me. I'm going up to my room."

And she did.

"You back her into a corner, Elise, and she's going to come out fighting." Sam took another helping of mashed potatoes. I suddenly couldn't eat another bite. What I had eaten settled heavily in my stomach.

"She hasn't been honest with me."

"You haven't let her."

chapter 9

The storm outside formed a perfect backdrop to the mood in the house.

Okay, God, if You planned for us to have supper together, couldn't You have worked things out a little differently? Maybe then Sam wouldn't be up to his elbows in canceled checks and Bree wouldn't be in seclusion in her room. And I wouldn't be sorting through the stack of gardening magazines next to the bed, waiting for nine o'clock to roll around, when I could justify going to sleep.

I couldn't remember a time when I'd openly questioned God. For some reason, it didn't seem right, given the fact that He was in control and I, well, I'm not.

Mmm. But you try to be, don't you, Elise?

Restlessly, I pushed that thought away. What was happening to me? Cranky flashes. Tears over broken pickle jars. I hadn't cried since Shadow died. I'd heard someone say that tears watered wrinkles and made them grow but smiles smoothed them away. I had taken that advice and made sure I smiled more than I frowned.

"Mom?"

Bree knocked lightly on the door at the same time she pushed it open. She had a box in her hands. Oh, no. *The Box*.

"I found this by the attic stairs." She slipped into the room and put it down next to me on the bed.

"Annie Carpenter was collecting stuff for the church rummage sale."

"And you're donating this?" Bree took out the tiara and put it on her head. It listed slightly to one side.

"No, it got mixed up with the other boxes by mistake."

I remembered the pageant and wondered if sharing that humorous tidbit might put a smile back on Bree's face. "Someone called me today about being in a pageant..."

"The Proverbs 31 Pageant?"

"You've heard of it?"

"Are you kidding? I entered you in it!"

In a teenage sea change, Bree squealed, her arms went around me and we tumbled back against the pillows.

"What do you mean *you* entered me in it?" I gasped, coming up for air.

"Mom, I can't believe this! What did they say?" Bree took the tiara off her head and put it on mine. "You're going to compete, right? Of course you are. I didn't want to tell you that I'd filled out an application for you, because I didn't want you to be disappointed if you didn't make the preliminary round—"

"Whoa," I said, a word that I knew Bree would understand. "How did this happen? I thought it was some sort of telemarketing scam."

Bree looked shocked. "You were nice to the woman who called, weren't you?"

I hid a smile. She sounded more like a mother at that moment than a soon-to-be college freshman. *You remembered to say thank you for the birthday gift, didn't you?*

"I was nice. It would have been better if I'd had a heads-up before getting the packet of information and a phone call five minutes later."

"You got the packet!" Another squeal. Bree hugged a pillow against her chest. "Where is it?"

"On the counter by the phone." Right next to the freshman orientation schedule you haven't looked at yet.

Bree was already out of the room and flying down the stairs. She returned a few minutes later with my packet of information. And the emergency bag of M&M's that I keep in the freezer for PMS days and the rare Katharine Hepburn movie.

"I found out about the pageant from Mrs. Kramer at church a few months ago," Bree said. She opened the bag of M&M's and poured them out on the quilt between us.

"She mentioned that you'd won a pageant in high school and you fit the Proverbs 31 criteria perfectly, but a woman had to be *nominated* for the pageant because, you know, the whole Proverbs 31 woman *thing* is that you're kind and gracious and humble. That kind of woman wouldn't nominate herself, would she? So, I nominated you. And sent in your picture."

"But…" It was the only word I could manage, given the circumstances.

Bree didn't seem to need me to say anything, because she was tearing happily through the information packet. "It says right here that only one woman from each state goes on to the national competition. To make the preliminary round, a woman is judged on her contributions to church and community…priorities…hobbies."

Bree's voice faded in and out as she chose to read some words to herself and some out loud to me while I tried to make sense of it all without bursting Bree's bubble, which I found myself extremely gifted at lately.

"Judging at the state level involves a one-on-one interview, judging of a personal journal, and evening gown competition." Bree paused for a second to laugh.

I held my breath. *Don't you dare say swimsuit competition!*

"Each contestant will be expected to give a five-minute presentation on something close to their heart in the realm of faith, family or community." She winked at me. "Five minutes! Piece of cake, Mom.

"The winner at the state level will go on to compete at the national level the following summer. The winner will receive $10,000 to be donated to her favorite charity." Bree's eyes widened. "Wow. I'm your favorite charity, right?"

I tried to straighten the tiara, which had slipped down over my left ear. "I don't think you qualify, sweetie."

Bree pretended to pout for a second, then she started reading again. I used the silence to sort through the pieces of Bree's excited ramblings and piece them together to figure out just what all of this meant.

A beauty pageant for Christian women.

That's what it meant.

I couldn't sleep. Maybe the caffeine from Bernice's killer coffee, the two rows of fudge brownies or the quarter pound of M&M's I'd eaten with Bree were to blame. Or the fact that I was suddenly a contestant in the Proverbs 31 Pageant.

I could hear Sam's gentle breathing as he slept next to me. He still didn't have a clue what was going on. Bree had made me promise that she could tell him in the morning. For some strange reason, my daughter was more excited about me being in this silly pageant than she was about going to college. My daughter, the classic tomboy, who was wearing cowboy boots to church when the other little girls were wearing white leather sandals to show off their Pepto-Bismol pink toenails. The same daughter who paused occasionally by the TV while I watched a pageant, snorted disdainfully and judged all visible cleavage as *fake*.

When it came right down to it, I didn't have the heart to tell Bree that I wasn't interested in being in a pageant. Those dreams had vanished before they'd even fully taken shape. Still, I decided it wouldn't hurt to *pretend* to be thinking about it. Bree and I needed something to connect us again. It may as well be this.

I had heard vague references to the Proverbs 31 woman. You couldn't go to a women's ministry luncheon or workshop without someone making reference to *her*—the Christian woman's equivalent of a superheroine.

Since I couldn't sleep anyway, I turned the bedside lamp on and paged quietly through Sam's Bible, looking for her. As I read through the passages, something began to squeeze my heart. No wonder women uttered a collective sigh when meeting her face-to-face. She could have been the poster child for the Women's Hospitality Committee, mission sewing circle, PTA and Mother of the Year.

Something Bree had mentioned came back to me. Mrs. Kramer, beloved church secretary, thought that *I* fit the whole Proverbs 31 criteria. I began to pick apart the verses, feeling pretty good about myself.

Yup, there it was.

The heart of her husband trusts in her. (Sam trusts me.)

She looks for wool and flax.

And works with her hands in delight. (Okay, no sheep, but gardening has to count!)

She rises while it is still night. (Farmer's wife—hello!)

Not afraid of the snow… (I have a really warm coat.)

Makes linen garments. (We already established the fact that I don't sew, but buttons count, right?)

So far so good. I do look to the ways of my household, I take very good care of Sam and Bree and the odd assortment of critters. I sell veggies at the farmers' market in the fall.

Charm is deceitful and beauty is vain, but a woman who fears the Lord, she shall be praised.

And suddenly I was scared, borrowing one of Bree's favorite expressions, spitless.

chapter **10**

By the time Sunday morning rolled around, I had decided to tell Bree that I wasn't going to be in the pageant. My conversation with pageant coordinator Shelby Hannah had played a part in that decision but it was a conversation with Sam that had clinched it. The conversation with Shelby had me convinced that the only thing I would qualify for was a pageant for the Proverbs 31 phony. The one with Sam had left me in tears. Again.

I knew Bree had told him about the pageant. Even though I couldn't hear the words, I had heard their voices down in the kitchen the next day, blending like two instruments in an orchestra, Sam's low alto sax playing against Bree's lyrical flute. Just by the notes, I knew what she was saying and found myself holding my breath, wondering what Sam was going to think about the whole thing.

When I went downstairs, Bree was gone and Sam was by the door, pulling his boots on. Lady was waiting patiently for him on the other side of the screen door.

"Bree left already?"

"The O'Briens have a sick cow," Sam said. "Kevin paged her a few minutes ago."

"I suppose she told you the news."

Sam just looked at me.

"About the pageant." I laughed lightly, tossing the isn't-that-the-funniest-thing-you've-ever-heard line at him. He let it drop on the floor between us. I couldn't read his expression, which was unusual. It reminded me of Bree that night at the dinner table, when I'd been fishing for information about her and Riley Cabott. I tried again. "So, what do you think?"

"You've always wanted this." A shadow passed through his eyes as he turned away. "Maybe this is what will make you happy."

He took advantage of the next moment—the one when my mouth fell open like a surprised trout and my vocabulary was temporarily depleted—to make his escape. I was so shocked I didn't even try to call him back to explain what he'd meant. Tears stung the back of my eyes in response to his words.

You *were what I wanted,* I was suddenly tempted to yell. *Didn't I prove that when I gave up everything to stay here in Prichett and become a farmer's wife?*

The Sunday-morning drive to church was quiet. I didn't want to tell Bree about my decision yet. The pageant had connected us by a tender thread and the truth was, I wasn't in a hurry to sever that connection. Sam hadn't brought up the topic of the pageant again. With stubborn ceremony, I'd packed my old tiara in the box and stashed it in the trunk of the car. I was going to give it to Annie for the rummage sale. No doubt it would wind up in a little girl's dress-up box, filled with outdated satin bridesmaid's dresses, plastic beads and feather boas.

"I won't be able to go to Sunday School, I have an ushers' meeting." Sam finally spoke.

I felt a tiny poke. Just enough to draw a drop of resentment. Sam wasn't fighting fair. Usually we went to an adult Sunday School class together. I was content to sit next to him, my eyes trained on whatever Scripture passage we were studying. It had been that way for years. People looked to Sam to answer the tough questions and I smiled as though I knew exactly what he was talking about. If for some reason Sam couldn't go to Sunday School, I'd stay at home and meet him at church for the worship service later. Now he'd deliberately cut me loose, like a boat released from its moorings.

Plan B. Hide in the kitchen and fuss with the coffeepots if spotted. When I walked into the foyer with Sam and Bree, we were immediately caught up in the Sunday-morning crush.

"I'm going to talk to Jamie, Mom. I'll see you after Sunday School." Bree darted away and I headed toward the kitchen.

"Elise!"

Annie Carpenter's voice cut a cheerful swathe through the hum and I slowed down, waiting for her to find an opening through the tangled skein of giggling junior-high girls that separated us.

"I was hoping you'd be here." She linked her arm through mine. "I'm starting a new Sunday School class today. Just for women."

No, no, no. "I usually go to class with Sam…"

"But he has an ushers' meeting this morning." Annie nodded. "That's great. It'll give you a chance to sit in on my class and I could really use a familiar face in there." Suddenly, she swiveled and directed us into the kitchen. Turning to face me, her eyes searched mine. "I can't believe I'm this nervous, Elise. Will you pray with me?"

Two men walked into the kitchen, on a mission to find a cup of coffee, but Annie didn't pay any attention to them. She had already bowed her head and closed her eyes, waiting. Waiting for me to say something.

Say something! It wasn't like prayer was a completely foreign language to me. I prayed. Snippets of prayer that no one except God heard. But I wasn't usually asked to pray out loud. Especially for something specific like the butterflies in Annie Carpenter's stomach.

"Um, Dear Lord, help Annie not to be nervous about leading the Sunday School class. Give her Your peace. Amen."

Annie opened her eyes and laughed. For a moment, I thought she was laughing at my prayer. But then she put her hand on my arm and gave it a squeeze. "Thank you, Elise. I feel better already! I knew when I saw you that God put you right there, knowing I'd need a little encouragement."

God had sent *me* as the answer to Annie's prayer? *Me?* I was messing things up left and right lately, so I had my doubts. But now I was truly stuck. No hiding in the kitchen now. No plan B. I was beginning to suspect that God had something against plan Bs.

The Sunday School room was set up with round tables instead of rows of chairs like a regular classroom. Each table had a plate of muffins and a carafe of coffee in the center. I figured that Annie had instigated the changes I was seeing.

"Do you want to take my place?" Annie whispered in my ear as everyone stopped talking and looked at us.

I knew she was kidding because she didn't look the least bit nervous anymore. Her eyes were sparkling and the smile on her face wasn't the brittle plastic kind. She had the same expression Bree had when she was about to show Buckshot at the fair. Delight. Anticipation. Somewhere between the kitchen and the classroom, Annie's nervousness had evaporated.

"Welcome, ladies." Annie took advantage of the momentary silence that had fallen to step up to the whiteboard at the front of the room. "Help yourselves to a cup of coffee and some muffins and we'll get started."

Although there were empty chairs at some of the tables, I chose a table by myself. The other women had Bibles. I hadn't brought mine because I always looked on with Sam.

"Did you ever notice that Jesus took everyday items and used them to teach spiritual truths?" Annie asked. "Salt, lamp stands, grapevines, sheep. People could relate to them because they were ordinary things in their ordinary lives. Well, I brought something today that I think we can all relate to." She reached behind the narrow podium and pulled out a television remote control. "But what kind of spiritual truth can we possibly get out of this?"

"Don't set any worthless thing before your eyes," Margaret Stone piped up. "Television today is full of worthless things, if you ask me. I heard about a program where women try to land a rich man...."

I felt sorry for Annie. Margaret was like a horse that sets its bit and bolts. There was no stopping her until she was good and ready. And that usually took awhile.

"That's a very good observation." Annie did what no one else had ever had the gumption to do. She sweetly interrupted Margaret. "Does anyone else have anything they'd like to share?"

Margaret was so surprised she stopped in mid-sermon and sat like a tree stump. I guess everyone else was surprised right along with her because suddenly every woman in the room turned into a tree stump.

Annie smiled. "It's the buttons on the remote control that we're going to talk about today. Think about the fast forward button and the rewind button first. We women can struggle in two different areas. Some of us have a hard time living in the moment. Everything is *when*. *When* I'm married, *when* I have children, *when* my children start school. You fill in the blanks. The trouble with wanting to fast forward your life is that you miss out on what God has given you today. The rewind button is just the opposite. Women who press the rewind button in their lives can't stop looking over their shoulder at their past. If only I'd stayed single, had had children, *hadn't* had children, had gone to college. Both of these buttons are dangerous because they rob us of something very important."

Annie paused and waited, apparently hoping that someone would clue us in as to what that important thing was. I glanced at Margaret. Both cheeks were puffed out, like she'd stuffed an entire muffin into her mouth at once. Her face was pink but I wondered if it was lack of oxygen (she has a very small nose) or if she was still in a state of shock that her soapbox had been pulled out from underneath her.

No one said a word. Annie looked at me. Why was she looking at *me*? This wasn't the way Sunday School class was run. I was used to listening, not participating. I know I have a reputation of being reserved, which has saved me from situations like this in the past. No one needed my opinion, not when there were outgoing, walking reference Bibles in the class. Unfortunately, I got the feeling that no one had told Annie *the rules.*

Her next words convinced me of that.

"Elise? What do you think?"

The problem was, I wasn't able to think. Hearing my name turned my brain into a chalkboard. I was suddenly transported back to junior high school, with Ms. Foley towering over me.

Elise, if you spent half the time on your algebra as I'm sure you do staring at yourself in the mirror, you'd be my best student.

"Being content."

My brain formed the words and my mouth dutifully said them out loud.

"Yup, contentment." Annie wrote that on the board with a bright blue marker and underlined it. "Thank you, Elise. Being caught up with past mistakes, regrets, unfulfilled dreams takes our thoughts off today and can lead to regret or bitterness. And today is God's gift to us, to use for whatever purpose He has. The same thing happens when we're so focused on our tomorrows. Proverbs 31 describes a woman who smiles at the future. You can only do that when you trust God with each of your tomorrows and are content with where He's put you today."

Annie's marker performed a miracle. When she underlined the word *contentment,* every woman in the room was suddenly anxious to share. Except me. There was a nagging sense of *something* trying to rise to the surface of my heart but I stirred it back in. She'd quoted Proverbs 31. A coincidence. No doubt about it.

I glanced at the clock. Less than five minutes. Next Sunday I'd be safely next to Sam—

"Elise Penny!"

The door opened and Mrs. Kramer tottered in. At the sound of her voice, everyone stopped talking. Again.

Her gaze bounced from table to table until it rested on me. "There you are! Congratulations. Bree just told me the news."

Bree, please tell me you didn't.

"What news?" Annie asked.

"She didn't tell you?" Mrs. Kramer shook her head and tsked at me. "I'm not surprised. Our Elise is such a humble woman."

I swallowed hard.

Don't say it, Mrs. Kramer.

"Elise was chosen to be the Wisconsin delegate for the Proverbs 31 Pageant!"

"I haven't decided yet—"

I was surrounded by women. Hugging me. Patting my arms. Asking me a hundred questions, most of which Mrs. Kramer fielded as deftly as a Hollywood agent.

By the time everyone finally spilled out of the room, I felt like the favorite teddy bear in a preschool classroom. Only Annie remained. She paused to tuck a strand of hair behind my ear that had worked its way free during the hugging.

"Oh, I can't wait to see how God uses this, Elise."

I managed a smile. That was funny. I could.

chapter **11**

After church, I tried the classic duck-and-dodge maneuver. And failed. By the time the service was over, everyone from Pastor Charles to four-year-old Lindie Hurder knew I was the Proverbs 31 woman. I calculated that by three o'clock in the afternoon everyone in Prichett would know, too.

Bree stood on my left, happily telling the captivated circle around us the story of how she'd filled out an application for the pageant and sent it in. I just wanted to go home. It was going to be hard to tell everyone now, especially Bree, that I wasn't going to get involved in the pageant.

When I caught a glimpse of Annie by the front door, I suddenly, thankfully, remembered the box in the trunk of the car.

"Excuse me, everyone. I have to talk to Annie for a second." I made a break for it.

Annie was talking to her husband, Stephen, and this was the first time I'd gotten a good look at him. He had longish brown hair (how that got past the deacon board I'll never know) and wire-framed glasses that made him look like a radical young college professor. His arm was curled around Annie's waist and as I got closer, he brushed a kiss against her forehead.

I hated to interrupt what looked to be a private moment, but two more women were heading in my direction, eyes bright with excitement, and I needed to utilize my chosen escape route. Fast.

"Annie, I have another box in the car for the rummage sale."

"I can't believe you found something else to donate," Annie teased me. "Stephen, this is Elise Penny. The woman I've been telling you about."

That was unnerving. Just what had she told him? This is the lady who refuses to help me coordinate the rummage sale? I shook away my paranoia as Stephen extended his hand.

"It's nice to meet you, Elise. I've already met Sam. I have a lot of respect for him. He's real."

He's real. I hadn't heard anyone described as real before and wondered briefly what it meant. *Obviously the opposite of phony.* No time to dwell on that spiteful voice.

I began to ease away from them, inching toward the double doors. "It's nice to meet you, too."

Annie smiled up at him. "I'll be right back, hon."

Sidestepping some stragglers in the parking lot, I was three steps ahead of Annie when I heard her laugh.

"Elise, I can't believe you can move that fast in high heels. I guess that'll come in handy when you're on stage at the pageant."

Immediately it was as if someone shifted me into neutral. "I'm not going to be in the pageant," I whispered tersely as I unlocked the trunk and pulled out the box.

"Why not? This isn't your tiara, is it?" She glanced down at the box and frowned suspiciously.

For some reason, I was hoping that Annie wouldn't recognize *The Box*.

"Yes, it's my tiara, and it's silly to keep it," I said. "Remember what you said a half an hour ago? It's silly to dwell on the past."

"But…" Annie caught her lip in her teeth as she stared at the box.

"That's why I'm not going to participate in the pageant," I muttered. "I'm almost forty years old. I'm not going to parade around on a stage, pretending I'm eighteen. My *daughter* is eighteen, for goodness' sake."

Annie was still frowning.

"Here comes Sam. We have to get home before dinner burns." I had a chicken in the oven on timed bake.

Annie gave me one more searching glance and nodded. "Elise? I was wondering if you'd be willing to be my mentor?"

Her what? "Your what?"

"My mentor. I thought that maybe we could get together once a week to talk…maybe pray."

"Me?" I croaked the word in disbelief.

"You have a lot of qualities that I admire. Maybe if I hang around you enough, some of your wisdom will rub off on me." She touched my shoulder and laughed.

Wisdom? "I don't know…"

"Pray about it," Annie said simply.

"I will." I nodded distractedly as Bree and Sam reached the car. I didn't want Bree to see *The Box.*

I'm not sure if Sam was still in a mood or if Bree's chatter filled the silence that had fallen between us. I decided to take a risk and see where Sam was on the relationship barometer. I took his hand. For a second his fingers were slack, then they softly traced the valley between my thumb and index finger. Out of the corner of my eye, I saw him exhale silently but it didn't seem as if he was releasing some burden. More like he'd just taken on another one.

I woke up in the middle of the night and realized I hadn't told Bernice about the pageant. If she heard about it from someone else first, she'd never forgive me. The salon was closed on Sundays so there was still a slight chance she hadn't heard the news. Hopefully I could make it to the Cut and Curl before her eight-thirty appointment spilled the beans.

I made sure I got there at eight the next morning, hoping that I'd have half an hour to fill her in on the details.

The salon was dark. I rapped on the window but the lights were off and there was no sign of Bernice. I could see the glowing red eye on the coffeepot, but it was empty. I hurried around the back of the building and took the stairs that wound up to her apartment two at a time. Worry had started to cloud my breathing, making it come out in short little puffs. Every day by eight Bernice was in the salon, recreating the intricate dance steps of her morning routine.

I rang the bell.

Nothing.

"Bernice?" Hesitantly, I tried the handle but the door was locked. "Helloooo."

I was just about to press my ear against the crusty paint when the door opened a crack. "Elise?"

"Of course it's Elise." Now that I could see her eye blinking at me, my worry faded into exasperation. "Did you oversleep? It's after eight."

I heard the chain slide against the lock and the door opened but Bernice wasn't there. I got a clear view of the back of her fuzzy purple robe as she walked away, though.

"Are you sick?" I asked the question cautiously because Bernice definitely wasn't acting like Bernice.

"Yes…no." She pulled a tissue from the saddlebag-sized pocket of her robe and blew her nose.

"I got worried when I didn't see you downstairs." I followed her to the breakfast counter that bisected the kitchen from the living room, where the remains of a weekend long pity-party stretched out between us. Pizza sauce and melted cheese were glued to a paper plate. Empty Tootsie Roll wrappers were sprinkled everywhere like confetti. Two video rentals. I discreetly read the titles. *Casablanca* and *Roman Holiday*. Uh-oh.

"So what brought you into town so early?" Bernice asked.

"Oh, no. You first," I said, waving my hand toward the pizza box. "This definitely takes priority over my news."

Bernice shrugged. "Typical weekend at Bernice's place," she said. "Some delivery pizza and a couple of videos."

I cleared my throat. "Um, *spongy* videos."

"Spongy?"

"You know, *spongy.* Sad. Romantic. The kind you cry all the way through."

"Can't a girl eat junk food and watch videos without her best friend jumping all over her?" Bernice asked irritably.

"Not if that girl is still in her bathrobe when she's supposed to be at work. That's grounds for serious friendship intervention."

"Elise, you're like the ice queen with everyone in this town. How come I'm the lucky one who gets to see the real you?"

"Because you're a transplant, like me."

"You're not a transplant anymore," Bernice said, her eyes narrowing as she smiled wickedly. "When you've lived in Prichett more than ten years, then you're officially *not* a transplant. You're a lifer. Might as well have been born and raised here."

A little voice inside my head shrieked, "Take it back!" But she was probably right. A lifer. It was a depressing thought.

"You're just trying to suck me into your pity-party."

"You're the one who crashed it."

"That means you're a lifer, too," I pointed out.

"My ten years aren't up until next month." She smiled in satisfaction and pulled a slice of pizza out of the box.

"How long has that been sitting out? Don't eat that!" I plucked it out of her hand. "I hate to tell you this, but you've lived here more than ten years."

"No. Ten years in August."

"It seems longer."

"Maybe it's time to move on. Become a transplant somewhere else."

Bernice said the words so casually that they didn't register for a few minutes. I laughed, even though I felt uneasy. I'd never seen Bernice in a mood like this before. But then again, I couldn't remember a time when I'd felt so restless before, either, with cranky flashes igniting inside me like summer lightning. Maybe there was something in Prichett's water supply…

"How are things with Bree?"

"Bernice…"

"Let's just pretend for a few minutes that you aren't seeing me with my hair pasted against my head, wearing a bathrobe that's twenty years old, hiding out in my apartment with a stack of spongy movies, okay? We can talk about me later."

I let her have her way. "Things are fine at the moment."

"So you're okay with her and Riley dating?"

"No!" How had I forgotten about that little situation? I knew how. The pageant. "We sort of got sidetracked."

"By what? A cloud of locusts descending on your corn?"

That she could even joke about that made me wince. "By the Proverbs 31 Pageant."

"The what?"

"Bree entered me in a pageant. And I made the preliminary round. Don't ask me why."

"Because you're beautiful?"

"There is that." I wadded up a greasy napkin and tossed it at her.

The phone rang, a tinny, slightly muffled rendition of a song from *The Sound of Music*. "Hold on a sec." She dug around in the pocket of her robe and pulled it out. "Yes, I'm sorry, Mindy. Have a cup of coffee at the café. I'll be down to open up in fifteen minutes. I'll even throw in a free manicure for making you wait…really, I'm sorry."

Bernice shoved the phone back in her pocket and suddenly looked as if someone had snapped their fingers and shaken her out of a trance. "It's almost nine o'clock!"

I rolled my eyes.

"I've got to take a shower." Bernice took off like a rare purple bird, robe flapping against her legs. "Let's have lunch. I want to hear everything about the pageant."

The phone on the wall rang this time and Bernice paused

just outside the bathroom door. "Let the machine pick it up. It's probably another satisfied customer."

Bernice always had a quirky message on her machine that she changed several times a month.

Hello, this is Bernice. I'd love to talk to you, but only if you aren't a telemarketer or a long-lost relative who's short on cash. Please leave your number and I'll call you back.

Beep.

"This message is for Bernice Strum. I have information about a child born at St. Therese's Hospital in St. Paul, Minnesota. Please call me back as soon as possible."

The voice was a young woman's, as thin and crackly as the paint on Bernice's door. "That's strange." I said the first words that popped into my head and waited for Bernice to agree with me.

Bernice didn't answer. I looked at her and saw the color had drained out of her face, leaving her skin a pasty gray.

"Bernice?" I jumped up and scrambled to her side. "Who was that?"

Bernice smiled wanly. "My past."

chapter **12**

"Come and sit down."

"Mindy—"

"Mindy can wait." I was afraid that if Bernice didn't sit down, she was going to fall down. And Bernice wasn't the fainting type.

"The weird thing is, I was just thinking about her this weekend," Bernice said, shuffling into the living room and collapsing in the chair by the window. I perched on the arm, reluctant to move too far away.

"You're looking for your birth mother?" I ventured, trying to make sense of the short message the woman had left.

Bernice made a choking sound and I couldn't tell if it was laughter or the jump start that would release a flood of tears. "I think my daughter's looking for *me*."

Two thoughts collided. The first one was that I'd known

Bernice for ten years and she'd never told me that she'd had a child. The second was *why* hadn't she told me. I groped for the right words but couldn't find any.

Bernice took a deep breath. "I've got to get down to the shop. Mindy's bladder is like a colander and if she drinks too much coffee, I'll have to stop cutting her hair every five minutes while she runs to the bathroom."

"You just had some upsetting news," I said slowly, feeling my way through this like someone stumbling down a dark stairwell. "I'll tell Mindy that you aren't feeling well this morning. Hey, I'll even cut her hair if you want me to."

"I can't ignore my customers." Bernice pushed to her feet, her movements slow and precise, and I could see the change in her expression. She'd shifted from stage one—shell-shocked—into stage two—survival mode. "But could you open up the salon and keep her company for a few minutes until I get there?"

"Sure." I would have agreed to anything.

"The key is hanging on the hook by my door."

There were a hundred questions that I wanted to ask her. I was only brave enough to ask one. "Are you going to call her back?"

"Ellie, I can't." She squeezed my arm and repeated the words, maybe to convince herself more than me. "I can't."

Strangely enough, it was Annie's words from the day before that chased through my mind. *I can't wait to see how God uses this.* I knew I couldn't say them out loud. I didn't *want* to say them out loud. Coming from Annie, they had sounded right. She was a pastor's wife. She was supposed to be fluent in Bible and encouragement. Bernice and I didn't talk about our faith. Or lack of it. Because of little comments she'd made over the years, I sensed that Bernice had mixed feelings about God. She mentioned His name once in awhile, as if she believed He was there, but always with an edge in her tone. Like a person who mentions an estranged family member. I felt like I was letting Bernice down, but at the moment I couldn't offer anything. I was in a similar state of disbelief from that brief message we'd heard.

I opened the salon and listened patiently to Mindy's complaints about how much she had to do and how she was going to be way behind schedule now. I told her that Bernice wasn't feeling well but when I saw her horrified expression, I realized that was the stupidest thing I could have said. Everyone in Prichett knows Mindy is a first-class hypochondriac and now she was probably imagining any number of diseases that Bernice was going to pass on to her through her scissors.

To make matters worse, the bell over the door jingled and Jill Cabott came in, smiling delightedly when she saw me. Then she moved right into my personal space and hugged me.

"Elise, I saw your car parked outside. Bree told me about the pageant. You must be thrilled."

"Pageant?" Mindy hadn't heard yet and honestly, I actually *saw* her nose go out of joint.

"Elise is going to be in a beauty pageant," Jill said, more than happy to fill her in.

"A real pageant? Like Miss USA?"

"Well, she's a *Mrs.,* isn't she?" Jill said. She'd let go of me but was still hovering at the edge of my space. "This is called something else. Some number…"

"The Proverbs 31 Pageant." I sighed.

Bernice came in, looking like a rug that had been slung over a clothesline and left out in the rain. I wanted to save her from Mindy. And Jill Cabott. And every other appointment she had written in her book for the day.

"You look terrible," Mindy said nervously, ready to bolt.

"I'm fine." Bernice's smile was stretched so tight I was afraid it was going to fly off her face and ricochet around the room.

"Well, this is the most exciting thing that's happened to this town in a long time," Jill went on. "Imagine, someone from Prichett. In a pageant!"

Mindy allowed Bernice close enough to clip the cape around her neck but I could tell she was holding her breath. Her cheeks were tinged with pink and her eyes were bulging. She finally exhaled. "You'll need a special dress, won't you, Elise?"

I'm not going to be in the pageant! That did it. I was taking out a full-page ad in the newspaper to make the announcement once and for all. After I told Bree. For now, I had to play along.

"I suppose I would."

"My niece Greta designs clothes."

My eyes met Bernice's in the mirror. Greta was sixteen and dressed like a bag lady from Transylvania. Black baggy clothes, combat boots and enough leather accessories to get PETA's attention.

"I'm sure she could come up with something real special. It might help her career as a fashion designer, too. She has to design something to get a scholarship to some fancy college in New York."

"Sounds like a win-win situation to me," Jill said cheerfully. "Well, I've got to scoot. Just wanted to say congratulations, Elise."

The good-Jill ambassador swept out the door. I closed my eyes. Another cranky flash was upon me. When I opened them, Bernice was patiently listening to Mindy recite her to-do list. I started to wonder if I'd fallen through a time warp and the last hour hadn't really happened.

"Do you want me to stay for awhile?" I asked.

Bernice glanced at me. "Come back at noon."

A daughter. Did she look like Bernice? Did she have Bernice's strong cheekbones and pale-green eyes? How old was she? *Who was her father?*

I realized that some of questions Bernice could answer and some of them she would be asking, too.

"Thanks, Ellie."

The words reached me just as I opened the door.

We'll get through this, Bernice. Don't worry.

The warmth of the July sun that I'd basked in earlier now felt oppressive. We were in for, to borrow Sam's expression, a scorcher. In less than sixty seconds, my white cotton shirt melted to my skin and the back of my neck began to itch.

Now it was almost ten and I stood in front of Bernice's shop, undecided as to what direction to take. I'd been in such a hurry to get to Bernice's that I'd left my purse sitting by the door. I wasn't sure if it would pay to go back home and then drive back to town less than two hours later.

A car pulled alongside me and the window purred as it went down. "Excuse me, ma'am."

The car was a BMW—a perfect match for the couple who sat cradled in leather, staring at me. "Can you tell me where we can find a decent restaurant in town?"

Today's oxymoron is: Decent Restaurant.

"You passed it. Sally's Café." Sally's was your typical small-town diner. Black Formica tables. Vinyl booths unashamedly patched with duct tape. A long counter with wobbly stools that were guarded like family church pews by the retired farmers who claimed their places every morning.

I could see the woman, who was about my age, make a face. "Isn't there anything else?"

"You could drive to Munroe. It's about half an hour from here."

"I'm hungry now!" A plaintive voice wailed from the back seat. A boy about ten years old made his presence known as he practically crawled into the front seat to glare at me. As if it was *my* fault that Sally's was the only restaurant in Prichett.

"Sally's makes up lunch buckets," I said in a moment of inspiration.

"What's a lunch bucket?" He looked at me suspiciously, as though he thought I was about to explode with laughter and gasp, *"Got you! No such thing as a lunch bucket! Enjoy the half hour car ride to Munroe!"*

"Sally makes the lunches and puts them in plastic buckets so you can eat in the park." I secretly hoped that Sally was still doing that. It had been a remarkably creative move on Sally's part. Remarkably creative and a shrewd business maneuver. With no fast-food restaurants in Prichett and a small contingent of freed school children in the summer, Sally had come up with the concept of lunch buckets. Basically, she ordered colorful sand pails wholesale, filled them with the standard hamburger, greasy French fries and a cookie from the bakery. She raised the price two dollars and effectively divided two groups of natural enemies: the tobacco-chewing farmers who lined the counter at the café and the mothers who thought tobacco-chewing was a disgusting habit and didn't want their hamburger-crazed children exposed to it.

"I want a lunch bucket!" the boy wailed.

I took a step back. Now the mother was glaring at me.

"The park is right over there." I pointed.

"You mean those three trees across the street?" the woman asked sarcastically.

Actually, there were six. But I didn't hold the sarcasm against her. She had to travel with a whiney child in ninety-degree heat and manage not to sweat.

"Let's get a lunch bucket," the man said, injecting just the right dose of enthusiasm into his voice. The window began to scroll back up. "Thank you." He winked at me. It wasn't a flirty wink. I knew the difference. He reminded me a little of Sam. The calm in the midst of life's storms.

I suddenly needed my flower beds. Warm soil. Fragrant blossoms. No people in my personal space. I'd block out the sun with my umbrella-sized straw hat and lose myself in the garden. A prescription for sanity.

Then I heard it. An ominous tapping. Down the street, a teenage boy was on a ladder, changing the letters on the old theatre marquee that hung over the sidewalk. The theatre had closed when Bree was a baby, driven out of business by the one in Munroe that could show four different movies at the same time. But the marquee lived on like a medieval town crier, announcing every birth, anniversary and community happening. Over the years some of the alphabet had mysteriously disappeared, so a person had to be up on Prichett's own form of hieroglyphics to make sense of it.

He already had CONGR TUL TIONS running crookedly across the top. *Please tell me no.* Someone *must* have had a baby over the weekend. The message slowly came to life as I stood frozen on the sidewalk. ELISE PENN Y (the y slid to the right) PRO VERBS 3 W OM N

chapter 13

"Hey!"

I walked quickly up to the boy. He had red hair and an explosion of freckles across his face. It would be a safe assumption that he was a Frith. "Who told you to do that?"

"Do what?"

Definitely a Frith. "To put *that* on the sign."

"The mayor." He shrugged.

The mayor. The Prichett grapevine had been busy.

"I want you to take it down. *Right now.*"

He gaped at me as if I'd asked him to commit a murder right there on Prichett's Main Street. "I can't do that, Mrs. Penny."

"Listen…you're a Frith, right? Which one?"

"Austin."

"Austin, the fact is, I'm not going to be—"

"Elise!"

Just the person I needed. Candy Lane. *Mayor* Candy Lane. I'm not kidding. That's her name. She was the first woman ever voted in as mayor, but Candy didn't *look* like a mayor. Probably because her other job is working at the feed mill. I think the reason why she won the election was because people figured she'd run Prichett like she did the feed mill, with steely-eyed fairness and practicality. It didn't matter that she was short and square, with skin that looked like she used sandpaper on it instead of moisturizer. Or that she habitually wore corn-dust-streaked overalls and a backwards baseball cap. I wondered what the BMW couple would say if they met her. Maybe they already had. Candy zeroed in on unsuspecting tourists like a bomb-sniffing German shepherd. They ended up with an unscheduled tour of Prichett (fortunately that didn't take too long) and either a slice of lemon meringue pie from Sally's or a five-pound bag of bird seed. Take your pick.

"Hi, Candy. I was just asking Austin to take this down."

I knew how to deal with Candy. She was a straight-on kind of person. No point in beating around the bush.

"Not a chance." Candy grinned and in a very un-mayor-like way, she turned her head slightly and spat.

Austin's mouth fell open in awe.

"Could you just wait a few days?" I heard myself plead. *Dignity, Elise. Where is your dignity?* "I'm not sure…"

A horn honked. I looked over my shoulder and there was the Country Lane Veterinary Clinic's truck. Bree. The truck hitched in the street as it came alongside us and then roared away. But not before we heard Bree whoop. "Way to go, Mom!"

"Your daughter seems excited."

Now Austin was looking at Bree in awe, a wave of scarlet washing into his face and momentarily blotting out his freckles.

"She's the one who entered me in the pageant," I explained, trying desperately to come up with a plan B, C or D.

"I s'pose there'll be reporters and TV cameras coming around," Candy said.

"What? I don't think so. It's not like the Miss Universe Pageant or anything." I wondered if I could sneak back under the cover of night and take the letters down without Candy suspecting it was me.

"Still," Candy mused, "it'll get people's attention, won't it? We should have a parade…"

A parade?

The entire world suddenly shifted on its axis. I saw the gleam in Candy's eyes. She had finally found something that she thought would put Prichett on the map: me.

I took refuge in the park. Thankfully, the BMW couple and their son must have decided to take their lunch buckets to a park with more trees. I avoided the merry-go-round and instead chose one of the horse-shaped gliders. I think Bree had named this one Torch, because of its rusty-red color. There were three horses and she'd pick a new favorite each time we came to the park, but their names never changed. Torch, Trigger and…I felt a moment of panic when I couldn't remember the third one's name. Tonto. I breathed a sigh of relief. There were some memories that I didn't want to slip through the cracks of time. Like every one connected to Bree.

From where I was perched, I could see the yellow-and-white circus-style awning of the Cut and Curl. Bernice had a daughter but no memories of her growing up. I still couldn't believe she had a child. A daughter. I tried to imagine the circumstances that had forced Bernice to make such a heart-wrenching decision. I tried to imagine what it would be like not to have Bree in my life—even though motherhood had extracted my heart from my body, leaving it exposed and vulnerable but still beating.

"Hi."

Thinking about Bernice, I had somehow missed Bernice. She stood in front of me, arms crossed over her chest. I knew what she was trying to protect: her heart, extracted from her body, exposed and vulnerable but still beating.

"Is it noon?" I felt a moment of blind panic at having missed our meeting. I blamed the look in Candy's eyes after she sauntered off. Parade. *They'd have to chain me to the float…*

"It's only eleven-thirty." Bernice reached out and pushed on the nose of the horse next to me, setting it into motion. "I called the rest of my customers and canceled out for the rest of the day."

"Sit down."

"I don't think this relic will hold me."

"If it'll hold me, it'll hold you. That's Tonto, by the way."

"Bree named it?"

"Yup."

"That girl was born horse-crazy," Bernice said with a laugh, then the words turned on Bernice and attacked, bringing tears to her eyes. "How ironic is that, Ellie? I know everything about Bree and nothing about my own daughter except her age."

"How old is she?"

"Twenty-one this December twenty-fifth."

Christmas Day.

"You could know more about her," I ventured quietly. "And she must want to know you or she wouldn't have called."

"I gave her up. I don't deserve to know her now."

The strength in Bernice's words surprised me. It was as if she'd judged and sentenced herself and was rejecting a complete pardon. "That's silly," I blurted out. Because it was. "There must have been a reason—"

"If you call pride a reason," Bernice shot back at me. "She'd never forgive me if she found out why I gave her up for adoption. It wasn't because I was young and alone and knew she'd have a better life with two parents who loved her, Elise."

"Then why?" I whispered.

For a minute, I didn't think Bernice was going to answer me. Then, she sat on Tonto and rested her forehead on the bar that held him in place. "I didn't want to tell you this. I didn't ever want you to know what kind of person I am."

"I know what kind of person you are," I said, suddenly exasperated. "We've been friends for ten years, Bern."

"No." Bernice shook her head.

Those scars that I'd seen when I'd met Bernice weren't scars at all. They were festering wounds. And like the only witness at an accident scene, I was drawn in, feeling helpless and afraid of what I was going to see. And what I'd have to do. *God, I hate to be the kind of person who calls on You in a crisis, but I can't help it. We need You here. Bernice needs You. I need You.*

Bernice fixed her gaze on a point somewhere in the distance. "I grew up in California. After I graduated from cosmetology school, I got a job at a salon in Beverly Hills. The owner, Nell, was like your favorite grandma. She was sixty years old and losing her own hair, but she could work magic with anyone else's. It became kind of the *thing* for actresses to come in and have their hair done by Nell. I paid attention and pretty soon, I started to get my own clients. One of them worked at NewVision Productions and put in a good word for me. The next thing I knew, I was fixing the hair on some of the biggest names in Hollywood and their agents were calling me in the middle of the night to schedule emergency appointments. That's when I met Alexander Scott."

I tried not to look shocked. Alexander Scott's acting career had been buoyant for years. No doubt a combination of his rugged good looks and the fact he chose action-adventure films that audiences never tired of.

"Exactly. Alexander Scott. So there I was. Frizzy brown hair, big turquoise glasses and looking like a moose turned loose among a herd of gazelles," Bernice said, but she was smiling. "He asked me out to dinner."

Was Bernice telling me that Alexander Scott, *Alexander Scott,* was the father of her child?

"Elise, I felt like I was living a fairy tale for a few months, but then it started to sink in. He was just using me. I wasn't pretty and I knew it. I don't know what kind of game he was playing, but I knew I had to end it. If you haven't experienced Hollywood, you can't imagine the kind of surreal life it is. Alex was already making a name for himself and he was followed constantly by the press. He didn't take me out in public because he claimed he wanted to spare me that, but I knew it was because I wasn't leading-lady material. I just cut their hair. I fell in love with him but I decided to break it off before he did. And to tell you the truth, if by some miracle he really did care about me, I didn't want *that* kind of life. I wanted the white house. The picket fence. I wanted to be known only by a handful of people—the people that mattered to me—not the whole country. I wanted a *smaller* life."

Bernice paused and smiled and I could see affection in her

eyes. "I wanted to be you, Elise. You have everything I've ever wanted. You're beautiful, you have a husband who can't take his eyes off you, a wonderful daughter, cozy house, a front-porch swing. You even have the dog, for crying out loud. I wanted to hate you when we first met, but instead you became my best friend. Go figure."

She wanted my life. And I had wanted hers. I had the white house and the picket fence. I had the small town. And I had yearned for so much more.

chapter 14

"Did you ever tell Alex that you had a child?"

A part of me was still in denial. The story she was telling me sounded like the plot of a movie of the week. Or maybe Bernice was suddenly going to double over with laughter as a camera crew jumped out from behind the bushes and yelled, "Gotcha!"

"I left while he was on location in Texas. A week later, I found out I was pregnant. My parents wouldn't let me come home, not even for a little while. I was twenty-four and they said that since I was old enough to make that decision, then I was old enough to be responsible for it. I moved around a lot, looked up old friends and slept on their sofas until they got tired of me. By the time I was ready to have the…baby…I knew I couldn't provide for her. And I couldn't go back to Alex. He never tried to find me, never called to see if I was all right. That's when I knew it hadn't been real for him."

She hadn't told him. Alexander Scott, award-winning actor, had a child with Bernice Strum, owner of the Cut and Curl Beauty Salon in Prichett. I could see the anguish in Bernice's eyes. The guilt that hung over her like a cloud.

"Bernice, whatever happened between you and Alexander, you did what you thought was best for your daughter. You gave her *life*. Take a chance, call her."

"She'll ask me about her father." Bernice turned away. "What am I supposed to say? Your father is a well-known celebrity and if you pop up in his life, he's going to hate me for not telling him. Or he's going to think that I slept around and that she's someone else's child and he'll get a team of lawyers to fight it and—"

"Bernice." I interrupted her wild-eyed rambling. "One step at a time. We'll think about Alex later. Right now, think about your daughter. She wants to find out who you are."

"So she can tell me off for giving her up."

"Maybe."

Bernice glanced at me suspiciously, surprised that I had agreed with her.

"Can you handle that?"

Bernice squared her shoulders, looking as if she was about to face a firing squad—and thinking that she deserved it. "Yes."

"What do *you* want, Bernice?"

"I've always hoped…she'd find me."

"She did," I said simply. "So don't run away."

Pain flashed across Bernice's face.

An alarm went off in my head. "What haven't you told me?"

"He found me."

"Who found you?"

"Alex. A little over ten years ago. I was working in Chicago and he was filming there. One of the people I'd worked with was talking about me and he overheard them. It's not like Bernice is a common name, you know."

I drew a quiet breath. "So you ran away."

"I started over," Bernice corrected me. "Again."

"In Prichett."

"I grabbed a map, closed my eyes and put my finger on a dot. This was it. My small town."

I was surprised Prichett was even worthy of dot status, let alone that Bernice's finger had happened to land there.

"So, by accident or design, here I am. And I still don't have my white house and picket fence. Not that I deserve them."

There was that word again. *Deserve.* I knew there was nothing I could say that would breach the wall Bernice had built, each stone mortared with guilt. I was afraid that if I did say something, it would sound like the trite words in a ninety-nine-cent card.

"So, basically what you're saying is the rumors about you being Tammy Holowitz's cousin aren't true?" I ventured.

Bernice was silent and then she chuckled, her shoulders relaxing a little. "Imagine what would happen if *they* knew the truth."

"Maybe you'd be on the marquee instead of me."

"I saw that." Now Bernice's shoulders began to quiver. "Just promise me one thing, Ellie."

"What's that?"

"I get to do your hair and makeup."

We laughed together and somehow it must have opened one of the chambers Bernice had kept boarded up, because the sigh that swept out of her carried years of emotional debris. "If I call her, you'll be there, right?"

Another moment of sheer panic. In the past ten years, our friendship hadn't really stretched beyond chatty lunches, mutually beneficial gripe sessions and Sunday-afternoon porch-swinging-iced-tea-drinking silent conversations. Maybe that's why Annie Carpenter terrified me. I had a feeling she'd want to hold a microscope up to my soul whenever we got together and the irony was, I was more like Bernice. I showed people only what I wanted them to see. That Sam knew me and loved me anyway was nothing short of awe-inspiring. I wasn't willing to take the chance that someone else could, too.

"I'll be there," I promised.

"I think I need a nap."

As if connected, we both clambered awkwardly off our metal ponies. My leg muscles joined together in protest.

"You never got a chance to explain this whole pageant thing," Bernice said as we started to walk back to Main Street.

"I'm not quite sure how to explain it. Bree is ecstatic because she's the one who entered me in it. Sam is acting strange and won't talk about it. And Annie Carpenter can't wait to see how God uses it." I couldn't believe I'd added that last part.

Bernice frowned. "What do you mean, how God uses it?"

It was the first time Bernice had said the word *God* without sounding like the two of them were squaring off in separate corners of a boxing ring.

"He uses the things that happen in our lives."

"For what?"

For what? *You must know the answer to this, Elise. You've been going to church for years.* "For His purposes." I winced. That sounded lofty but cold. I tried again, wishing that I could say it in a way that would make sense. Like Annie with the remote control buttons in the women's Sunday School class.

The rewind button. Unfulfilled dreams. Bitterness. Regret. It was becoming clear that both Bernice and I had our thumbs on that button. "He wants us to love Him. And trust Him. The things He lets come into our lives either push us closer to Him...or further away, if we let them."

Bernice rolled her eyes. "Something else I messed up, then. Add it to the list, Bernice."

That wasn't supposed to happen. She was supposed to be

comforted by what I'd said. "You don't have to keep a list. That's what you give to God and He rips it up."

We had reached the sidewalk in front of the Cut and Curl and as we paused, I gave Bernice an awkward hug. She melted against me like candle wax. On Main Street. I patted her back, keeping an eye open for Prichett's informants. Blessedly, there was no one in sight but the mailman and he was terribly near-sighted.

"Just call me if you need anything," I said.

"I *hate* needing anything." Bernice muttered against my shoulder. "And El, I have no idea how to be a mother."

I suddenly remembered all the times that Bernice had watched Bree for me over the years—had patiently French-braided her hair with slender satin ribbons, spoiled her with ice cream cones and hung on every word she said. Taught her songs from Broadway musicals. I hadn't realized the significance until now. Bernice hadn't been able to raise her own daughter but she'd shared in the raising of mine.

For graduation, Bernice had given Bree a pair of red leather cowboy boots. She had even kept it a secret from me until Bree opened them. Sam and I had scraped up the money to buy her a computer for college, but I knew that someday, when that computer was outdated and sold for parts, those cowboy boots would still be in Bree's closet.

"I'll let you in on a secret, Bernice. Neither do I."

I went home, leaving Bernice to take a nap. Somehow I just knew that before she did, though, she'd play that message over and over until she could hear her daughter's voice in her dreams.

My emotions were heaped together like the compost pile in the backyard. I planned to sort through them by weeding my cottage garden. Guilt stabbed me when I realized it was well after noon and I hadn't accomplished a thing. No supper started. No laundry done. I realized I hadn't done any the day before, either.

Clancy loped toward me and by the expression on his face, I knew he'd been convinced he'd never see me again.

"Hey, Clancy." I dropped to my knees and let him barrel into me, squirming into my lap like a toy poodle instead of a chunky seventy-pound retriever. "What a morning! Did you have a morning like I did?"

His eyebrows said no, but that he was there for me.

I gathered together my gardening tools and stepped into my rubber clogs by the back door. The cottage garden had been something I'd worked on for three years now. An impressionist's canvas of bachelor buttons and cutting flowers, a tangle of climbing roses that I'd special-ordered from a catalog and clouds of delicate baby's breath. Over the years, the gardens had saved me from resenting Sam's long hours during the summer. I took as much pride in my flowers as Sam did in his tidy rows of tasseled corn and frilly soybean plants.

Weed. Weed. Weed. Flower. Weed. Flower.

A car door slammed and I wanted to crawl behind the baby's breath and hide. I grabbed Clancy's collar before he went to greet whoever was at my door. His eyebrows lifted, questioning my decision, but then he flopped down beside me and rested his chin on my knee. The doorbell rang twice.

There was nothing more than I wanted but to be alone but maybe it was Annie. Or Bernice.

"Elise, there you are!"

I froze in shock as Calvin Richardson ambled around the corner of the house. I was even more in shock when he grinned and lifted a camera and snapped my picture. Calvin was the editor/reporter/photographer for the weekly newspaper in Prichett. He always had a pipe clamped between his teeth and permeated the surrounding air with the smell of apple-flavored tobacco.

"What are you doing!" I squawked, leaping to my feet.

"Getting a picture of the Proverbs 3 woman," he said cheerfully. Another flash.

"That's Proverbs 31," I hissed, no doubt sounding *nothing* like the woman described in that particular chapter.

"Oh, I'll have to make a note of that." His pipe bobbed up and down thoughtfully. "Let's get one more. Maybe you could hold one of those roses between your teeth."

"Do I look like I want my picture taken with a rose between my teeth?"

Calvin was a bachelor, so I could tell by the confusion on

his face that he wasn't sure of the correct answer. Sam would have instinctively known and would be in the next county by now. Even Clancy, canine but male, obviously had it figured out. Belly skimming the grass, he slunk away and disappeared under the porch. "Um, no?"

"Exactly."

"I thought we should get a few shots of our beauty queen in her natural setting, that's all." Calvin put his hands slowly behind his back, as if I'd forget that he was holding a camera and he'd just taken two pictures of me up to my elbows in dirt with sweat dripping from every pore.

"My natural setting," I repeated. "This is my natural setting, is that what you're saying?"

"Um." Now Calvin began to sweat. "Yes?" He looked hopefully at me.

Oh, if only that camera had a leather *strap* attached to it...

I giggled. Where that giggle originated, I wasn't sure but it bubbled up like spring water and had a curious effect on Calvin. He began to take tiny backward steps. "I can come back some other time."

"No. Here. You're right, Calvin. This is Elise Penny's natural setting." I plucked a rose from the tangle behind me and bit down on the stem, lifting my arms above my head like a prima ballerina.

Calvin's pipe sagged between his teeth. He looked around, his eyes wide with panic. He cleared his throat. "I have a better idea, Elise. You come down to the newspaper tomorrow and I'll get a nice picture of you against the corkboard by my desk."

I collapsed on the ground after he left, the rose still between my teeth. Clancy dared to venture over, delighted to see me indulging in one of his favorite pastimes—rolling in the grass.

I was glad to know that the only ones who witnessed my temporary moment of insanity were Clancy and God.

chapter **15**

I closed my eyes and could see the headline and article now.

Elise Penny, Proverbs 31 woman, has officially dropped a stitch. Last seen rolling on the grass with a rose clamped between her teeth....

Something suddenly blocked out the sun. I opened my eyes and squinted.

"Mom?"

The something that had blocked out the sun was Buckshot, who didn't seem to think it was the least bit strange to see me stretched out on the grass in front of his hooves when I was usually upright, clothed and in my right mind. I couldn't say the same about Bree, though, who was sitting on his back, staring down at me in disbelief. And tucked behind her, his arms firmly around her waist, grinning like an idiot, was Riley Cabott.

Like giving birth, I was pretty sure I wasn't going to get out of this situation with any dignity intact. I sat up and casually plucked the rose out of my mouth, amazed that the words that came out sounded almost…normal. "I thought you were working today." Good. All is right with the world.

"Kevin gave me the rest of the day off." Bree's eyes ran a quick, veterinarian-in-training scan from the top of my head to the tips of my clogs. I wasn't sure what she was looking for. Maybe signs of rabies. Or distemper.

"Hi, Mrs. Penny."

I glanced at Riley again and rose to my feet. I was still at a slight disadvantage because Buckshot is almost sixteen hands high, but it made me feel a little better. At least my eyes were level with Riley's kneecap instead of examining the sole of his boot.

"Mom, this is Riley."

"I remember. We met the other day."

I hadn't realized that Buckshot could comfortably take two riders. I was used to seeing Bree on his back, flying down the edge of the fields that bordered our property. Buckshot had been a gift for her thirteenth birthday—a fifteen-hundred-pound package with a big red bow taped between his ears. They'd been a team ever since. I wondered if he minded sharing her with Riley Cabott.

There was something about Riley that set him apart

from the other boys who had been interested in Bree over the past few years. And that's why his interest in Bree worried me. In the first place, he wasn't a boy. He was a young man. He had a certain air of confidence and strength about him that I sensed would appeal to Bree. She was confident and strong-minded herself, and she'd never had time for local boys who put on an "aw-shucks" persona.

"We're going to take Buckshot to the pond to cool off, then Riley's going to help Dad this afternoon." Bree tucked her chin and flashed him a quicksilver smile. "And I'm going to make a pie."

Pie. The world slipped on its axis once again. If it tilted any more, I was going to slide right off and end up bobbing helplessly around in a bowl of stars.

"I knew you were my favorite cowgirl," Riley said.

I expected Bree to push him off Buckshot's back and send him sprawling into a rosebush. Instead, she laughed. Laughed as though he'd just given her the highest compliment a beautiful, talented, valedictorian pre-vet major could be given. *I* wanted to push him off Buckshot's back into the rosebush. Cowgirl, indeed!

"Mrs. Penny? I wanted to say congratulations. My mom told me about the pageant."

If Riley was hoping to score some points with the eccentric, rose-studded mother of his favorite cowgirl, he had played the wrong card. I opened my mouth to inform him and his mother and everyone else in Prichett once and for all that *I wasn't going to be in the pageant* but Bree jumped in.

"Mom won some titles when she was my age," she told him, exaggerating slightly. It had only been one title and definitely nothing to brag about, although I'd been willing to at the time. "But she had to give all that up because she got pregnant with me the first year she and dad were married. Now, she'll finally have her chance." A wink at me. "I'll be back in a little while to start the pie, Mom."

Clancy watched Buckshot saunter away and he whined. I nodded my permission for him to go with them, even though he'd come back soaking wet and smelling like gym socks marinated in algae. Distractedly, I replayed Bree's words in my mind.

Now she'll finally have her chance.

I wondered if Bree thought that *she* was the reason my life had taken a detour from the original path I'd set. There was a trunkload of irony in that, I realized. I'd put the blame squarely on my *mother* for moving us to Prichett and setting my life off course.

Her looks are going to take her places.

All she has to do is walk into a room and everyone notices her.

No doubt about it. She's going to make the boys turn red and the girls turn green.

I'd started hearing those kind of comments when I was ten. By the time I turned fifteen, I dreamed about being a model or an actress. Stylish clothes. Limousines.

And even when my mother sat me down at the end of my freshman year of high school and told me she'd taken a teaching position in Prichett and that we were moving, I clung stubbornly to those dreams.

"Why do we have to move? What's wrong with your job here?"

"There's nothing wrong with my job," my mother had said quietly. "I just feel like we need a change."

"I don't need a change! I love Chicago."

"You'll love Prichett, too. It's a beautiful little farming community. Like a postcard."

"A farming community." Immediately I discarded the word *beautiful* and shook the words *farming community* in her face like a dirty dishcloth. "Mom, just wait a few years until I graduate, then you can move anywhere you want to. Please?"

"I've already accepted the position."

"I'm not going. There's nothing in *Prichett* for me."

"You might consider the fact that there may be something in Prichett for *me*."

The truth was, I hadn't considered that. Didn't want to consider it. Mom was just Mom. She'd been widowed when I was two and had never dated. She poured her time and energy into her students and into me. And she may have been soft-spoken, but she was no pushover. Less than a month later, our little car was bulging with our possessions as it rattled along in the wake of the moving truck.

We didn't know anyone in Prichett. No shirttail relatives. No friends. Not that I wanted any. I was counting the days to graduation and I told everyone who cared to listen that Prichett was not home, it was just a wayside stop on the road to my future. Like a gas station.

My ongoing lament about Prichett became a source of conflict between me and my mother. I constantly compared our new life in Nowheresville to our old life in Chicago. For the most part, Mom listened with a patience that was probably born out of guilt for having uprooted me in the first place. But one evening she'd had enough. And that's when the truth came out.

She interrupted me mid-tirade and transformed from sympathetic mother to passionate teacher right before my very eyes. "Elise, I wanted you to see that there are things in this life with *substance*. If we had stayed in Chicago, you would have only become more shallow and self-centered. You would have stopped caring that all the attention you get is based on your looks instead of who you are on the inside. I could see it happening."

"You said we came here for *you!* Now you admit it, you wanted to take me away from the things that are important to me…" I sifted the words *shallow* and *self-centered* out of my anger and didn't give them the attention they deserved.

"Those things aren't important. And the fact that you can't see that means that I failed anyway."

"So does that mean we can move back to Chicago?"

"Oh, Elise."

All these years later, I still winced at the memory of Mom's shattered expression. I dropped to my knees to attack the weeds in the flower bed again. Even after that conversation, I hadn't changed my thinking. Prichett was simply the obstacle course I had to maneuver to obtain my freedom. Mom never viewed Prichett as an obstacle course. My secret hope that she'd get tired of small-town life never bore fruit. She'd never had any interests or hobbies when we lived in Chicago, but she joined the library foundation and the historical society and met with a group of teachers for coffee at Sally's every Saturday morning.

Prichett had brought out the best in my mother and the worst in me.

"Mom, are you all right?"

Bree suddenly careened around the side of the house and flopped to her knees beside me, panting.

"I'm fine."

"Fine?" she repeated. "You were lying in the grass with a rose in your mouth."

"I was just trying to get rid of Calvin Richardson."

"I'll bet it worked," Bree said and I could see she was still skeptical. "Do we have any apples?"

"There are some in a bowl in the kitchen."

"Enough for a pie?"

"Breanna Penny, the only time you come into contact with a pie crust is when you're eating it."

She grinned. "That's why I was hoping you'd help me."

"Is this to impress Riley?" I asked, although I was sure I already knew the answer to that.

"You're always complaining I don't show enough interest in cooking," Bree said innocently.

"Baking," I corrected. "Pies fall under the baking category."

"Whatever." Bree shrugged.

This was the daughter I knew and loved.

"I just thought Riley could maybe stay for supper tonight, since he's helping Dad."

I hesitated. I didn't want Riley staying for supper. I didn't want him helping Sam. Or riding double with Bree. Or eating homemade apple pie at my kitchen table. I didn't want to pretend to be polite to someone who called my daughter his favorite cowgirl.

"Mom, we're not going to elope after supper if that's what you're worried about."

"Very funny." Why would she even joke about something like that? Now I *was* worried. "Let me get cleaned up, then I'll help you bake a pie."

When Sam and Riley came in a few hours later, I suspected a conspiracy at work.

"Ellie, we didn't have much time to talk over the weekend," Sam murmured in my ear as he leaned over my shoulder to snitch an apple slice. His hair was still damp from the shower and I breathed in the scent of the Stetson cologne that Bree bought him every year at Christmas. "Let's go out for dinner tonight. Just the two of us."

I was tempted to remind him that he was the one who hadn't wanted to talk. But I didn't. He buried his face against my neck and kissed me, sending my pulse into a happy skip.

"But I have a roast in the oven." I'd stuck it in the oven while Bree sliced apples.

"The kids can eat it."

"We can't leave them alone." Riley and Bree. Alone. With a homemade apple pie that Bree would take credit for, even though all she'd done was peel the apples.

"El, Bree has been sneaking over to the Cabotts' all summer. I think it's a good thing that she finally brought him over here. It means she trusts us with this."

"Trusts us with *what?*" I pushed away from Sam. He wasn't making any sense.

"You have to let Bree make some decisions of her own, that's all I'm saying."

"Are you telling me that *Riley Cabott* is a decision she's made?" I whispered tersely.

"For now." Sam reached out and unlocked the fingers I'd clenched together at my side. "He's a nice boy, Ellie, give him a chance."

"Can I just give him a piece of pie?"

Sam's lips twitched. "I suppose that'll do for now."

chapter **16**

"So, I guess you're the local celebrity now."

"I don't want to do this, but I don't know how I can get out of it now." I sighed and twirled the straw around in my glass of iced tea. I'd been relieved when Sam had driven to a nice restaurant in Munroe instead of going to Sally's. "If it had been anyone but Bree who'd sent in the application, that would have been the end of it."

"The Proverbs 3 woman." Sam smiled in amusement, letting me know that he'd seen the marquee.

"Have you read that chapter?"

"El, how long has it been since you've read the inscription inside your wedding band?"

I knew there was an inscription on the gold band Sam had slipped on my finger the day we were married. He'd even quoted it softly to me the first morning we woke up together as husband and wife. For the life of me, I couldn't remember what it was.

I tugged my wedding band off and read the tiny flowing script.

An excellent wife, who can find? For her worth is far above jewels.

Maybe Sam should have just skipped down to the next part. "Charm is deceitful and beauty is vain…."

"How did you know I would be an excellent wife?" I asked in amazement. "I was eighteen years old, Sam. What did you see in me?"

"I guess the same thing you saw in me," Sam said. "My future."

That was true. As much as I hated Prichett and couldn't wait to shake its provincial dust off my shoes after graduation, I'd weighed that against a life apart from Sam. Even if it meant staying in Prichett, I couldn't leave him. I was so in love with him that if he'd told me he planned to irrigate the Sahara Desert, I would have gone with him with a shovel.

"You didn't seem too thrilled about the pageant," I offered slowly, reluctant to bring it up but needing to know the source of the remark he'd made in the kitchen that day.

But Sam didn't open up like I'd hoped he would. Instead, he looked away from me, as if he wanted to hide another drop of emotion that might accidentally leak out. That scared me. Bernice had swept years of guilt and regret into the bare corners of her heart so no one would see them, covering them until a phone call had lifted up the edge and exposed everything.

Was Sam hiding things from me, too? I didn't want there to be any shadows—nothing that would push silences and secrets between us. I knew couples that it had happened to. Those were the ones who ended up so far apart that it seemed the natural thing to begin to walk away in the opposite direction. Alone.

The waitress, a young woman with a bored expression and a plastic name badge that told us her name was Gwen, deposited our plates in front of us. "Anything else?"

"Coffee would be good." Sam smiled at her and she came to life. A spark flickered in her eyes and her shoulders rose out of their slump. Sam had that effect on people. If there was a Proverbs 31 man, Sam would win hands down.

"Coming right up."

She hurried toward the row of coffeemakers next to the kitchen. From neutral to drive. Incredible.

"It's not about the pageant, El," Sam said, picking up the thread of our conversation. There was one weighted moment between us. "Bree is having second thoughts about going to Madison."

If Sam had suddenly produced a two-by-four and smashed the cheap centerpiece on the table it would have had less of an impact on me. *"What!"*

Sam grabbed my hand and looked me right in the eyes. "I just said she's having second thoughts. She's young. She isn't sure what she wants to do."

"Bree has wanted to be a veterinarian since she was twelve," I said, aware that there were people all around us and keeping my voice low to match Sam's. "The only change in the equation that I see is Riley Cabott."

This was a nightmare. *Another* nightmare. *God, You promised not to give us more than we can handle. Well, I'm getting close to capacity here.*

Gwen returned with the coffeepot and a smile on her face that clearly said Sam was her hero. "Here you go."

"You should pour a cup for yourself," Sam told her. "You've probably been on your feet all day."

Gwen nodded vigorously and I half expected her to pull up a chair and join us at our table. "If you need anything else, just holler."

After she left, Sam eased his grip on my hand but didn't let go. "Bree loves the farm. She's always loved the farm."

"What difference does that make?" I asked. "She can be a veterinarian and still love the farm."

I saw the answer on Sam's face.

"She wants to *farm?*"

"She's not sure."

"Well, obviously she talked to you about this," I said, struggling against the hurt that came from knowing Bree had gone to Sam instead of both of us. Instead of *me*. "What did you tell her to do?"

"I told her to pray about it."

"She doesn't need to pray about it! It's pretty obvious that God expects her to head in the direction where her abilities are. She loves animals, she has a four-point grade average and…she's *special*. There is a whole world out there that needs Breanna Penny and what she has to give."

"And you think Breanna Penny would be wasted in Prichett."

"Of course she would—"

"And you wouldn't want her to make the same mistake you did and stay."

Not only did I realize at that moment that Sam and I were wading into a full-blown-are-you-ready-here-goes-the-bell *fight,* I realized that it wasn't going to be a fair one. "Sam, that's totally different."

"Is it?"

Was it? Of course it was. I didn't look at Sam as a mistake. "Bree is smart…"

"And obviously anyone with the IQ of an earthworm can run a farm. Intelligence isn't a prerequisite."

"You're twisting my words around," I said, wondering who had replaced my beloved Sam with *this* man. "Don't you want *more* for Bree?"

"More than what?" Sam asked. "That's where we part company, I suppose. I don't want to dream Bree's dreams for

her. That's not my job. God has a plan for her life and I sure
don't want to get in the way. You blamed your mom for
years because she dragged you to Prichett and ruined your
plans for your future, El. A part of you probably still wishes
that you had left when you had the chance."

"That's not true." Tears stung my eyes and I blinked
them away.

"Not everyone thinks that Prichett is the end of the
world," Sam continued. "Some people would love to live in
a place where people say hello to them on the street and take
care of them when they're in trouble."

I wanted a smaller life. That's what Bernice had said. She
had deliberately chosen the small town instead of the glam-
orous life that I'd spent hours daydreaming about when I
was a teenager. But even in that small town, she hadn't let
people take care of her. Not even me. She'd kept her hurts
a secret and hadn't let light or air get to them and aid in the
healing process. What was it about me that the people I was
closest to couldn't confide in me? Not my best friend. Not
my daughter…and, it became clear, not even Sam. Not if
he'd thought all these years that a part of me regretted marrying him.

But this was Bree we were talking about, not me. Maybe
she just had cold feet at the thought of leaving home. Most
kids probably felt that way. Once she was settled in, she'd be
glad she left. She'd meet people, get involved in some activities. I couldn't imagine her being content to work alongside Sam on the farm for the rest of her life.

"You work long, hard hours and it's already taking a toll on your health. Every year you're at the mercy of the weather. Is that what you want for Bree? Really?"

"She hasn't made up her mind yet," Sam said. "She just wants to think things through a little more. Bree knows what farming is about. She doesn't look at it the way you do, Elise. She never has. You tried your best to keep her from being interested in it, but you may as well have tried to stop the sun from coming up. She doesn't want you to be upset and she doesn't want you to blame Riley."

"That's what this whole dinner was about, wasn't it?" I asked. "You were supposed to take me out and tell me all this."

After a moment, Sam nodded.

"Why couldn't Bree just tell me herself?"

"Why?" Sam actually laughed at the question. "You've had your hand on Bree's elbow since she was born, directing her here, directing her there. She knew exactly how you'd take this news."

Oddly enough, I realized we were still holding hands. Through this entire mess, through Sam's bitterness and my supercharged atomic emotions, we hadn't let go of each other.

"El, it's time to take your hand off her elbow and let her figure out her next step."

"Everyone will think…" I pulled back the words even as they tried to rush out.

"Everyone will think what?" Sam frowned, trying to draw them out of me. "No one will think anything."

"That's not true and you know it. It's been that way for years. Those people wait for you to *fail*. They'll think that Bree is scared to go out into the real world. Just like this pageant. Everyone acts so excited and all the while they're secretly hoping that I trip down the stairs in my high heels."

Now Sam was staring at me with a who-are-you expression on his face.

"I can't believe after all these years you really think that," Sam said quietly, pushing his plate away. "Not that it should matter what people think, but everyone in Prichett loves Bree. No matter what she does with her life, whether she's a waitress at Sally's or the president of a bank, they're going to love her. And you know something, Elise? I can't believe that you've lived most of your life around here and you somehow missed that. You belong to them. They knew that the day we got married but I guess the difference is, they've never belonged to you."

I couldn't argue with him on that. He was right. And I hadn't wanted them to.

chapter **17**

The house was quiet when I woke up the next morning. I hadn't even felt Sam get out of bed at five. Or heard Bree humming in the shower before she left for work. I closed my eyes and pulled the quilt back over my head, wondering if this was what depression felt like. A stubborn resistance to engage in another day.

"Elise?"

It couldn't be. Annie Carpenter's cheerful voice floated up the stairs. "Sam told me to come on in. I brought cinnamon rolls."

I sat up and stared at the clock. Nine. I never slept until nine. Not even when I was sick with a hundred-and-three temperature and had spent half the night sitting on the tile floor of the bathroom.

"I'll be right down."

Okay, God. I'm engaging. All right already. I decided that Annie Carpenter must be on God's active reserve. When He needed her, she was there—with a smile on her face and a plate of cinnamon rolls in her hand.

In record time, I pulled on a T-shirt and a denim jumper and twisted my hair into a knot. When my foot hit the first step, I could smell cinnamon and frosting and strong coffee.

Annie was pirouetting around the kitchen, looking for something. "It's a beautiful day. Not too hot. There's more of a breeze out here than in town, though."

There were three plates on the table and I wondered if Sam was planning to join us. Or maybe Bree.

"There's a woman on your porch," Annie said, as if I'd wondered it out loud. But I was sure I hadn't. Had I? I didn't trust myself anymore. After all, I'd been sure my daughter was going to be a veterinarian.

"A woman?" I hurried to the front door and looked through the screen.

Bernice.

I cast a panicked glance over my shoulder at Annie, who was filling coffee cups with a serene smile on her face. And then back to Bernice, who was sitting on the porch swing, looking anything but serene.

What was I going to do with *both* of them? I hadn't wanted to get out of bed and now I was hosting an impromptu gathering on my front porch.

"Bernice." I eased the door open and poked my head out. "Are you all right?"

She pushed out with her feet and sent the swing into motion. "The coffee smells good."

"Did you close the salon again?"

"Here we go," Annie sang out behind me. She'd found a painted tray that I kept on top of the microwave but never used. As if she'd been practicing for years, she held the tray high on one hand and eased around me.

And headed straight for Bernice.

"I'm Annie Carpenter." She set the tray down on the wicker table and handed Bernice a cup.

"Bernice Strum."

"The Cut and Curl." Annie slid a cinnamon roll the size of a bicycle tire onto a plate and gave it to Bernice.

Bernice still had that shell-shocked look on her face. I'm not sure what had put it there. Either Annie feeding her like a protective mama sparrow or the fallout from the phone call she'd gotten yesterday. I tried to ease in between them. No such luck. Annie handed me a cup of coffee and a plate that barely contained the gargantuan cinnamon roll. The edges began to wilt over the sides and white icing dripped between my fingers.

"I'm practicing," Annie announced. "The rolls. Every month I try something new and keep working at it until I get it right. What do you think?"

While Annie waited, Bernice took a bite. So did I.

"Mmmm."

"Gooumphhd."

"I won't let the dough rise so high next time," Annie said as she perched on the railing. "I could only fit six in the pan instead of twelve."

Somehow, I was going to have to get rid of Annie and keep Bernice. But how?

"I didn't call her yet."

The words came slowly, drawn from Bernice's soul like an empty cup tied to a fraying rope and hauled out of a dry well.

Annie looked at Bernice, then at me. She put her plate down. *Now she'll leave,* I thought in relief. *She can see that Bernice is upset. That she needs to talk to me.*

"I got a call yesterday from the daughter I gave up for adoption twenty years ago," Bernice told Annie, in the same tone of voice she might have said, "nice weather we're having."

Annie stood up and I expected her to beat a safe retreat to her car. She slid into the swing right next to Bernice.

Oh, please, don't start reciting Scripture verses, I pleaded silently. *You don't know Bernice.*

"I would give anything to get a phone call like that some day," Annie said simply.

I sagged against the porch railing and coffee sloshed over the side of my cup. Annie had to be making it up. Was this allowed in some sort of mysterious, pastor's wife handbook? To make up stories so you can get people to spill their guts?

"My mom kicked me out of the house when I was fifteen, and I'd found out I was pregnant. I stayed in a home for unwed mothers and then gave him up for adoption." Annie tucked her cheek against Bernice's shoulder. "I pray that someday he'll find me. That I'll get that phone call."

Annie Carpenter. Fresh-faced youth pastor's wife. Eyes as innocent as a toddler's. If I'd had to pick Annie's past from a multiple choice, it would have been the one that said something like: stable, loving home. Attended church from the womb. Christian school. Christian college. White wedding dress.

"Aren't you the pastor's wife?" Bernice asked, confused.

"Youth pastor." Annie nodded. "You know what, Bernice? We all meet Jesus in a different place. Some of us meet Him sitting on our mother's lap. Some of us meet Him in church. And some of us meet Him while we've got our head in a Dumpster."

"I think I've been ducking around corners, trying *not* to meet Him," Bernice said.

"That's just silly," Annie said, although there wasn't any condemnation in her tone. Just the opposite. "He loves you with an everlasting love."

An everlasting love. Coming from anyone else, it might have sounded cheesy. From Annie, it sounded like…truth.

"Elise told me that we either let things push us away from God or into His arms," Bernice said.

I remembered saying that, but I sure hadn't thought Bernice would.

"Elise is a wise woman," Annie said, sounding so certain that I almost believed her. "He loves you, whether you love Him back or not. Because He can't *not* love you. And you can trust Him with your heart and your secrets and your dreams. I know, because the day I trusted Him with mine, He made me new. I was wearing rags and He gave me His robe to wear instead."

I'd heard a lot of sermons about God's love over the years, but never on my front porch. And never delivered by a messenger quite like Annie. Bernice had a look on her face that reminded me of Clancy when I got home from the grocery store and unpacked a box of dog biscuits. Hope.

I don't think I know You like Annie does, Lord. I don't even think I know how.

"I'm going to call her," Bernice said. "Will you be there when I do? Both of you?"

Somehow, I knew that wasn't the decision Bernice had made when she'd camped on my porch swing. Annie had changed her mind.

You sent Annie here this morning, didn't You, God? For Bernice.

I felt a stab of envy. Servant envy. When I'd seen Bernice on the porch swing, I had plotted to get rid of Annie, almost accidentally sabotaging God's plan in the process. Some Proverbs 31 woman I was turning out to be. Maybe I should send Annie in my place. It had taken Bernice ten years to tell me she had a daughter. She'd known Annie Carpenter less than ten minutes.

"I still don't know what to say if she asks me about her dad." Bernice scraped at the nail polish on her thumb. The rest of her fingertips were already bare. She'd told me once that she used to smoke but she'd discovered a hundred other creative cancer-free ways to deal with stress. It looked like she'd stumbled upon another one.

Annie looked at me.

"Alexander Scott," I said baldly, hoping Bernice didn't mind. After all, she's the one who brought it up in the first place.

Bernice groaned.

Annie laughed. "Who said small town life is dull?"

I think that would have been me.

"I'm ready," Bernice said.

"You're going to call her now? From here?" The cup in my hand began to wobble.

"Before I lose my nerve."

"Let's pray first," Annie said.

The way she said it, the words came out as easy as a Lamaze coach saying, "breathe." She didn't know that I preferred silent prayer. And between just the two of us—me and God. But I didn't want to wade into this alone. I slid a glance to Bernice, expecting to see her chin sagging to the floor at the word *prayer*. Her eyes were closed. She had an expectant look on her face.

When Annie put out her hand, I didn't hesitate to take it. We formed a small circle right there by the swing, surrounded by sunshine and the smell of cinnamon. I struggled to form an articulate prayer in my head and began to panic when nothing profound came to mind. In fact, I was so engrossed in receiving an A on this prayer pop-quiz that I totally missed what Annie had said.

And suddenly, there was silence. It was my turn. I shut off my mind and opened up the valve to my heart, hoping there was something there. The strange thing was, when I changed channels, it suddenly didn't matter if it made sense. Or sounded like a coffee-table devotion. I was pretty certain it *wouldn't*. "Help us to be women who trust You with everything. Help us smile at the future."

There it was. Two short sentences. But I meant every word. I expected that Annie would say a final amen, but instead, Bernice's ragged sigh was our benediction.

"I'm sorry," Bernice whispered.

I peeked at her and saw the tears tracking her cheeks. She wasn't talking to me. Or to Annie. And I knew that Bernice had just met Jesus on my front porch.

I paced a circle around the kitchen table as Bernice dialed the phone. Annie was washing the breakfast dishes, up to her elbows in airy white suds. She'd used about a half cup of dish soap and I didn't stop her. Something told me she liked a lot of bubbles.

"Hello." Bernice was talking to someone.

I paused in my pacing and shot a look at Annie. She had her eyes closed.

"This is Bernice Strum. Is this the person who called me on Monday?"

I had an overwhelming urge to run to the barn and pick up the other phone. There was nothing more frustrating than trying to fill in the blanks of a one-sided conversation.

"Heather." Bernice looked at me and mouthed the word again. *Heather.* Her daughter had a name.

An hour ticked by as Bernice learned about her daughter. Finally, I glanced at the clock and reluctantly turned my attention to the morning chores I had neglected.

"I've got to sneak out and get the eggs or they're going to be frying in their shells," I whispered to Annie.

"I'll come with you."

We were almost to the chicken coop when I finally voiced the question that had been nagging me. "Did you really have a baby when you were fifteen?"

Annie's eyes widened and then she chuckled. "I wouldn't make something like that up."

"I just can't picture it." I unhooked the wicker basket from the wall.

"Oh, can I carry that?" Annie's excitement brought her up on her toes. I handed her the basket.

"It's a testimony to Him that I'm not all marked up from my past, like a window full of messy fingerprints. I definitely had my head in the Dumpster, searching for scraps, when I met Him. When did you meet Him, Elise?"

Just now on my front porch, I thought. *Like Bernice.* Maybe it was a little different. Bernice had been playing duck-and-dodge with God for years, too guilt-stricken to step out and say hello. For me, it was a wave-across-the-street kind of relationship. The difference between recognizing someone and knowing how their arms feel around you. Knowing that they have a dimple in their cheek that comes out when they smile or a mole between their shoulder blades.

Annie knew something that I was just beginning to figure out. God wasn't an absentee father—the kind who is always away on business and occasionally breezes in to ruffle your hair and ask you how you're doing in school. He was right there with me. Loving me. I'd known it in my head, but my heart was finally starting to catch up.

But I couldn't tell Annie the truth. Not yet. I was just coming to grips with it myself. "Oh, you know, a while ago." *An hour?*

"I'll tell you a secret, Elise, but you can't tell anyone yet." Annie broke into a waltz around the chicken coop, using the basket as her dance partner. "I'm pregnant."

chapter **18**

"Annie, that's great! Is Stephen excited?"

"He's thrilled. We were hoping to start a family right away but it's been harder than we thought." Her eyebrows skated together over the bridge of her nose. "The first time was the first time. You know what I mean?"

I knew what she meant, and I tried to imagine Annie at fifteen, her boyish frame filled out with baby. It still didn't seem possible. I wondered if Sam knew. He'd been on the committee that had hired Stephen Carpenter. Did they know about Annie's past? Would it have mattered?

"It's like a second chance. Oh, look. Here's an egg. Oops!"

Hazel, my best layer, ruffled her feathers until she doubled in size and Annie shrunk back. Believe it or not, as harmless as chickens look, they can sport an attitude.

"Just put your hand in the box and she'll move out of the way."

"I pray for my son every day," Annie said. "I know he's not my son anymore, but I'll always think of him that way."

We collected the rest of the eggs in silence and Annie handed me the basket. "You better carry this now. I'm sort of a klutz."

Bernice was sitting on the porch swing again, waiting for us. Her feet were pulled up and her head was buried in her knees. The swing jerked back and forth, in tune with the sobs that shook through her.

"Bern." I tried to peel her face away from her knees. "What happened?"

"Cosm...ology."

"Cosmic biology." Annie repeated.

What on earth did that mean?

"Cosmet...ogy."

"Comet meteorology?" Annie patted Bernice's knee.

"I think she said cosmetology," I whispered.

"Cosmetology." Bernice lifted her head, her eyes filled with tears and wonder. "What are the chances of that?"

"God," Annie said with a smile and a shake of her head, as if that explained it all.

And the weird thing was, it did.

It was almost lunchtime and my routine continued to careen down an unknown path. My days were generally choreographed like a synchronized swimmer and I wasn't used to unexpected company in my kitchen, my gardens or my chicken coop. Annie and I needed to hear all about Bernice's daughter, though, and I wasn't about to sow some well-placed hints that I needed to "get things done."

I sent Annie to the vegetable garden on a mission to find something for lunch. Bernice still sat on the porch swing, but now the swing went back and forth with a gentle, upbeat glide as if it sensed Bernice's mood. I wondered what would happen if *I* sat on it. It would probably crash through the floor of the porch and end up in the spidery part of the basement.

I was anxious to hear what Bernice and Heather had said to each other but Bernice seemed content in the silence. Every Christmas, I took out the box of hand-blown glass ornaments my mother had given me and sorted through them, one by one. I'd hold them up and study them, turning them this way and that to see how the light would bounce off the different colors. Somehow I knew that's what Bernice was doing with every word Heather had said.

Annie swept past us and went into the house, emerging moments later with our lunch.

"I found a place to sit."

Obediently, we followed her to the willow tree in the backyard and sat down in its shade while Annie served us bowlfuls of sun-warmed spinach and cucumbers drizzled with lemon juice. Instead of my everyday flatware, she'd pulled the tiny silver forks out of the wooden holder on the wall. Bree called them the "vacation forks." They were a shiny reminder that occasionally a Penny had left the farm and taken a token trip somewhere. My fork had a tiny replica of Mount Rushmore on it.

"Heather lives in an apartment with her best friend," Bernice finally said, pausing slightly over the name as if savoring the sound of it. "She is going to cosmetology school in the fall. She took some time off to travel after high school. She went to Europe. I can't imagine that's safe. What do you think *they* were thinking when they let her do that?"

"It's a good thing for kids to see the world," I said in Heather's defense. And maybe my own.

"She's a city girl," Bernice said. "She was raised in a suburb of St. Paul. Her dad is a pediatrician and her mom is...her mom stays home. Does a lot of charity work, Heather said. They didn't mind that she found me and, um, she wants to meet me."

The last part of Bernice's sentence somersaulted over itself.

"Are you going to?"

"I think I'd rather take things slowly." Bernice looked away from me. From my question. "For now we'll just talk on the phone. Send some e-mails back and forth."

"Don't be afraid, Bernice," Annie said.

"I'm not afraid!" Bernice scowled at Annie. Just as I was about to play peacemaker, "More salad, anyone?" she gave in. "I'm terrified, okay?"

"It's okay to be terrified. Because now you've got someone to run to. He's your strong tower."

"Really?" Bernice looked hopeful but skeptical, as if she suspected that Jesus had stayed on the front porch swing instead of moving to the willow tree with her.

Annie clapped her hands together in her lap. "This is going to be fun!"

They stayed until the middle of the afternoon and when they left, there was a gaping hole in my day. I didn't have holes in my day. Anything that remotely resembled a hole was filled with pruning and snipping and weeding and admiring. I stared at my flower beds and absently patted Clancy on the head. With Bernice and Annie gone, all that stretched in front of me were my own problems. I decided I liked tackling other people's problems better.

I know that the Bible says that you aren't supposed to let the sun go down on your anger, but it had been so tightly curled in my hand when I flopped into bed the night before that I couldn't shake it free. Not that I'd been completely willing. I had to have something to hang on to and that seemed as good as anything.

Now you've got someone to run to.

It wasn't a familiar or comfortable feeling to run to God. I felt more like a child who shimmies shyly up to her father and tugs on his pant leg for attention.

"Mrs. Penny?"

I turned around and saw Riley Cabott standing several yards away. He was wearing blue jeans, a gray T-shirt and a

cowboy hat that shaded half his face. I hadn't seen him or
Bree when Sam and I had gotten home last night. The only
evidence that they'd been there at all was a half-eaten apple
pie and a sticky pool of melted ice cream by the sink. That
had been fine with me. Sam and I were barely speaking but
there was an avalanche of words building inside me that
would probably have been unleashed on Riley Cabott's unsuspecting head if I'd found him in my kitchen. And now
here he was.

The anger I felt when I looked at him surprised me. No
matter how much Bree denied it, I blamed him that Bree
was rethinking her decision to go to college.

"Bree is working today," I said tightly, keeping the words
behind a wall of self-control even as they hammered to be
released.

"I know." Riley pulled his hat off and looked me right in
the eye. "I came to talk to you."

Lord, I can't do this. Not right now.

"Riley, I don't think—"

"Just for a minute."

Good manners prevailed. My mom would have been
proud. I didn't answer but turned and headed toward the
porch. Clancy, ever sensitive to the downtrodden, waited for
Riley and fell into step with him. The swing was waiting
patiently.

"Sit down." I let those two words out and clamped my
lips down before any more escaped.

He didn't, but I didn't hold it against him. I wouldn't have, either. He slapped his cowboy hat gently against his thigh and sent a puff of dust into the air.

"I don't want you to think that it's because of me that Breanna is having second thoughts about college."

He'd read my mind.

"She knows I think she should go to Madison."

"I guess it doesn't matter what either of us think then, does it?" I said.

"She loves the farm. Buckshot."

And she thinks she loves you.

"Bree has wanted to be a veterinarian for years," I pointed out. "I don't think that kind of dream can change overnight."

Yours did. I didn't want to acknowledge that traitorous thought at the moment. My mom had loved Sam from the day she'd met him. She hadn't questioned my abrupt departure from my plans to go back to Chicago and become a model—to slide into fame and fortune as easily as I'd slide into a pair of expensive shoes. That was different, I argued silently with my rebellious thoughts. *Bree* is different. She's brilliant. To stay in Prichett would be a *waste.* That was the barrier that Sam and I hadn't been able to tear down between us at dinner the night before.

"She and I got in a big fight last night after you left," Riley said. "I'd be surprised if she doesn't hang up on me when I call her tonight."

"Maybe you should give her some time to cool off then," I suggested. "If you care about Bree, the best thing to do would be to give her some time to think. She's never had a serious boyfriend before. It could be that her feelings for you are clouding her decision, whether you think they are or not."

He studied me as if he knew right where I was headed with that. What if my mom had said that to Sam? I winced. At least Sam had had some stability. His parents couldn't wait for him to take over the farm. Riley milked cows and spent his weekends playing cowboy at team-penning events.

"All right. If you think that's what I need to do." He pushed his hat back onto his head, pivoted and down the steps he went.

I blinked. *All right?* That was it? I'd expected him to dig his cowboy boots stubbornly into the dirt. The fact that he didn't tempted me to call him back. But I didn't. His tires churned up miniature dust clouds as the truck rolled down the driveway.

One thought pushed its way into my head. I still hadn't talked to Bree. She knew I was against her changing her plans for college. And now I'd just chased her boyfriend away. Somehow, I had a hunch our next conversation wasn't going to be a cozy one, huddled together on my bed, sharing a bag of M&M's.

"What's for supper, Clance? Pork chops?"

He beat his tail against the porch in approval.

"We'll just have to start supper now, won't we?"

I gave up the idea of working in my flower beds and went inside. The phone rang and I sighed.

"Hello. Penny residence."

"Good afternoon, Elise, this is—"

"Hi, Shelby."

I was beginning to recognize Shelby Hannah's voice. I wondered what she looked like. With that serious "young professional" tone, I imagined someone in a navy-blue skirt and blazer with one hand always on her Palm Pilot.

Just when I started to forget the reality of the pageant Bree had gotten me into, there it was, hanging over my head like the little black rain cloud in a *Winnie the Pooh* story.

"I just wanted to remind you about your journal. You have to have it to me two weeks before the preliminaries. That means the deadline is coming up fast. And I'll need to have a summary of your speech, too."

"Journal?" I repeated faintly.

"Elise, have you read through your packet?" Shelby's voice took on the schoolteacher edge again.

"I skimmed it."

I heard a funny cough on Shelby's end. "All right," she said briskly after a moment. "We want everyone to keep a journal that records their daily activities. Nothing too fancy, just a page or two for each day. This gives the judges an idea what you are involved in, what your life is like. What your interests are. Photos are good, too. You mentioned that you like to garden. A good journal entry would mention time you spent gardening and a picture of what you grow."

"Flowers," I murmured.

"Perfect." A gold star from Miss Hannah. "I'm sure you have your platform by now," she went on. "So just e-mail the summary of your speech to me and we're all set."

"Will an envelope and stamps work?" I pulled a frozen block of pork chops out of the freezer.

"What do you mean?"

"No computer. No e-mail."

"Mail the old-fashioned way. Not a problem," Shelby said with the barest hint of a chuckle. "I can't wait to meet you, Elise."

I hung up the phone and pressed the package of pork chops against my forehead, which suddenly felt hot. I had to keep a journal. A month ago, that would have been easy. Nice neat entries of my well-mapped-out days. Baking. Gardening. Long walks for exercise. Planned-out meals. I looked at the clock and saw it was almost four. Thank goodness for microwaves with a defrost setting. I hoped I could figure out how to program it.

It was a good thing that Shelby hadn't needed the journal entries for the week before. Let's see. First gray hair. Brilliant, formerly *obedient* daughter decides not to go to college, becomes Riley Cabott's favorite cowgirl instead. Have picture taken by small-town paparazzi, drenched in sweat and chewing on a rose. Best friend receives phone call from child she gave up for adoption twenty years ago and meets Jesus on my front porch. First major argument with husband in, mmm, *many* years…

Definitely Proverbs 31 woman stuff.

Yes, indeed.

chapter **19**

I threw the pork chops in a roasting pan with some fresh sage and half a bottle of cooking wine that I'd found in the pantry, then spent the next hour straightening the house. Shifting pillows. Dusting. Stacking magazines next to the sofa. And all the while, the acid in my stomach was bubbling like a spring. I lined the boots up in the hallway. Tugged at a wrinkle in the drapes. Then I realized what I was doing.

I was preparing for a storm. Just like Sam has done a thousand times when he knows bad weather is on the way. Check the fences. Move equipment inside. Close windows. Tighten anything that's loose. Protect anything that might rust. We've had some impressive thunderstorms in the county and over the years, even I've learned to guess their intent by the tint of color in the sky and the way the wind feels on my skin. But this storm wasn't outside. This storm was coming in the shape of my eighteen-year-old daughter.

"What happens happens," Sam would say when he came inside, stripping off his rain-soaked coat. "But at least I did my part."

What was my part when it came to Bree? That's what I wasn't sure of. If she was simply suffering from cold feet, shouldn't I make her stick with her plans? She'd find out after the first week that college wasn't as bad as she'd imagined. As friendly and outgoing as Bree was, I knew she would love the opportunity to make new friends, get involved in clubs. She was a natural leader.

She loves the farm.

Sam's words from dinner the night before came back to me. It seemed like a hundred years had passed since that conversation instead of twenty-four hours. No matter how much I wanted to support Bree, I didn't think I could support a decision that would keep her on the farm.

Don't ask me to, Lord. I can't do it. You've given her so much… I know You don't expect her to throw it all away.

The front door opened. Bree or Sam? I listened for the movements in the hallway. Bree's were quick and light, Sam's always slow and measured.

I sank onto the love seat in the living room.

"Mom?"

I exhaled softly but it didn't help. There was still a brick sitting on my chest. "I'm in here."

Bree stepped around the corner. Her shirt was spattered with something that looked like canned peas. I took one look at her face and knew something terrible had happened.

"What's wrong?"

Bree walked across the room on legs as wobbly as a newborn colt's and dropped down beside me. I didn't even scold her about the fact that she hadn't taken her boots off, or that whatever was all over her clothes was now smeared on the upholstery. Had she talked to Riley? Had he broken up with her because of me?

"One of the Cabotts' horses had a twisted bowel." Bree's eyes filled with tears and her fists curled and pounded against the cushion. "Kevin had to put her down."

"I'm sorry," I whispered.

"I just hate that part of it, Mom," Bree groaned. "I just don't think…"

I can do it. Silently, I finished the sentence for her. "Think of all the good that Kevin does," I said, trying to be encouraging. "All the animals he's saved. He even got Buckshot through that bout of colic last fall."

Bree stared at me and the tears in her eyes suddenly dried up. "What do you want for me, Mom?"

"What do you mean?" I stalled.

"What do want for me?" Bree repeated.

I want you to be happy, was the first thought that swept through my mind. But then something inside me rejected that. What was *happy* anyway? Something that borrowed its shape from everything around it. Not necessarily stable. I needed more time. This was obviously a trick question. "This is about the talk you made Dad have with me last night, isn't it?"

"I didn't *make* Dad have that talk with you," Bree said. "It was his idea. He said you'd listen, that you'd keep an open mind. Did you?"

A flap came untethered from my heart. I suddenly realized I shouldn't have been straightening couch pillows. I should have been tying down my emotions. Because they were all surfacing, ready to lash out at my daughter, and I felt helpless to prevent them.

The teaching of kindness is on her tongue.

Where had I heard that? It didn't matter—I grabbed onto the words and clung to them. Kindness. Kindness.

"Mom?" Bree touched my knee.

"I tried," I said, and I could actually feel my lips quiver, fighting a battle with what I wanted to say and what I knew I should say. "I'm *trying.* I'm sorry you didn't think you could tell me about school. I want you to be able to tell me everything…anything, without having to worry that I'm going to get mad at you. You are just so…there's so much *to* you and I want the whole world to see it. Not just Prichett. I'm afraid that if you stay here, you'll just be a shadow some day."

"A shadow?" Bree frowned.

I didn't know how to explain to her what I saw in the people who lived in Prichett. Caught up in the smallness of their lives. Arguing over which pesticides were the best, which tractor dealer had the best prices. Maybe the thing Sam had accused me of was true—the town *didn't* belong to me.

"I love living here," Bree said. "I love knowing that this farm has been in the family for a hundred years. A *hundred years,* Mom! Dad's great-grandpa built the old summer kitchen from stones he picked out of the field. I like knowing that what we do is important."

"Corporate farms are taking over." I tried to inject some logic into Bree's passion. "This farm isn't that big compared to some of the others in the area. Who knows where we'll be in ten years?"

It didn't work.

"I'm not saying I want to farm," Bree said. "And I'm not saying I want to be a veterinarian."

"Then what *are* you saying?"

"That I want to feel like it's my decision," Bree said. "And if I decide to take some time and think about it—pray about it—that you let me. That's all I want for right now, Mom. For you to *let* me."

I didn't know if I could. "How much time?"

"Mom!" Bree collapsed against the cushions and squeezed her eyes shut.

"I'll try." That was all I could promise, but it must have been enough because Bree smiled.

"I'm going to take a shower."

"Throw your clothes in the laundry tub on the porch."

"I might just throw them in the garbage." Bree rose and stretched the way Diesel did after he'd napped in a patch of sunlight. Just as she reached the door, she paused and glanced back at me. "Did Riley call?"

"No." Guilt gnawed briefly at my conscious.

"He thinks I should go to Madison, too. He says I'm too smart to stay in Prichett. What an insult to you and Dad. And to his parents. Like the only reason a person would stay in Prichett was because they didn't have any other options." Her eyes flashed and I caught a glimpse of Breanna Penny, warrior princess.

I thought of the people I knew who had chosen to come to Prichett. Bernice. Annie and Stephen. My mother.

"I don't suppose that's true," I murmured.

Bree wrinkled her nose. "Shower." Once again, she took a few steps. Then paused. "Mom? Thanks. I thought you'd really freak out. I mean, I know you're not thrilled about all this, but it means a lot that you're willing to try." She used my word.

I nodded, unable to speak while something inside me busily smoothed out rough edges and tied neat little knots in my loose emotions.

"If Riley calls, tell him I'll call him back after supper. He wasn't there when Violet died. His mom said she hasn't seen him all day. I know he's going to take it hard because they bought Violet for him when she was a yearling."

I could just picture my journal entry: Sabotaged daughter's budding romance with young cowboy whose favorite horse just died. Daughter finds out and not only does she *not* rise up and bless me, she never speaks to me again.

Bree was quiet during supper and I could feel her exhaustion. Five o'clock mornings and long days with Kevin were beginning to brush shadows under her eyes. Once in a while, I caught her looking at the phone. She excused herself halfway through dessert and disappeared to her room.

Sam took his second cup of coffee and a piece of cake out to the porch. I never quite understood his need to be outside. You'd think after working under the hot sun all day, he'd be happy to be in the house. I followed him and perched on the railing. Lady had already commandeered the empty space beside him. The porch swing had had a busy day. I thought I could still smell cinnamon lingering in the air.

"Does the deacon board know about Annie Carpenter's past?" I asked.

Sam anchored his coffee mug between his knees and stared at me. Not even during our argument the night before had I seen such an expression of anger reflected on his face.

"Are people gossiping about her?" he demanded.

"No!" I felt the need to assure him. Quickly. "She was over this morning and she told me…and Bernice."

"She did?" There was doubt in his tone and I bristled.

"All she said was that she'd…she'd gotten pregnant at fifteen and had given the baby up for adoption." I shooed Lady off the swing and sat down. "You knew about that?"

"I knew," Sam said shortly. "She and Stephen told us during our interview with them. Stephen is very protective of Annie but she insisted that we know. She said that there might be times when God would ask her to use her story to minister to someone and she didn't want it to be a problem for Stephen if people found out."

To minister to someone. Like Bernice.

"Can you tell me the rest?"

Sam hesitated only a moment and then nodded. "She was a teenage runaway. One night she got into some trouble, got arrested. A police officer broke every rule and took her home with him. He volunteered part-time at a Christian youth center so he had a way with kids. He and his wife ended up becoming her foster parents. I guess she'd been in several different foster homes before she ran away. Her mom had kicked her out of the house when she found out Annie was expecting." Sam's voice softened on the last word. "She gave her life to the Lord and after she graduated from high school, she went to a Bible college. That's where she and Stephen met. Apparently, Annie didn't think she'd be a good minister's wife, but Stephen convinced her that all she needed to be was *his* wife. We're their first church and we're blessed to have them. As far as I'm concerned, everyone has things in their past that shouldn't be held against them. In Christ, aren't we made new—"

"You don't have to convince me," I interrupted.

Sam flushed. "Sorry," he said, ducking his head. "I just can't imagine anyone finding a bad thing to say about Annie Carpenter. I'm surprised she told you and Bernice about the baby, though. Stephen says it's not something she talks about very often. Too painful, he said."

I tried to imagine Annie as a runaway. I knew some people who had been scraped against some pretty hard surfaces during their lives and it always seemed to show in their eyes. The survivors. But not Annie. Her eyes were as clear and honest as a child's.

"She must have thought we needed to know," I said, struggling with whether to tell Sam about Bernice's daughter. He and I didn't have secrets between us, but this one wasn't mine to share. "She wants me to be her mentor. Can you imagine?"

"Sure." Sam didn't hesitate the least little bit.

"I have no idea what that means, really."

"I think it means she respects you." Sam held out his fork, which held the last bite of cake. For some reason, I felt like crying. Again. He never forgot to offer me the last bite. I hated it when there was a distance between us.

"I'm thinking about it," I said. "But I think as far as Annie's concerned, it's a given. She keeps turning up when I least expect it."

"That's good for you. Sometimes you get too caught up in your routine."

"I didn't know I had a routine."

Sam just looked at me.

"All right, maybe I do. Just a little one."

"Did you and Bree have a chance to talk?"

"You were sitting at the dinner table with us."

He nudged me with his elbow and gave me a look.

"I told her I'd try to give her some time to think, but I can't help the way I feel. I *want* her to go to college," I said, my frustration seeping through. "There is nothing here for her, Sam. Why can't she see that?" Bree may have been passionate in her tribute to the farm, but I was just as passionate in my belief that she was meant to do more with her life.

"El, look." Sam put his face against mine, so our eyes were at the same level. I breathed in the smell of the soap he used.

"Look at what?"

"Just look."

I looked at the barn. Everything seemed to be in order. Then at the fence, checking post to post to see that the electric wire was in place. Then at the horses—Buckshot and Belle, our old draft horse—who were standing shoulder to shoulder, their heads low. Nothing amiss. Sam was still waiting. I could feel it. I shifted my gaze from the yard to the fields. And then I saw it. The sun was melting into a puddle of pink and gold over the corn. There were wisps of lavender clouds and puffs of smoky blue ones.

"Almost as pretty as you," Sam murmured in my ear. "I wouldn't call this *nothing,* would you, Ellie?"

I had to replay our conversation to figure out what he meant, then stumbled over it. Sam had been hurt with that thoughtless comment that I'd made. I hadn't meant to hurt him. Part of me wanted to argue that there were beautiful sunsets in a lot of places, not just over the Penny farm. But instead, I rubbed my cheek against his shoulder and that's when I noticed the old summer kitchen in the distance, painted with soft evening shadows.

Before Bree had mentioned it, I'd forgotten that that had been its original purpose. Most of the time, we referred to it as the old coop, because at one time, Sam's dad had kept chickens in it. Now it was empty, as far as I knew. Or maybe there were tractor parts hiding in it. Either way, it was such a familiar part of the landscape that I didn't even pay much attention to it. There had been a time several years back that I had planted spring tulips along the foundation and thrown in some daylily bulbs, just for color.

"Did your great-grandpa really build the summer kitchen with rocks from the field?"

Sam chuckled. "What made you think of that?"

"Bree mentioned it."

"Yup. It's what he used to lure Grandma Alice to the farm. She was a city girl like you, you know."

I hadn't known, but then, I'd never paid much attention to the old farm stories.

"It's pretty sturdy for being almost a hundred years old," Sam said affectionately. "Dad said Great-Grandpa told her that every rock he hauled out of the field stood for one year that they'd be together."

"Did she ever count them?"

"The way the story goes, she told him that it would take forever to count that many rocks. To which Great-Grandpa said exactly so. She married him the next month."

"You Penny men," I said softly. "You do know how to butter up the ladies. It must run in the family."

chapter 20

I wasn't even surprised when Annie called the next morning. I tucked the phone between my ear and my shoulder while I finished washing the breakfast dishes.

"Hi, Elise." Annie's exclamation point was gone.

"Are you all right?"

"Just a little sick to my stomach this morning," she said. "I think Stephen meant well when he told me that I needed to praise God in all things, but I threw a wet dishcloth at him."

Men. Sometimes their timing was a bit off. I made a mental note to tell Sam that when he met with Stephen, he should bring that up.

"I won't keep you, but I wondered if you'd be willing to donate a bouquet of flowers for a wedding later this afternoon," Annie said. "I noticed you have some beautiful roses growing by the house. The couple, you might know them from church, doesn't have any money, really, and Pastor Charles and Jeanne and Stephen and I are trying to make things a little special."

"Who's getting married?"

"Esther Miller and John Crandall. They're both in the nursing home. That's where they met."

I didn't remember a John Crandall, but Esther Miller had to be close to ninety! I remembered when she sang in the choir. She was so petite the ladies in the sewing circle had had to use a child's pattern for her choir robe.

"We're having the service right in the chapel at the nursing home and serving coffee and cookies afterward. There won't be many people there, but Jeanne and I are planning to decorate a little bit this afternoon."

I thought about my Vanilla Perfume roses, the ones that had just started to bloom a few weeks ago. Ordinarily, I didn't cut my flowers but I decided I could part with one or two. Gathered with some baby's breath, I was sure they'd be adequate for the kind of wedding Annie was describing. "I can pick a few roses for her."

"That would be great...ah, Elise. Can I call you back later?" Annie's voice was thin and held a note of panic.

"Sure."

The phone went dead in my ear and I smiled. Morning sickness. I'd had the same experience with Bree, followed by three months of fatigue that had propelled me to the sofa every afternoon for a long nap.

I tucked a pair of scissors in my pocket and went outside. So far, we'd been blessed with a long stretch of hot, sunny weather. It was good for the corn, but there came a point when the crops needed a good soaking rain, too. Irv Howard's little blue car turned into the driveway. Not only was Irv the postmaster, but he also personally delivered the mail. The light on the top of his car was blinking its official mail-delivery blink. Except that Irv drove with the light on even when he *wasn't* delivering mail. There had been several letters to the editor about that particular quirk of Irv's and the mayor had had a talk with him, but it hadn't done any good. Irv liked people to know that he was with the U.S. Mail.

"Hi, Elise!" He stuck his arm out the window and waved at me. "Just had to give this to you in person."

"What's that?"

"The newspaper." Irv winked a watery eye at me. "You made the front page."

I snatched the paper out of his hand. I was going to kill Calvin Richardson…but then I decided it probably wouldn't look very good recorded in the journal I had to keep for the pageant.

"Doesn't surprise me a bit," Irv said. "You are the prettiest gal in the county. Always have been. Do you think you can sign my paper for Winnie? I know she'll want to put this up at the post office."

Sure, right next to my wanted poster.

My face stared back at me from the front page. My face took up *most* of the front page. Apparently it was a slow week in Prichett for news. It wasn't the photo Calvin had snapped the afternoon that *I* had snapped (Thank you, God). It was a picture he had dug out of the archives from when I'd won the Miss Sweetheart contest.

Former Miss Sweetheart Becomes Proverbs 31 Woman.

Irv coughed lightly and waved another newspaper at me.

"Irv, are you sure you want me to sign this?" I asked. "I mean, I'm just a contestant in the pageant. I haven't won."

Irv looked affronted. "It doesn't matter that you haven't won yet," he rumbled. "You will. Those judges aren't blind. Here's another one for Winnie's sister in Myrtle Beach…" He slipped another newspaper to me.

I felt silly, but I signed my name more carefully than usual. Irv had come prepared—the pen he'd given me had metallic gold ink that sparkled on the newsprint.

"And one for Winnie's sister in Seattle."

I handed him back one newspaper and he snuck another one into my hand. I was beginning to wonder how many sisters Winnie had.

"I'm sure they don't care—"

"Don't care!" Irv rolled his eyes, as if that was unimaginable. "You are so humble, Elise. That's what Winnie says, too."

I suddenly remembered the times in high school when I'd pretend to be taking notes during fifth-period history class when all the while I was filling up notebook pages practicing my autograph. I was sure there would be a time in my life that I would be asked for it. This certainly wasn't what I'd had in mind back then. I smiled.

"That's the smile that's gonna win the pageant," Irv said confidently. "One for my brother in Houston. If you don't mind."

I signed another paper.

"This one's yours," Irv said. "Better get down to the newspaper and pick up a couple extra for yourself this morning. They were selling faster than slices of Sally's sour cream raisin pie."

"Thank you, Irv."

"Winnie said we should take a drive to Madison and watch the pageant in person. She's got a cousin there. A second cousin, if you want to be picky. Family is family to Winnie, though. She's got more cousins that a dog has fleas. Makes up for the fact that I don't have much family at all…."

Irv lost me there. I started skimming the article. Somehow, Calvin had gotten more information about the Proverbs 31 Pageant than I had. Somewhere inside Calvin was a frustrated investigative reporter. He mentioned how long the pageant had been in existence, how many contestants were chosen from each state and what the criteria for the judging was. He devoted two paragraphs to my background, mentioning that my mother had been a schoolteacher in Prich-ett before she died and that I'd married Sam Penny shortly after high school. Toward the end of the article, he actually reprinted Proverbs 31 and wrote down my accomplishments. He interviewed Sally and Candy Lane and Mrs. Kramer, church secretary extraordinaire, who took credit for starting the entire thing.

I've no doubt Elise Penny will win the pageant. She is a farmer's wife and no one works harder than they do. She's raised a beautiful daughter, she grows prize-winning roses and cans her own vegetables. She goes to church every Sunday. Elise is sweet and quiet, too. Hard to find those qualities nowadays. Of course she's going to win.

That was Mrs. Kramer's quote.

Elise Penny is a respected member of this community.

That was from Mayor Candy Lane.

Elise Penny always buys local. She doesn't eat a whole piece of pie when I give her one, either. Always leaves some on the plate. That shows me she's got a lot of self-control. Especially when you're talking about my pies…

That was from Sally.

I didn't know whether to laugh or cry.

"I did have a stepbrother that came out of the woodwork a few years ago, but I think he just wanted money. Seemed a little shady to me."

I tuned back to reality just as Irv finished wrapping up his family saga.

"Ah, Irv, I better get going. I have a few things to do in town."

"Yup, remember to grab up some more of these newspapers before they sell out," Irv said, with a sharp salute. "See you tomorrow."

The little blue car sped away, light blinking. I walked slowly back up the driveway and read through the article again.

"Lord," I groaned out loud. "You see what's happened here, don't You? Look who they think I am. They think I'm *her!*" I waved the paper at the sky. "And do you know why they think I'm *her?* Because I've worked hard at home, and taken good care of Sam and Bree…and worked with my hands in the gardens. But here is the truth, Lord. I'm quiet because I *don't want to talk to them!* And I may seem sweet and full of wisdom but *they can't see what's inside me!*" I stomped up the steps to the house to get my purse. "I married Sam. Not the farm. Not Prichett. Sam. And I don't want to change my mind about *them* because that would mean that I've got to be content here. And *like* it. And I don't want to like it, Lord, because that would mean that they've *won*. The brainwashing would be complete. I'd have to accept that there is never going to be any *more* for me than what I have right now."

I grabbed my purse and walked back outside. My hydrangea bush was sulking in the sun by the corner of the porch, where I'd planted it two years ago. It was mid-morning and already the leaves were wilted and feverish.

"I'm not moving you," I told it. "I want you where people can see you when they come up the driveway."

I went around the side of the house and hesitated in front of my rosebushes. With Irv's impromptu autograph session, I'd gotten sidetracked and hadn't cut the roses for Esther's wedding. Taking a deep breath, I snipped off two of my roses, mumbled an apology, then cut some baby's breath from the back of the patch.

My words dried up on the way into Prichett, but that didn't mean I'd settled anything with myself. Or God. Still, it felt good to know that He was listening. Somehow, I just knew that He'd *heard*. And that He cared.

I was afraid that the Cut and Curl would be closed again, but the open sign was in the window when I got there. I sighed in relief.

"Hi, El."

Bernice was cutting a little girl's hair while her mother hovered protectively beside the chair. Bernice had a special chair for children to sit in when she cut their hair. It looked like an elephant and even though Bernice had painted it a cheerful antibiotic pink, I'd even seen little boys perched in it with big smiles on their faces.

"Hi." I helped myself to a cup of coffee and sat in a chair by the window, right underneath the air-conditioning vent.

"I didn't expect to see you in town today."

"I have an errand to run. Annie's helping with a wedding at the nursing home this afternoon and she asked me if I could donate a few roses."

Bernice's eyebrow rose. "A wedding at the nursing home?" She held up a small mirror in front of the little girl's face. "All done. What do you think?"

"Do I get a sucker?"

"You sure do. You sat very well, Amber." Bernice unclipped the cape and shook it out. "I think you'll be too big for this chair the next time you come in. You're getting to be quite the little lady."

I saw Amber's expression—awe—and her mother's expression—dismay. I could sympathize. *They outgrow the elephant chair too fast, don't they?*

"One of the nice things about growing up," Bernice said, "is even though you outgrow the chair you never outgrow suckers." She took the big plastic container of suckers off the counter and let the girl pick one. Then Bernice took one, unwrapped it and popped it in her mouth. The girl giggled. Bernice offered one to the mom, who accepted it hesitantly.

After they left, Bernice poured herself a cup of coffee and used the sucker to stir the cream in.

"Esther Miller and John Somebody are getting married today," I said, picking up the thread of our conversation.

"I know Esther," Bernice said. "She's eighty-six years old."

"I thought she had to be in her eighties."

"Wow."

I thought that word just about summed it up. "How are you doing?"

"Shaky." Bernice sat down beside me. "Heather e-mailed me last night. She really wants to come for a visit."

"And?"

"I haven't answered yet."

"Bern!"

"I know, I know. But look at me, El. Do I look like mother material to you?" She ran a hand through her hair, which now sported gold highlights.

"See, you haven't officially been a mother for a week, and already you're swimming in guilt. There is your criteria. You're one of us." I stood up. "I can stop back again after I go to the nursing home, but I don't want the roses to sit in the car too long."

"My perm just cancelled, so I'll come along. If we're talking, then I'm not thinking."

"What you just said."

Bernice laughed. "Let me put a sign on the door and I'm right behind you."

chapter **21**

Golden Oaks Nursing Home was a half mile from Prichett, an L-shaped brick building that had been an elementary school before the consolidation.

"These places depress me," Bernice said with a shudder.

I couldn't argue with her. Not that I'd had much experience with nursing homes, but it seemed to me that the air inside was always heavy, as if crowded with memories.

"I hope Annie is here," I murmured. "I have no idea where to go."

We stepped into the front lobby and I could hear the ripple of a piano and the sound of singing from somewhere in the building.

"Can I help you?" I didn't recognize the young woman behind the front desk but her nose looked familiar. Maybe a Lafferty. Or a Cooke.

"I'm bringing some flowers for a wedding this afternoon. Is Annie Carpenter or Jeanne Charles here?"

"You're Elise Penny, aren't you?"

Behind me, I heard Bernice stifle a laugh.

"Mmm-hmmm."

"I saw your picture in the paper this morning. Congratulations!" Her gaze shifted and she started moving things around on her desk.

Don't ask me. Don't ask me.

"Would you mind signing this? How about something like, 'To my friend Audrey Cooke, a fellow beauty queen.'"

Bingo. She was a Cooke.

"Fellow beauty queen?" Bernice ventured.

"I was the runner-up for 4-H princess when I was twelve," Audrey said, glaring at Bernice over my shoulder.

"Sure," I said quickly and scribbled my name underneath the photograph. At least I wasn't signing a picture of myself with a rose between my teeth.

"Mrs. Charles is in the chapel and Annie Carpenter is in the party room." Audrey took out a pair of scissors and began to snip carefully around the photograph. "Last door on the right at the end of the hall."

"Thank you."

"Kind of uncomfortable to be a celebrity, isn't it?" Bernice murmured in my ear.

"Tell me Sally hasn't framed that picture already and hung it on the Prichett's Pride and Joy Wall."

"Okay, I won't tell you. If you think this is bad, you should have been there when a busload of high-school girls stumbled on me and Alex one afternoon. Literally. We were at the beach and their volleyball hit me in the back of the head. A couple of the girls ran over to apologize and when they recognized Alex, that was it. They didn't have any paper, of course, so he signed hands and shoulders and even a foot, if I remember right."

At one point, I would have thought it sounded fun. Now I wasn't quite so sure. I found myself uncomfortable with all the attention the pageant was creating.

"Watching him with all those gorgeous, tanned girls made me realize the competition I was up against," Bernice said. "That's when I decided to quit the game."

"Do you ever think you didn't give him enough of a chance?"

"A chance?"

"You know. If he loved you, no one else would have mattered. Ever."

"I was just plain, uninteresting Bernice." She refused to look at me. "I'm sure he didn't love me. Not like that."

"Elise!" Annie must have heard our voices because she poked her head around the corner of the doorway. She hugged me and then turned to Bernice. "I woke up at two o'clock this morning and prayed for you."

"Thank you," Bernice said formally.

I could see Bernice was going to have to get used to Annie's open-hearted communication.

"The roses are beautiful! I'll let you give them to Esther."

I hadn't noticed the woman sitting in a chair by the window until she stood up. If anything, she looked smaller than she had the last time I'd seen her. She was wearing a beige linen skirt and white blouse, paired with tennis shoes.

"Elise Penny." Her eyes sparkled with life and she rose up on her tiptoes. I bent down slightly and felt the brush of her lips against my cheek, and caught the unmistakable scent of Chantilly. My mother had worn Chantilly. She bought herself a new bottle every year on June eleventh. That had been her and my father's wedding anniversary.

"And Bernice Strum. I love your hair, my dear. You look like Audrey Hepburn in *Breakfast at Tiffany's.*"

Bernice blinked and stammered out a thank you.

"I want you to meet someone." Esther tucked her hands under our elbows and walked us over to the window where a man sat in a wheelchair, the lower half of his body covered by a cardinal-red afghan. "John, this is Elise Penny and Bernice Strum. Elise brought me some beautiful roses for my bouquet."

"A pleasure to meet you." His voice was low and pleasant.

I realized two things. This had to be Esther's soon-to-be-husband. And he was blind.

"Just smell these," Esther said, taking the roses from me and holding them close to John's face. "There's two of them, the most beautiful shade of buttermilk. Kind of a creamy white. And there's baby's breath, too. As light and delicate as lace."

"They can't be as beautiful as you," John said.

"Well, of course you'd say that! You can't see this wrinkled old face," Esther teased, then turned to us and said in a loud whisper, "Should I tell him I'm wearing sneakers to the ceremony?"

"Sneakers?" John shook his head. "I hope you aren't planning to run away and leave me at the altar, because these wheels are faster. You wouldn't make it to the door."

"Sorry. You're stuck with me." Esther kissed him.

Annie returned, armed with a roll of pink crepe paper and some tape. "Jeanne thought maybe we could tape some streamers around the room."

For the first time, I looked around the "party room." It wasn't much bigger than our bedroom at home. A rectangular table was pushed against one wall and a dusty silk ficus tree sulked in the corner. There were two brass wall sconces (one of them had tilted slightly) and the only color came from a braided rug someone had positioned by the door.

"Mr. Crandall, it's time to go back to your room for your medication." A nurse swept in but cast Esther a warm smile. "The next time you see him will be in the chapel, Esther. I'll personally make sure he gets there on time."

Esther dropped another kiss on John's head and I saw her murmur something in his ear that made him grin.

"I don't think I can wait until four o'clock," Esther said after they'd gone. She settled into the chair by the window. "The first time I was a bride, I was seventeen. Homer and I were married for fifty-two years. I never thought I'd love anyone again. Then John moved in across the hall from me six months ago. For a week, I didn't even see him because he kept his door closed. But I heard him. Every morning while the breakfast trays were being delivered, he'd sing 'Amazing Grace.' One day, I decided to join in. And the next day. And the day after that. Then, the day after *that,* he stopped singing."

She paused and Bernice, Annie and I all waited impatiently for her to finish.

"I'm sorry. I'm boring you young ladies. I tend to ramble on—"

"What happened?" Bernice interrupted.

"Oh, you want to hear more?"

"Yes!" All three of us spoke at once.

"I asked a nurse about him and she told me he'd had to go to the hospital. Pneumonia. Even though I didn't know him, I prayed for him. And every morning after I prayed, I sang 'Amazing Grace.' One morning, he started to sing with me. He was back." Esther smiled blissfully. "We met that afternoon for the first time."

"Was he blind then?" Bernice asked.

"Yes, he was," Esther said, her cheeks pinking slightly. "The nurse mentioned something about him being blind, but to tell you the truth, I hadn't noticed. He has the most beautiful voice. I could listen to it for hours. Now I get to listen to it for the rest of my life. The Lord is good, isn't He? He put me here to cheer people up and then He blessed me with a husband. I think sometimes that God's favorite word is *surprise!*"

I blinked back the tears that burned my eyes. Annie slipped her arm through Esther's and rested her face against Esther's shoulder.

"I wonder if you'd like me to fix your hair," Bernice said. "For the wedding. It would be my gift."

Esther touched her hair. Unlike most women her age, Esther's silver hair was long, braided on either side of her face and held in place with a barrette at the nape of her neck.

"You have plenty of time," Annie coaxed. "We still have to decorate."

"I've never been one to refuse a gift," Esther finally said. "Thank you, Bernice. I'm overwhelmed. I knew this day would be special, but the flowers…now a new hairdo. I don't know why I'm always surprised when God does these things. He is so lavish in His love, it takes my breath away. It really does. Just when we think something has ended, He always shows us a new beginning."

"I'll run back to the salon and get my things," Bernice said. I noticed her hands were shaking as she picked up her purse. "It won't take me more than ten minutes."

"She's brand-new, isn't she?" Esther asked.

"Uh-huh," Annie replied with a grin.

"I can always tell." Esther smiled and her gaze moved to me. I felt a jolt of panic. They were speaking a language I wasn't fluent in and when Esther looked at me, I knew she'd figure it out in a heartbeat. But all she said was, "Do you know what I love about roses? There is so much more to them than beauty. Even if you close your eyes and can't see what they look like, you know them by their fragrance."

I mumbled in agreement and told Annie to wait on the streamers and went to the front desk to use the phone. Sam had bowed to technology and bought a cell phone the summer before, but I'd never called him.

"Sam?" There was a lot of background noise and I could tell he was out in the field. "Can you do me a favor?"

"Yup." He didn't even ask what it was first.

"I need you to cut some flowers and bring them to the Golden Oaks. As soon as you can."

"Esther and John are getting married this afternoon, aren't they?"

Leave it to Sam to know that when I'd just found out a few hours ago. "Do you have time?"

"Not a problem. What should I cut?"

I silently revisited my gardens. There was one Memorial Day in bloom that I'd coddled and admired. It was the same shade of pink in Esther's blush. "Sam...just surprise me."

"I can't imagine why they're getting married," Audrey Cooke muttered when she took the phone from my hand. She lowered her voice. "I mean, look at John Crandall. He's in a wheelchair and he's *blind*. I can see what he's getting in the deal—someone to push his wheelchair around, but I can't figure out what *she's* getting."

A new beginning. I didn't say the words out loud, because somehow I knew Audrey wouldn't understand.

"I need to use the phone one more time," I said, struck with a sudden idea. I dialed Sally's number at the café. "Sally, this is Elise. How many pies do you have made up today?"

"Three cherry, one banana cream and a pecan."

"Can you have someone deliver them to the Golden Oaks by four o'clock?"

"What's the occasion?" Sally wanted to know. "By the way, I put your picture on The Wall this morning."

"Esther Miller and John Crandall are getting married this afternoon." I ignored the reference to the Prichett's Pride and Joy Wall. Technically, it wasn't even a wall. It was a narrow space above the coffeepots where news clippings of local people were framed and hung, mostly members of the high-school football team and the occasional trophy bluegill.

"John Crandall? No kidding."

"You know him?"

"Heard of him. His youngest daughter lives over by Munroe. She said he was a music professor at some expensive college out in New York. Too bad that he wound up at Golden Oaks."

"I don't think he'd say that."

"I'll send the pies over. No charge. Consider them a wedding gift." Sally was silent for a moment. "I'll bring them myself. Do you think they'd mind if I stayed?"

"I think they'd like that."

When I got back to the party room, Annie was staring miserably at a tangle of crepe paper in her hands.

"I don't think this is my gift."

"Forget the crepe paper. Sam is bringing some more flowers. And let's light those candles in the wall sconces. That'll be pretty."

"Bernice came back. She and Esther are locked in Esther's room. I could hear them giggling when I walked by."

"How are you feeling?" I asked.

Annie patted her stomach. "Good. For now. Ask me again when they bring in the cookies and punch."

"Sally is bringing some of her pies over. Not as traditional as a wedding cake, but a step up from cookies."

The door opened and Bernice peeked in. "All clear?"

Annie and I both nodded and Bernice ushered Esther in. Not only had she styled her hair in soft waves, but she'd done her makeup. Esther's skin almost glowed. She'd changed into a pale-pink dress, but she still wore tennis shoes.

"I don't know what she did to this old lady," Esther said. "But I don't look a day over seventy-five!"

Bernice fussed with Esther's hair. "I just wish John could see you."

"He sees me with his heart," Esther said. "That's what matters."

chapter **22**

Somehow, in just the space of a few hours, Esther and John's tiny guest list had stretched to twenty-five. Sam not only brought flowers, he also brought Bree. She put three years of piano lessons into practice and offered to play while Esther walked down the aisle. Sally brought the pies and three of her favorite customers, who were upset that she was taking their dessert. So they tagged along. I'm not sure where the rest came from. Some of them were nurses. Audrey snuck in and a few times during the ceremony I saw her pull a tissue out of her pocket and dab at her nose. Not that I blamed her. I could even see tears glistening in Sam's eyes when John surprised Esther and sang to her before their vows, which they'd obviously written themselves.

"It doesn't matter if we're given one day or a hundred

years," Esther told John. "Every moment with you is a gift from God that I promise to cherish."

I squeezed Sam's hand.

I love you. He mouthed the words to me.

Usually I didn't get mushy at weddings like some people did. This one was different. Not just because the bride and groom were in their eighties, but because of the expressions on their faces.

"We aren't going to have enough pie for everyone," Jeanne whispered to me after the ceremony. "I had no idea this many people were coming."

Sally overheard.

"You'd think a minister's wife would know the story of the loaves and fishes," she said with a wink. "You pray and I'll do the rest."

We found out that Sally had a hidden talent. She could slice ten pieces of pie from a pan that normally yielded eight. Sally was wasted at the café. She could have been the CEO of a major corporation.

Bernice was the unofficial wedding photographer. She always kept a disposable camera in her purse and she flitted around, taking more pictures than the paparazzi on Oscar night.

"The flowers look beautiful, Elise." Pastor Charles stood beside me, balancing a plate and a cup of coffee in one hand.

"Thank you." I didn't know what else to say.

When I'd told Sam to surprise me, he'd done a good job.

I wasn't sure there would be any flowers left when I got home. Audrey had found some vases and a mismatched array of baskets in the kitchen, which we'd filled with armloads of baby's breath. Sam had even cut a dozen of my strawberries-and-cream Asiatic lilies. Those were on the pie table. At first I thought he'd left my single, one and only Memorial Day rose, but then I found it at the bottom of the paper sack he'd brought the flowers in. The stem was snapped off in the middle but the rose itself was still in perfect condition.

"Oh, Mom, we can't use that one, can we?" Bree noticed what had happened and she tried to console me with a hug. She knew how much time I spent in my gardens.

"I think we can." I cut the rest of the stem away and slipped out of the party room. John's door was right across the hall from Esther's and I tapped on it quietly.

"Come in."

"It's Elise, Mr. Crandall. I brought you something. A boutonniere for your jacket."

He was sitting in his wheelchair, already dressed in a charcoal-gray suit and tie.

"Do you mind if I pin it on?"

"Please do."

He sat quietly while my fingers fumbled with the straight pin. I adjusted the rose on his lapel and then stepped back, admiring the softness of it. "It's my favorite one, a Memorial Day. It's light pink. Um, kind of like the color Esther's cheeks get when she blushes."

"Thank you for making this day special for her." John lifted his hand and I reached out and gave it a gentle squeeze.

"Oh, I'm pretty sure *you're* the reason this is a special day for her."

People lingered over their pie until Sally announced she had to get back to the café for the supper crowd. Some of the nurses reluctantly drifted out of the room to go back to work and Sam came up behind me.

"I've got to get back. Bree wants to go home with me if that's all right with you."

"Sure." I looked around for Bernice. "I'm going to stay and clean up, then I'll get a ride back to the Cut and Curl with Bernice. My car is parked there."

"Should I throw a few steaks on the grill?"

"My hero." I wrapped one arm around his waist and kissed his cheek. "How did you know I didn't start supper?"

"Just a lucky guess," Sam said. "I can see you've been busy today. Should we load up the flowers to take home?"

I shook my head. "I told Audrey to give them to people who aren't feeling well."

Sam laughed.

"What?"

"You."

"What about me?"

"Sometimes I've wondered if you love those flowers more

than me," Sam said teasingly. "All the time you spend on them, fussing over them. I get jealous sometimes."

I rolled my eyes. "I could leave you here to cheer up the residents, too."

"I'll see you at home." He wiggled his eyebrows at me and I gave him a gentle push toward the door. Men.

"Stephen is making me go home," Annie said. "But I feel terrible, leaving you to clean up."

Annie did look a little pale and Stephen looked a little anxious.

"Don't worry about it. We'll be here another fifteen minutes at the most," I told her.

Stephen gave me a grateful look.

"Well, we're off to our honeymoon suite," Esther said.

Bree had decorated John's wheelchair with the pink crepe paper and taped a Just Married sign to the back of it.

"Your boutonniere must have fallen off," I told him, noticing it was gone.

"Look, dear," Esther said. "It's right here. Safe and sound." The rose was pinned to the collar of her dress. "John said I blush this exact shade of pink. How do you think he knows that?"

"I have no idea."

John smiled up at me and off they went.

"Ready to go?" Bernice asked me a little while later. The cleaning crew had been whittled down to just her and me.

"I think that's everything." I blew out the candles and wiped down the table.

Bernice was quiet when we drove back to the salon.

"That was some wedding," I said, trying to jump-start some conversation.

"Do you believe what she said about new beginnings?" Bernice asked.

Okay, Lord, this isn't the conversation I planned to jump-start! "Yes," I said cautiously.

"Because lately I've been feeling terrible about leaving Alex the way I did. I know I ran away like a scalded cat. I didn't have the guts that Esther has. She may not even get to celebrate her first wedding anniversary but she's marrying John anyway." Bernice pulled over by the curb. "And you gave up a modeling career to stay here in Prichett with Sam. That took guts, too."

I hadn't thought that marrying Sam qualified as being a particularly gutsy move. "It would have been gutsy to head to Chicago at eighteen and become a model. Staying here was easy."

"No. Modeling would have been the easy thing for you. Becoming a farmer's wife—that was the gutsy thing. You took a risk and you got the fairy tale."

I could have argued the point about life in Prichett being a fairy tale, but at that moment Bernice's car bumped against the curb.

"I keep forgetting to ask you how the pageant prepara-
tions are coming along."

"I have to keep a journal so the judges can see that I do
more than watch television and eat bonbons."

"I never even wanted to keep a diary," Bernice confessed.
"You never know when it could end up in enemy hands."

I thought about the diary I'd pushed under the pile of
socks in my dresser drawer. The one I'd kept when I was a
teenager and hadn't had the courage to read again. "I also
need to send a summary of my speech."

"You're going to be a busy girl."

"I have a feeling that's what they're looking for. Have you
read Proverbs 31? The woman is definitely a type-A. She
was multi-tasking before there was a word for it."

"Well, I'm going to stick a Lean Cuisine in the microwave
and go to bed early. I'm glad I don't have to record that in a
journal."

I read between the lines. "And you're going to call
Heather about visiting you?"

"Talk to you tomorrow." Bernice neatly dodged my question, grabbed her bag of rollers and left me standing on the
sidewalk. I let her go. I knew where she lived.

When I got home, I took a quick detour around the
house to look at my flowers. Which were no longer there.
Sam must have used his pocket knife to cut a swathe through
the baby's breath. There were only a few left that had somehow evaded the siege and they looked naked and pitiful by

themselves. There was only a stem where my Memorial Day had bloomed. Sam had left one bud from my Buttercream rosebush. I took my nail file out of my purse and carefully cut it. Maybe Annie would like it. I'd noticed she kept admiring them at Esther's wedding. Then I remembered that Shelby Hannah had told me to include a picture of my flowers when I sent the journal in. Maybe I could find one from last year....

Clancy thumped his tail when he saw me but there was no way he was leaving his spot next to the grill, where the aroma of beef steak wafted into the air along with the smoke. And I'm sure he was aware that Lady had taken up surveillance under the truck by the barn, planning her next move.

I hung my purse on a hook by the door and I could hear Sam and Bree talking.

"What's going on?" I sidestepped boxes and chunks of foam packing as I followed their voices to the den.

Bree's computer—which we'd decided to keep safely packed away until her first day of college—was out of the box and taking up the entire top of Sam's desk. Their heads were close together because they were sharing the chair.

"I'm just showing Dad a few things," Bree said.

Sam looked nauseous. "I don't know, honey. They say you can't teach an old dog new tricks."

Bree snorted. "It isn't hard. You're still keeping all your financial records on *paper,* Dad! I can set you up with a program so you can keep track of the farm accounts, right down to the last cucumber you sell at the stand."

Sam glanced at me, his expression dazed.

"I thought you weren't going to take your computer out until you got to school." I felt the familiar tension grab my spine and squeeze.

"I just think that we could be more efficient if we used a computer to keep track of everything," Bree said. "No offense, Dad, but you're the only one who can read your writing and you jot everything down on *legal pads.* That's like, from the Stone Age."

"I don't know anything about computers and I don't have time to set something like this up," Sam said slowly. I could tell he didn't want to say anything that would dampen Bree's enthusiasm. "Maybe this winter—"

"I could do it for you." She crossed her arms.

That simple sentence seemed to suck all the air out of the room. I was afraid to ask her just exactly what it meant.

"Bree, it would take both of us," Sam said. "Like you said, I've got a system that works for me—even if it is from the Dark Ages." He tugged on the end of her braid. "We'd have to sit down together…"

"Mom could help me."

My jaw came unhinged. "What?"

"You must have an idea of how Dad keeps the books," Bree said. "We can set up the simple stuff first until Dad has more time after the frost. To compete with the corporate farms, we have to move this farm into the twenty-first century. Part of that includes disks, not paper."

"That's your computer for college." I couldn't seem to get my thoughts dislodged from that particular rut.

"You'll have to buy your own eventually," Bree told me.

Now Bree wasn't simply asking me to give her time. Now she was asking me to take an active role in ditching college and staying on the farm. I thought of the enormous challenge to move the Penny farm from paper and file folders and bulging desk drawers to computer.

I took a deep breath and prayed. "I'll help you."

"Great." Bree's eyes were sparkling. "Because I've decided to go to college for Agriculture and Business—and then I'm coming back."

chapter **23**

When I stopped by Annie's the next day, it took her a few minutes to come to the door. Just when I thought she wasn't home and turned to go back to the car, the door opened cautiously, just a crack, then all the way.

"Elise. Come in." Annie had one hand pressed against her stomach. She was still in her pajamas. Her long red hair was in two braids and she looked just like Pippi Longstocking.

"You're sick again, aren't you?"

"Is that for me?" Annie spied the vase I was holding. During the night, the rose had come to life, beginning to uncurl at the first seam.

"I thought it might cheer you up."

She gave a short chirp and hugged me. I was getting used to Annie's hugs. They came without warning like a summer shower. "Can you stay? I couldn't even look at coffee this morning, but I made some peppermint tea. Someone told me it's good for touchy stomachs."

"For a few minutes." I'd never been inside the duplex before, but was surprised at how barren it was. The way Annie had fussed over my "country decor," I was sure her home would have been filled with homey touches. It wasn't. In fact, it wasn't even what my mother called "early attic," with bits of the flotsam and jetsam that most newlyweds acquired from friends and family.

I followed Annie into the kitchen. It was painted a welcoming yellow, but that was it. The space at the top of the cupboards, where most women would have put baskets or a collection of some sort, was empty. The chrome table with its Formica top had a damaged surface and I was surprised she hadn't covered it with a cloth or placemats.

"I felt better last night, but I think I can definitely call this all-day sickness," Annie said. "At this point, morning sickness would be a blessing. I wasn't sick at all with…my first baby."

"I'm sure every pregnancy is different." I'd only had one, so I was repeating what I'd heard from other women.

"Let's sit in the living room," Annie said, carrying my cup and hers. "Stephen made scrambled eggs this morning for me and the smell is still making my stomach do flips. He meant well." She sighed and I smiled. Sam had taken over some of the cooking during my pregnancy, too. He loved bacon and I couldn't even say the word without feeling my insides tilt. He confessed later that a few times a week, he'd sneak over to his mom's house and make himself a few slices.

I sat down on a love seat and Annie curled up in a glider rocker that looked brand-new. There were no pictures on the walls here, either. The smell of fresh paint still lingered in the air, so I guessed that Annie hadn't had time to put any up yet.

"I see you're getting ready for the baby." I nodded at a stuffed bear flopped in a basket, clustered with some other things. A Raggedy Ann doll and copy of *Goodnight Moon.* Maybe Annie had already found out this baby was a girl.

"Nope, everything in there is mine. Stephen bought them for my birthday." Annie smiled winsomely. "I didn't have what you'd call an average childhood. No birthday parties, no sleepovers, no friends over. Just an alcoholic mother and a dad whose name she never bothered to tell me. When I met Stephen, I was a new believer but I was still lugging around an awful lot of things from my past. I knew I was supposed to love and forgive my mother, but she'd kicked me out of the house when I was a teenager because I was pregnant and she'd found a new boyfriend. I blamed her for taking things away from me that I could never, ever get back again.

"I met Stephen at Bible college and we started hanging out together a few months into my sophomore year. He found out it was my birthday and he gave me the Raggedy Ann doll. He said his sister had one and it was her favorite, so he asked his grandma to make one for me. It was a weird gift." Annie paused and laughed. "I told him that, too. I mean, I was twenty years old, but I kept her. She was cute and no one had ever given me a doll. On my next birthday, he planned a surprise party with some of our friends and he gave me *Goodnight Moon*." She paused and then said deliberately, "That's when I broke up with him."

"You broke up with him? Because of *Goodnight Moon?*"

"No, because of what he said after I opened it. He told me he couldn't erase my past, but he wanted to give me back some of the things I'd missed. I couldn't stay with him after that. I knew he wanted to be in full-time ministry, but I was sure that God wasn't calling me to be a pastor's wife. God definitely said, *'Surprise. Yes, Annie, I want you to be Stephen's wife.'* And at first I said no. I even thought about dropping out of school so I wouldn't have to see Stephen every day. I planned to be a teacher, so I could pinpoint kids who were at risk like I'd been."

"So, the gutsy thing was to stay with Stephen?" I thought about the conversation Bernice and I had had the day before, when she'd told me that marrying Sam had been more of a risk than becoming a model.

"That's one of the things I like about you, Elise. You say words like *gutsy*. I think that the gutsy thing is going with God's plan for us—every time," Annie said. "Our plans are always second-best. Always geared to what we think we need. What we want. It's the path of our own desires. I'll take God's plan any day. He knows me and He loves me and whatever I have planned, well, His plan is better. I don't think it always feels safer, but it's definitely better."

"But if you didn't ask God what path you should take to begin with, then how do you know if you took the right one?" I asked.

"I think that's where contentment comes in. Wherever you are, you remember that Jesus said this is what you should do—love the Lord your God with all your heart and with all your soul and with all your mind and love your neighbor as yourself. That's the secret, don't you think? You can do that where you work, in church, in the kitchen, even in prison.

"I know I could have been a good teacher, but I love having the freedom to be real with the kids in the youth group. I don't have to hint at my faith or hide it. I'm starting to get phone calls from girls asking me to help them with something they're struggling with. And Stephen, he's not perfect, but he's perfect for me. It's like God wrapped him up with a big bow and said, 'Here you go, Annie. The two of you can do more things for My kingdom together than you'll ever be able to do alone.'"

Contentment. Maybe that was the elusive thing that I'd never been able to grasp. Then again, maybe I hadn't tried. Ever since I'd married Sam, a part of my heart continued to restlessly wait for something *big* to happen. Something magical that would transform my rather mundane life into a special one. Prichett had always chafed against my dreams like a pebble in the toe of my shoe. Now I fantasized about the day when Sam would retire and we'd finally move to a place where time didn't tick by at a snail's pace and life didn't revolve around the harvest.

There had been a point in my life when it had almost happened. When Bree was in pre-school, we'd almost lost the farm. Secretly I'd hoped that Sam would see how precarious farming was and would get out while we could. I dreamed about the two of us going back to Chicago together and starting a real life someplace where there were stores open past nine o'clock at night and where Bree could take ballet lessons.

Then one night I felt Sam's body start to tremble after he thought I was asleep. He was crying. And I'd realized that fulfilling my dream would mean the death of his.

See, Elise, you're either dwelling on the past or longing for the future. Maybe you should start concentrating on the here and now.

I thought of Esther and John's vows and the expression on John's face at the end of the ceremony when Esther leaned down and kissed him. He'd never see her face this side of Heaven, but it didn't matter. They had promised they would treat each day—and each other—as a gift from God.

"I'm really glad you came over," Annie said. "I admit I was feeling kind of sorry for myself."

For a moment I was confused, like I'd fallen into a time warp of some kind and Annie's voice had pulled me back.

"I should go." It didn't feel comfortable, shining a light into the shadowy corners of my heart. "I've got to stop by the salon and check on Bernice, then I'm going to go and salvage what I can of my flower garden."

"I'm praying for her and her daughter," Annie said. "Will you tell her?"

I glanced at the Raggedy Ann in the basket and thought that she and Annie looked a little alike. Then I felt an inner nudge.

Do you see?

It wasn't an audible voice, but it was soft and it was real, cutting through my own thoughts so clearly that it seemed someone had whispered the words in my ear. I held my breath, wondering if I should answer. Okay…

See what?

There was nothing. I'd imagined it. Annie took our cups to the kitchen but I stood in the middle of her living room, unwilling to move until there was an answer. It was official. I was losing my mind. I took a few tentative steps toward the kitchen and paused again. Then suddenly I knew.

Other than the basics of housekeeping, Annie didn't *know* how to make a house a home. She hadn't had one. She'd never learned to cook, so she picked something and practiced it until she got it right—like her mammoth cinnamon rolls.

"You and Stephen haven't lived here very long, so you probably haven't had a lot of time to decorate. I could help you if you want me to," I told her.

Annie just stared at me and I wondered if I'd offended her. Then she burst into tears.

Without thinking, I reached out and pulled her into a hug, patting her back.

"I'd love that," she burbled into my shoulder. "I'm so glad you decided to be my mentor, Elise."

Your mentor? Annie—I think you're my mentor.

My next stop after Annie's was the hardware store, which really wasn't just a hardware store. It was more like a-bit-of-everything store. There were times I'd gone in there and Mr. Bender had loaves of fresh bread for sale. Mr. Bender (I wasn't sure if he even had a first name) had inherited the store from his father, who had inherited the store from his father. He knew where everything was, mostly I suppose, because he spent eight hours a day shuffling up one aisle and down the other, straightening jars of mysterious metal parts and sorting through bins of nails just in case some hurried farmer messed them up. I hate to admit it, but over the years the soft shuffle of Mr. Bender's shoes against worn linoleum had become a comforting sound to me.

Bree had given me a list of things to buy to bring the farm into the twenty-first century and she'd fitted them all on half of a three-by-five card. Bree, like Sam, was definitely an optimist. And I had time now to wonder if I was a lunatic for telling her I'd help her.

Sam had resisted changing his style of keeping books for years. He must have had a moment of weakness. Or maybe he had secretly hoped that Bree would stay on the farm. Maybe he was even *praying* that she would. I decided I'd definitely have to talk to him about that. Prayer wasn't something I was taking lightly anymore.

I slipped into Bender's Hardware and listened. There it was. Shuffle, shuffle, shuffle. Aisle six. I have no idea how the store stayed in business. There probably wasn't a huge profit in nails and bread. I had a hunch it was because of loyal customers who had known the previous Mr. Bender and now helped the current Mr. Bender.

"Elise Penny. How can I help you today?"

The shuffling grew louder and he came around the corner, wearing the same uniform that he'd worn since the first day I'd seen him—a crisp white shirt under engineer-striped overalls.

"I have a list," I told him, just to see his eyes brighten. They did. I could have found the items by myself in a fraction of the time I knew it would take him, but it was worth it to see his expression of delight. There probably weren't many days that he actually got an honest-to-goodness list. His hand wobbled when he reached for it and I noticed his fingers were twisted from arthritis.

"Mmm-hmm. Yup. I have everything on here. Why don't you just have a cup of coffee and I'll be back in a flash."

I hid a smile, imagining shuffle, shuffle, *flash!*

I poured myself a cup of coffee from the pot on the windowsill and looked outside. Across the street, the marquee still proclaimed me as the Proverbs 31 woman. The numeral one was smaller than the numeral three and I wondered what they'd used to improvise. It looked like a black permanent marker. I found it hard to believe that no one had given birth over the weekend and turned me and the pageant into yesterday's news. One could only hope.

Mr. Bender shuffled back into view. "Computer paper. All I have is typing paper, Mrs. Penny. Think that'll do?"

"They're probably the same thing."

"Ink for your printer. I figured you meant black ink. I didn't get you the calculator on the list. Did you know that computers have a calculator right inside them?"

"No. Really?"

"Sure they do. It'll save you ten dollars."

"Mr. Bender, I can't believe you had all this. What did you do, add an office supply store to your inventory?"

"Gotta keep up with the times," Mr. Bender said seriously, ringing up the items on the ancient cash register. He handed the bag to me and pressed a peppermint candy into my hand. "Have a nice day."

I tossed the bag into the back seat of the car and decided to walk down to the Cut and Curl. It was getting close to lunchtime, so I knew Bernice might have a few minutes to talk.

"Checking up on me, aren't you?" Bernice asked when I walked in.

"What makes you say that?"

Her chair was empty and no one was waiting, so she was free to let her sarcasm show.

"I don't know, you used to plan your trips into Prichett for once a week," Bernice said with a shake of her head. "Now you've been coming into town every day. Kind of suspicious if you ask me. Come on in the back while I eat my sandwich. I'll even share my potato chips with you."

I *had* been in town a lot, come to think of it. "You aren't going to believe this. I'm going to help Bree put all the financial records for the farm on computer."

"You're right, I don't believe it. When did you get a computer? Does that mean you'll have e-mail?"

"It's Bree's computer." *The one she's taking to college.*

Bernice looked skeptical.

"She decided to go." I felt tears sting my eyes. "But she's changing her major to Agriculture."

I still couldn't believe how sneaky she'd been about dropping that particular bombshell on us. I felt as if she'd been testing my promise to try to understand her need to take some time with her decision. And that computer…

"What about Riley?"

I felt a twinge of guilt. "He came over the other day and we had a…conversation. He hasn't called again."

"What did you say to him?"

"Just that he should give Bree some…space…some time to think about what she wants."

"Elise Penny." Bernice looked horrified, which only made my twinge of guilt quadruple.

"I know, I have to get him back somehow." I gnawed on my lower lip. "I just haven't figured out how yet. Now, let's talk about *your* daughter for a minute."

The bell jingled and Bernice and I both peeked around the corner. A young woman stood just inside the door.

"A walk-in," Bernice muttered. "It figures. I should have put my Gone to Lunch sign in the window."

There was something familiar about the girl, but I couldn't immediately make a family connection. She was tall and slender like Bree, but her face was more angular, her features accentuated by a short, almost boyish, haircut. She wore a denim skirt and a white tank top. Every inch of exposed skin was tanned an even, golden brown. I studied her face again. I heard Bernice's soft gasp and then I knew why the girl looked familiar.

"Bernice?" I whispered.

"You be Bernice," she hissed.

I choked on a laugh. "I'm not going to pretend to be you!"

Bernice stood frozen beside me. I nudged her with my elbow. "Go on. She looks like she's about to shatter into a bazillion pieces."

"El, do you think this is one of God's surprises, or a new beginning?" Bernice asked, her eyes full of panic.

"Maybe it's both. Go out there."

Bernice inched into view and the girl stared at her.

"I'm sorry...I know I should have called first. Dad says I'm really stubborn sometimes. I just couldn't wait to meet you and I was afraid you'd say no and I didn't want you to say no. So here I am..."

Heather didn't get a chance to finish because Bernice moved then. She didn't take a step forward, just opened her arms. Heather flew into them.

chapter 24

Bree came home from work early and found me in the kitchen, frantically preparing a dinner worthy of the occasion. Bernice's new beginning.

She took a carrot stick from the relish tray and leaned against the counter. "Who's coming over?"

"Bernice and..." I hesitated. "Bree, I don't know quite how to say this...Bernice had a baby when she was younger and she put her up for adoption. Heather started searching for her and, well, she found her. And she's here. In Prichett. And they're coming over for dinner tonight."

"How old is she?"

"Twenty. Not that much older than you."

I watched Bree's eyes to gauge her reaction.

"That must have been hard."

"To have her daughter find her after all these years?"

Bree shook her head. "No, to give her up in the first place."

"Are you planning to be home tonight?"

Her forehead puckered slightly. "I don't have any plans."

There it was again. The twinge of guilt. Reminding me that I had some unfinished business. Riley Cabott.

"Good, since you and Heather are so close in age, maybe you could be the…" I searched for the proper word.

"Comic relief?" Bree grinned.

"Maybe more like an ice breaker. I have no idea how things have been going with them this afternoon."

Bree did something she hadn't done for a long time. She leaned over and kissed me on the cheek. "No problem. I'm going up to shower first, though. I don't want my first impression to be the aroma of cow manure."

I finished up the lasagna, buttered the garlic bread and mixed the dressing for the salad. I saw Lady outside and knew Sam couldn't be far away. When I walked out to the porch, I saw him hooking up the baler to the tractor. He must have cut the hay in the back field. It needed a good three days to dry before being baled and now came the chore of having to bale it all and put it up in the loft. I hoped he wasn't planning on starting tonight.

He saw me and smiled. That was one of the marvels of Sam—that he still smiled at me the same way he had when we'd fallen in love.

"I've got lasagna in the oven." After nineteen years of

marriage, I knew what bait to put on the hook to entice him home for dinner.

Sam shook his head. "I heard there's rain coming in late tonight so I have to get the hay in. But save me a piece, okay?"

I squinted up at the cloudless sky. "Did your achy knee tell you that rain was coming in, or was it a reliable source, like the weatherman?"

"My knee, of course."

I drew a deep breath. "Sam, I would really like it if you'd come in for supper tonight. Just supper. You don't have to sit around and make polite conversation—"

"Polite conversation with who?"

After all these years, Sam could always skip over my verbal wanderings and get to the heart of the matter.

I told him the whole story about Bernice and Heather.

He leaned against the baler, pulled his cap off his head and tapped it against his leg. A sure sign he was agitated. He glanced at the sky, then back at me.

"Of course I'll be there."

I went back in the house, checked for signs of Bree, and dialed the phone. There was one more thing I had to do.

"Cabotts'." It was a masculine voice but I couldn't tell if it was Old Dan or one of the Cabott boys.

"Could I please speak with Riley?"

"This is Riley."

"This is Elise Penny. Bree's mom." Just to clarify.

Silence.

"Riley, Sam needs help baling hay this evening. If you can come over, I'll throw in dinner."

"Is this *really* Elise Penny?" came the cautious response.

I couldn't help but chuckle. "Yes, it really is. Dinner is at five."

"Sure, I can help." There was dignity in his voice.

"We'll see you then."

Bernice and Heather arrived at quarter to five. I had a few precious seconds to spy on them from the window in the den. It was hard not to stare at Heather, especially because I could see the genetic blueprint of Alexander Scott in her perfect Hollywood nose and gorgeous cheekbones. I wondered if Bernice had told her who her father was.

Heather had changed into a pair of loose khaki pants with a drawstring waist and multiple pockets, but she still wore the white tank top, only now there was a crocheted shirt over it. It was a look one normally didn't see in Prichett. Definitely city. Definitely expensive.

She and Bernice were laughing about something as they walked toward the house, and the tension I had been feeling all day suddenly disappeared as I grabbed Bree's hand and we went out to meet them.

"I don't think I introduced you to Elise this morning," Bernice said to Heather, a horrified look crossing her face. "Did I?"

"It's nice to meet you, Elise." Heather smiled and shook my hand.

"This is my daughter, Breanna."

Bree was wearing a pair of cut-off blue jeans and a barrel-racing T-shirt that pronounced This Is How Cowgirls Dust. She had on the red cowboy boots Bernice had given her for graduation. City meets country. And both looked terrific.

Our daughters looked at each other and for a split second, didn't speak. In that weighted moment, I wondered what they were thinking. Then, Bree's easy smile surfaced. "Call me Bree."

Heather laughed. "It's nice to meet you." Then, knitting Bree's heart to hers for life, she asked, "Can I see your horse?"

"Go ahead," I told them when Bree looked at me for the okay. "We have about fifteen minutes until supper's ready."

"Shall we tag along?" Bernice asked casually, and I realized she didn't want to let Heather out of her sight yet.

Several yards ahead of us, the girls chatted together as if they'd known each other for years. Buckshot heard his beloved's voice and came toward the fence at a fast trot. Bree slid between the wires and crooned in his ear while Heather watched, a fascinated expression on her face.

"Do you want to ride him?" Bree asked, a wicked twinkle in her eyes.

Heather's mouth dropped open and Bernice started to protest.

"We'll take him in the round pen, bareback," Bree said. "He can carry both of us." She lowered her voice. "He likes to carry two riders…it makes him feel buff."

I unhooked the fence and Bree led Buckshot out by the halter, toward the mounting block by the barn.

"Are you sure this is safe?" Bernice whispered to me.

"Now, now, Mother," I teased.

Bernice turned a bright pink.

"She calls me Bernice," she whispered. "I told her that's okay. I don't expect her to call me Mom. That's for the woman who raised her all these years."

Bree made reins out of Buckshot's lead rope and I could see her giving instructions to Heather about how to get on. Heather probably had no idea what her pants were going to look like after she'd ridden bareback in eighty-degree weather, but I could see there was no going back. Both the girls looked like kids on Christmas Day.

"Mom? You know what we need?" Bree said.

She couldn't mean…

"Yup." Bree nodded. "We have to do this right."

I shook my head. "I'll be right back."

In the barn, I went to the pile of wood shavings that Bree used to line the floor of the box stall and took a handful of sawdust, trying to remember the last time we'd performed this little ritual.

Sam had started it. He had a whimsical side to his personality that never failed to surprise and charm me. When he'd bought Sunny, Bree's first pony, he'd lifted her onto Sunny's back and then dipped into his pocket and sprinkled sawdust in Bree's hair and in Sunny's mane.

Bree had squealed and I'd been dismayed. He had no idea how long it would take to wash that out during her bath!

"This isn't fairy dust," Sam had told her solemnly. "It's better."

Bree giggled.

"What's it for?" I asked, exasperated.

Sam and Bree both stared at me in shock. Sam had clicked his tongue, given Bree a look that clearly communicated the need to clue me in on the mystery of horse fairy dust and said simply, "So she can fly."

The first time Bree had taken Sunny to a horse show, she'd turned to Sam. "I need my fairy dust, Daddy. So Sunny and I can fly."

It had become a tradition.

Both the girls were sitting on Buckshot when I returned. Heather was in front of Bree but Bree was holding the rope.

I glanced at Bernice. "Whatever happens in the next sixty seconds cannot change your opinion of the Penny family," I warned her.

Bernice looked a little nervous, but she nodded.

I reached up and sprinkled sawdust on top of Bree's head first and then in Heather's stylishly sun-streaked hair. Buckshot's nostrils flared and he gave a soft snort to communicate his disgust with what he deemed to be an unnecessary ritual. He didn't need anything to fly, he could accomplish that on his own, thank you very much.

"Let's go!" Bree nudged Buckshot's sides with her legs. They started off at a leisurely walk.

Bernice and I leaned our elbows on the metal rails of the round pen.

"How did things go this afternoon?" I murmured.

"Painful."

"Root-canal painful?"

Bernice shook her head. "Pulling out a splinter painful."

I understood exactly what she meant. There was always that moment of lip-biting pain when you pulled out a sliver, but then there was that sweet moment of relief right afterward. You couldn't have one without the other.

Bree and Heather's laughter rang out as Buckshot's body loosened and then flowed into the rocking-chair smooth canter that had taken them to first place in Western Pleasure four years in a row. They passed us in a blur of sunlit hair and golden-brown skin.

I knew what Bernice was thinking, because I was thinking the same thing. This is what we could have had for the past ten years. The girls would have played together. Gone to high school together. Grown up together.

I touched Bernice's arm. "Don't look back. A new beginning, remember? Smile at the future." I couldn't help it.

I'd read Proverbs 31 so many times over the past few weeks that parts of it were becoming rooted in my heart. It was a strange feeling—growth. Fleetingly, I wondered what I'd look like when the process was over.

Bree finally brought Buckshot back to the gate and both girls were covered with dust and grime. Heather was almost doubled over, clutching her side from the cramp that she must have earned from her first bareback ride.

"Riding strengthens muscles you never knew you had," Bree told her with a laugh as she slid off Buckshot's wide back.

"Here I thought I was in such great shape from weight training," Heather panted.

"Mom, why is Riley here?" Bree suddenly grabbed my arm.

I looked at the house and saw him standing on the sidewalk, watching us, then I brushed a strand of hair off Bree's sweaty cheek. "Because I invited him for supper."

True to his word, Sam came in for supper, washed up quickly in the laundry room and treated Heather like a member of the family. I guess in a way, she was.

It was so hot, I scrapped the idea of a sit-down dinner in the dining room and we ended up carrying our plates out to the porch.

Riley, Bree and Heather clustered together on the swing, their plates in their laps, and I gave up trying to eavesdrop on their conversation. It was like following a pinball. I was glad there didn't seem to be any tension between Riley and

Bree. Beyond an initial awkwardness when they'd first said hello, things seemed fine between them.

I brought out a pan of brownies for dessert and saw Sam looking at the sky, a concerned look in his eyes. Following his gaze, I could see a line of dark purplish clouds lurking on the horizon.

Riley didn't take a brownie when I offered him one. He jumped to his feet and looked at Sam. "Is it just the back field you cut?"

Sam nodded.

"We'd better get to it, then."

"You're baling hay tonight?" Bree asked.

"Have to," Sam said shortly.

"We grow our own hay. If it gets rained on, it's pretty much ruined," Bree told Heather. "I'd better help, too."

"Does this involve a tractor?" Heather demanded.

"Yes, it does," Bree said. She took a brownie from me. Practical girl. She knew she could eat chocolate *and* bale hay—one didn't necessarily cancel out the other. "It also involves sweat, itchy hay and a lot of dust, city girl."

I gulped and Bernice's eyes widened. The two girls had known each other for two hours and yet Bree felt free to tease her as she would her best friend. Or a sister.

"Bring it on." The gleam in Heather's eyes looked so much like one I'd seen in Bernice's on occasion that it took my breath away. This really was Bernice's child.

Sam grinned. "Give her some clothes, Bree. The more the merrier."

I thought of all the work that baling and storing hay involved and the fact that now they would be in a race against the weather. *I am losing my mind, Lord.* "In that case, count me in."

"Mom!" Bree's eyes practically popped out of her head.

"Oh, please," I said irritably. "You act like I've never helped bale hay before."

Sam leaned over and whispered in my ear, "You haven't."

"Well, I'm a farmer's wife, aren't I?" I took another brownie for courage and then prayed for strength. "To borrow Heather's words, bring it on."

chapter 25

The sky was unnaturally dark by eight o'clock and a soft scarf of a breeze sailed in, pushing the temperature down. Bernice and I were on the hay wagon, dodging bales as they spat toward us and then piling them into neat towers. Several times, Sam hopped onto the baler and skipped across it with the finesse of a tightrope walker. I made a note to scold him later about that.

By ten, with the low growl of thunder moving closer, we sent the last of the bales up the conveyor belt into the loft. As if on cue, the sky opened up and emptied buckets of rain onto the fields.

Bree, Heather and Riley ran outside the barn and performed an impromptu rain dance. I was tempted to join them.

"Feeling a bit old?" Bernice asked with a sigh as we watched them.

"She's pretty wonderful, Bern."

"Her parents are gone this summer. Her dad's a doctor, you know that, but Heather said they went on a mission trip to the Philippines. They're Christians, El. God took care of her. It's like He wanted me to know that she was in His hands. Like He said, 'Bernice, do you see? All these years that you wondered, I was looking out for her, just like I was looking out for you.' She doesn't hate me, either. She just wants to know me." Bernice turned to face me but her eyes weren't filled with despair anymore. She looked as if she'd been given a precious gift on an ordinary day. "Is this what it's like?"

I knew what she was asking me. *Is this what it's like to love God? To be a cherished daughter? To be involved in the sweeping gestures of His love?* The moment called for honesty and I knew it. "I think this is what it's supposed to be like. I'm just beginning to figure that out myself."

Bernice nodded. "It's kind of scary." She didn't look scared, though. She looked...excited.

Annie had said God's path didn't always seem like the safest one. *Well, you always wanted adventure, Elise. Here you go, then.*

"Do you and Heather want to go to church with us in the morning?"

As far as I knew, Bernice had never gone to one of the churches in Prichett. It was one of the unspoken boundaries I'd never had the courage to cross. Until now.

"Heather probably goes to church." Bernice gnawed on her lip. "And Annie will be there, won't she?" I could see her, silently sorting through our church directory for friendly faces. "Sure, we should go. We'll go."

"We always have a big breakfast together on Sunday mornings. Why don't the two of you come over around seven?"

Bernice looked tempted. "Define big breakfast."

"Pancakes, sausage, scrambled eggs…"

"That beats a granola bar. We'll be here."

"Mom?" Bree and Heather poked their heads inside the barn but Bree must have been appointed as spokesman. "Is it all right if Heather stays over tonight? That way, Bernice won't have to sleep on the couch and we can watch a movie. Or two."

"Or three." Heather said with a smile.

I glanced at Bernice, not sure she wanted to be separated from Heather their first night together. "I don't—"

"I don't mind a bit," Bernice interrupted. "It's Saturday night. That's what Saturday nights are for."

"What happened to Riley?"

The girls exchanged looks. "We kicked him out. This movie night is a girl thing."

"Why don't you fix up the sleeping porch?" I suggested. "It's cooler out there than it is upstairs."

"That's a great idea." They disappeared and we could hear the shimmering echo of their laughter as they ran up to the house.

"Are you sure about this?" I asked quietly.

"Are you kidding? I love the idea of her and Bree getting to know each other. I guess I can share her."

"How long is she staying?"

"She didn't say. I think she was waiting to see how our first meeting went. Her parents know that she's here. Apparently, they had a quick background check done on me to make sure I didn't have any outstanding parking tickets or that I'm not a fugitive from the law. I would have done the same thing. She offered to help me in the salon." A small smile curled the corners of Bernice's lips. "Her parents hoped she would go into medicine, but it seems she discovered she has a knack for making people look beautiful."

"Did she ask about her dad?"

"No. I kept waiting for her to ask, but she never did." Bernice exhaled loudly. "I still don't know what to say about him. Not without making myself look like the poster child for low self-esteem—"

"Hey, none of that. You're a princess now, you know."

Bernice looked at me blankly.

"Daughter of a King?" I was beginning to sound like Annie.

"Mmm." Bernice closed her eyes, as if savoring the thought. "That's right."

Sam joined us and on the count of three, we made a dash for the house. In seconds, we were soaked to the skin. Nature's shower. It felt pretty good.

"We'll see you in the morning," I called to Bernice, who had veered off toward her car.

"Thanks for helping," Sam called.

"The girls hit it off, didn't they?" Sam asked as we dripped our way up the stairs.

"They sure did." Another gift. My arms were getting full but I had the feeling that God wasn't done yet.

I peeled off my wet clothes and put on a robe before I went downstairs. Heather and Bree were hauling pillows and blankets out to the sleeping porch that slanted off the back of the house. When Bree was little, the sleeping porch had doubled as her bedroom on hot summer nights. There was no bed, just an ancient, sagging couch shrouded in sun-worn chintz and the lumpy chair that matched it. Every summer, Sam replaced the windows with screens and if you closed your eyes, it felt like you were outside.

"It might rain in," I told them. "You don't have to sleep out here."

"We'll be fine." Heather bounced onto the couch and a smile of pure bliss lit up her face. "Wow. This feels like a cloud."

Bree tossed a pillow at her. "And smells like country air."

"I think I like country air. If I were you, I'd fix up that little stone house over by the apple trees and I'd live there forever. I'd ride bareback every day and I'd marry some handsome guy like Riley and have cute little dark-haired babies…."

I saw the expression on Bree's face. And I knew what put it there. I knew I could even safely discard the words *marry, Riley* and *dark-haired babies.*

"Mom!" She breathed the word at the same moment I started to shake my head.

"What?" Heather looked perplexed. "What did I say?"

A wide grin split Bree's face.

Little stone house. That's what you said.

Sam was in bed, reading, when I went back upstairs. I knew when to beat a safe retreat, and it had been at that moment—the moment when Bree had an epiphany. The summer kitchen. There was no way it was inhabitable.

"What's not inhabitable?"

"What?" I looked at Sam.

"You just muttered something about not inhabitable."

"I meant *uninhabitable*. The old summer kitchen. There's no way someone could actually live in it. There's no electricity. No plumbing. No…*anything!*"

"Who wants to live in the summer kitchen?"

"Heather just said if she was Bree, she'd fix up that little stone house by the apple trees and live there forever," I repeated. I didn't mention the part about marriage, Riley and dark-haired babies. As much as Sam liked Riley, Bree was still his baby girl. And if Heather wasn't Bernice's daughter and I hadn't fallen in love with her on sight, I'd be driving her back to Prichett for daring to put such a crazy notion in Bree's head.

Sam wasn't shaking his head. No, he had a *thoughtful* look on his face.

"Sam!" I squeaked.

"It's sound."

"No."

"Look how long it's been standing."

"You can't be serious."

"It'd take a lot of work."

"That's it, then. You don't have time for one more project."

"Riley's looking for some extra work." There was a wicked sparkle in Sam's blue eyes.

I buried my head under the pillow. "I can't hear you."

"I know someone who turned their old cow barn into a house. I read about it in one of those home magazines at the dentist's office."

"She's going to college. Remember?" I didn't want to come up for air yet. It would have been a sign of weakness.

Sam lifted a corner of the pillow and his voice found me, hiding and in denial. "But then she's coming back."

Bernice showed up at the door the next morning, dressed in a conservative skirt and blouse that had probably been hanging in her closet with the tags still attached to them up to an hour ago. And her hair was a soft shade of caramel.

"Wow."

"This is as close to my natural color as I could get." She tugged on a handful and let it slide through her fingers. "What do you think? Do I look more like a mom?"

I pressed my lips together. Maybe she didn't look more like a mom, but she definitely looked more…something. I had never realized it before, but the garish colors Bernice had chosen to dye her hair all these years had detracted from the exotic slant of her sage-green eyes and the sculptured planes of her face.

The real difference was the one I saw in her eyes. It was like old dusty drapes had been ripped down and replaced with sheers to let the light through.

Sam came up and whistled appreciatively. Bernice hugged him. Annie was rubbing off on all of us.

"I can eat breakfast but I don't think I can go to church," Bernice confessed in a low voice after she stepped away from Sam. "How will I introduce Heather? What if people ask her embarrassing questions and make her feel bad?"

"This is church, Bernice, not a courtroom," Sam said with a smile. "It feels pretty much like supper on the front porch. Doesn't it?" He turned to me as a reinforcement.

Supper on the front porch. No wonder Sam felt so much a part of things at Faith Community. I had never had that perspective. Maybe I'd never seen church as a courtroom, but I guess I'd subconsciously treated it like a spiritual runway, where everyone watched you and waited for you to trip on your heels. There was no way I could tell Bernice how faulty my own view of my church family had been all these years.

"You'll be fine," I said awkwardly, still blinking away the scales that had dropped from my eyes.

"Sit down and have some pancakes." Sam was the designated chef on Sunday mornings.

"Hi, Bernice!" Heather and Bree sashayed into the kitchen, their hair tumbled around their shoulders and still wearing their pajamas.

"See, she's still here. Not a figment of your imagination at all," I murmured to Bernice.

"You colored your hair." Heather noticed the change immediately. "You should have let me do it!"

"I couldn't sleep," Bernice confessed. "I either eat Tootsie Rolls or give myself a makeover when I can't sleep."

Maybe that explained why Bernice's hair color had become part of an ever-changing rotation that followed the hair swatch card at the salon.

"Pancakes." Sam said the word and on cue, we all found a chair at the table.

Lingering over breakfast, we were almost late for church. Sam and I were already in the car when Bree and Heather charged out of the house. They'd swapped clothes. Bree was wearing a trendy khaki skirt, a floral wrap-around blouse with poet's sleeves and ridiculously high sandals that tied at the ankle. Heather was wearing Bree's long denim skirt, the one we'd compromised on because it *looked* like blue jeans, a white T-shirt…and Bree's sassy red cowboy boots.

"I think I understand now why God only gave us one," Sam muttered.

"Why is that?"

"He knew one was all this heart could take. Can you imagine the trouble two would have gotten into?"

He had a point.

When we got to church, Bernice hovered in my shadow. Twice, I even stepped on her foot.

"Are you going to Sunday School with me?" Sam asked.

I shook my head. "We'll go to the one Annie teaches."

In less than ten minutes, people began to spot Bernice. And Heather. These were people Bernice had known forever. She'd cut, combed and permed ninety percent of Prichett's population for years but now she looked at them as if they were total strangers. Her breath started to sound ratchety.

"Supper on the front porch."

I heard her mutter the phrase under her breath.

Then Annie swept in—a rescuer in a parrot-green sundress. "Bernice, I just knew you'd be here this morning." A hug. "You must be Heather." Another hug. "Your eyes are the same shade of green as Bernice's." She started to tear up.

Automatically, I searched my purse for a tissue.

"This baby is turning me into a faucet," Annie whispered with a sniff. "I don't think I knew how to cry until I was a teenager. I'm definitely making up for it now." She looked at Heather. "I'm Annie Carpenter."

We walked to the Sunday School room together, shepherded by Annie's smile. By the time we got to the end of the hall, Bernice was no longer tripping along in my shadow. Her head was higher, her smile wider. And her arm was linked with Heather's for all the world to see.

chapter **26**

Shelby Hannah's phone call early the next morning reminded me of something important that I'd completely forgotten. I was supposed to be keeping a journal for the pageant judges.

"Don't forget to enclose some pictures." Those were the words that were ringing in my ears right before I hung up the phone.

My flowers. I sank into one of the chairs at the kitchen table. I'd forgotten to take pictures of the roses before Sam cut them for Esther's wedding. I hurried outside to survey the damage again. It had rained all day on Sunday and now everything that was left was flecked with mud. Not that there was much to take a picture of, just some woebegone clumps of baby's breath.

I went to look at the hydrangea bush by the front steps. The branches were still hunched over from the force of the rain and it didn't look like it was going to rally anytime soon. I'd just have to send them those pictures from last summer after all.

I'd never kept a journal before. Shelby explained that the judges weren't necessarily as interested in length as they were in honesty. I suddenly realized that nixed the idea of including pictures of last year's gardens.

I went back inside and rummaged around in the den until I found a spiral-bound notebook that hadn't been used. Now I just needed some inspiration.

Maybe you should wait until tonight, Elise. I mean, you're starting a little too soon to write an entry for the day. It's only nine o'clock in the morning!

The pressure was off. Except that Shelby had also reminded me that I needed to summarize my *platform*. I had an idea what she meant. In the pageants I'd seen on television, each contestant talked briefly about something that they cared about, a difference they wanted to make in the world.

I started to doodle in the notebook. Mmm, what to change? What to change? *Can I start with Prichett?* An hour later, I gave up and tossed the notebook on the desk. Right next to Bree's computer, which was humming contentedly.

"Don't get too happy," I told it. "You aren't staying."

From the window, I could see the summer kitchen in the distance. It was rather charming. From a distance. It reminded me of something you'd see in the English countryside. Gray-and-white stone, the foundation hemmed with daylilies.

Daylilies. They were a jumbled palette of yellow, white and orange and they trumpeted their bold colors like the brass section of an orchestra. Even the weeds hadn't been able to silence them. They weren't as beautiful as my roses, but they'd have to do.

I stepped into my rubber clogs, grabbed the camera and headed out to the orchard.

The door of the summer kitchen hung on its hinges and I ventured a peek inside. Just as I thought. Years of junk were layered like rock sediments, retelling the story of one hundred years of farming Penny land.

"There is no way this will ever be fit to live in," I huffed. "Is there, God." I realized it hadn't come out like a question. More like a statement. On this, God just had to agree with me.

The sun moved a fraction and ignited a piece of sheet metal by the window. Had God just winked at me? I backed away from the door and decided to concentrate on the daylilies. Much safer.

"Mrs. Penny. Hey."

Greta Lewis had materialized out of nowhere. Clancy sat beside her, his eyebrows happily communicating his pleasure at having been the one to track me down.

It had to be seventy degrees, but as usual, Greta wore black from head to toe. Two gold hoops were threaded through one eyebrow and there was a gold stud glinting in the crease of her nose.

"What brings you out here, Greta? Does your mother need some eggs?" That was the only reason I could come up with for her unexpected presence.

"Eggs? No." Greta dropped to one knee and untied the bandana (black, of course) from around her neck, folded it into a triangle and tied it around Clancy's neck. "There, now you're stylin'," she said and gave him a friendly nudge.

Clancy, never much for fashion other than a clear flea collar, thumped his tail and preened.

Greta looked up at me. "I brought your dress."

I swallowed. Hard. "My dress?"

"My Aunt Mindy said you needed an evening gown for this pageant you're in and that you'd let me design one for you. I have it with me but I need you to try it on to get the hem right. You're tall but you're a perfect size six."

"How did you know that?" I asked cautiously, wondering if my measurements were written down somewhere. Maybe on the Prichett Pride and Joy Wall?

"That's what I do."

Sure it is. Panicked, I wondered how I could get out of this. I was planning to shop in Madison for a dress. A *real* dress. The kind of dress I'd always dreamed of wearing but had never had the chance. Probably something simple yet elegant in a light periwinkle. No black. No chains.

"You brought my dress *with* you?" I asked, just to make sure I'd understood. A vague memory of an even vaguer conversation with Mindy at the Cut and Curl was beginning to return. She'd mentioned that Greta was interested in fashion. How she'd made the leap from my need for an evening gown to Greta showing up *with* an evening gown was beyond me.

"I found a great one at a rummage sale last weekend," Greta said. "It just needs a little work."

A rummage sale. Worse and worse. Some nightmare bridesmaid reject.

"Greta, I don't know…" Our eyes met and even though hers looked like they'd been framed with felt-tipped marker, they sparkled with life. She was excited about the dress. Somehow, I couldn't say the words that would strip that excitement away.

"Okay, let's take a look at it." Maybe it wouldn't fit. *Please, don't let it fit!*

"Your flowers look like a painting by Van Gogh," Greta said.

"Oh, that's right. I need to snap a few quick pictures."

As I was focusing, Greta stepped before the lens, a somber contrast to the joyous explosion of color behind her.

"Um…that's good. Smile."

She smiled. I snapped the picture. Now I had an interesting picture for my pageant journal. I could only imagine the caption. "My dress designer in my alternate garden."

We walked in silence back to the house and I spotted a rusty blue car parked in the driveway. She skipped toward it, with Clancy matching her bounce for bounce. Funny, somehow Greta Lewis just didn't seem like the skipping type.

"I'll be back in a minute," she called over her shoulder.

I paced around the kitchen. *A rummage sale, Lord! She can't be serious. I mean, who else is going to be wearing an evening gown from a rummage sale?*

Greta came in with a garment bag draped carefully over one arm. There was a backpack slung over her shoulder that contained goodness only knew what. "Some of the beading is loose, so be careful when you try it on."

Wonderful.

"You want me to try it on now?"

Greta nodded. "It smells good in here."

"Banana bread. Help yourself."

I ducked into the bathroom and slowly unzipped the garment bag. And caught a glimpse of purple. Purple! Every molecule of color drained out of my face when I wore purple. Purple was a pigment-sucking menace to my complexion.

I pulled the dress out and heard the soft rustle of the fabric. And the ping of beads hitting the bathroom tile. Greta must have heard them, too.

"Beads!" She barked out a reminder.

I let the garment bag slide to the floor. The dress was old. Vintage old. So old that it was…stylish. The fabric was the thin, slippery satin that only someone without a bump or wrinkle could wear. Tiny pearls were sewn randomly across the bodice and sprinkled over the skirt.

I undressed quickly, praying it wouldn't fit. There was a

moment when I pulled the dress over my hips that it hitched at my waist, but I managed to ease it over that particular danger zone without ripping it. Rats. The satin pooled at my feet. It fitted.

I dared to look in the mirror. Just as I suspected, I looked like a mime. But the dress. There was something about it. Something unexpected. Something classic and beautiful.

"How does it feel?" Greta called.

Strange words. Not, "How does it fit?"

I stepped out of the bathroom and came face-to-face with Greta. She frowned and studied the dress. Then she studied my face. I tried not to twitch.

"You look pale."

I nodded eagerly. She noticed. That had to be a good thing.

"But you have to wear purple. I read Proverbs 31 and it says she wears purple."

"Oh, I don't think—"

"I can come up with something. I'll bet you look good in pink, don't you?"

"I never wear pink."

"You should. Come into the natural light."

She meant outside. We stepped onto the porch and Greta dumped the mysterious contents of the backpack out on the porch swing.

"I'm trying to get a scholarship to a fashion design school

in New York." She knelt down and started to mark off the hem of the dress with the pins in her hand—without using a tape measure. "This dress is going to get me the scholarship."

"But this dress is already designed. Don't you have to create something of your own?"

"The dress has a design but what they're looking for is a concept. That's what I give it."

"You add to an existing design?"

"Right. Like your garden. The foundation of that old stone building was already there but you planted the flowers along the edge that you imagined should be there. The two blend together and that's the concept."

It actually made sense. But I still wasn't sure. I wasn't sure about paper-thin satin that ruthlessly outlined every ripple and bulge (and there were definitely more of those now than there had been when I was eighteen). I wasn't sure about purple. I wasn't sure about a dress that was probably pulled from a trunk in someone's attic. But I really wasn't sure how to tell Greta that I wasn't sure!

"So, the school accepts you based on a design…on a concept…you send them?"

"And an essay." Greta said the words around the row of pins she'd pressed between her lips. "After Aunt Mindy told me about the pageant, I found a Bible and looked up Proverbs 31. It's perfect. I decided to write the scholarship essay about her—the Proverbs 31 woman—then I can show them the dress I designed, too."

"What are you going to write about?" Now I was intrigued.

"Clothes say a lot about a person," Greta said, spitting out the last of the pins and poking them into the fabric. "The woman in the Proverbs wore purple linen. Purple dye was extremely rare and only wealthy people could afford it. The average person didn't wear linen, either. So, she's wealthy, she has servants, but that's not the most significant thing about her."

I have to admit that I'd skipped right through the linen and purple part of the chapter. I hadn't realized there was anything special about what she wore.

"People tend to judge you by your appearance, but it doesn't look that way in Proverbs 31. I mean, it mentions that she wears purple and linen, but then at the end it says that beauty is vain. Her clothes are a symbol of her value but they aren't the reason she *has* value. The most important things are that she fears God and what she does with her hands."

"You figured all that out on your own?"

Greta wasn't offended by the question that erupted out of my surprise. I mean, the girl was sixteen years old!

"That's what it says." The expression on her face told me that this wasn't rocket science. "I like her. If I lived back then, I would have wanted to hang out with her."

"Doesn't she sound too perfect?" I asked curiously. "Look at everything she does. It'd be hard to keep up with someone like that."

Greta shrugged. "I never got the idea that she'd make me feel like…" she caught the word she was about to say and struggled to find an acceptable substitute "…pond slime. Look at how she's described. Kind. Wise. Brave. Strong. She's not doing any of the things she does out of duty or to get noticed. She does them out of love. That's why she's so cool."

That was the second sermon delivered on my front porch by an unlikely messenger of the truth. God certainly was getting my attention in unexpected ways.

"So, this is what we're going to do," Greta said, not realizing that once again my world had tilted. Or maybe, it had been righted. It was getting hard to tell the difference. "I'm going to rip off the sleeves because they look too medieval, and I'm going to add some more sparkle. Not much, though, because it has to be simple. Then, I'm going to make a wrap for you out of pink satin so you don't disappear when you wear the dress. I'll come back next week and we'll check the hemline."

"I hope you get the scholarship, Greta."

Her lips flat-lined suddenly. "Me, too. I can't wait to get out of Prichett."

"Why?" Silly question. I'd been feeling the same way for years.

"I don't fit in with the other kids my age," she said. "Mom says that Prichett needs people like me to loosen its seams a little. I guess that's my lot in life at the moment."

I hid a smile. Now she sounded like a normal, disgruntled teenager. "Your mom is right."

"You're Bree's mom, aren't you?"

I felt a sudden stab of concern that Bree had been one of the people who may have shunned Greta. "Uh-huh."

"We had gym together last year. I like her. She isn't full of herself like some of the other girls."

"I like her, too."

We shared a smile.

"So, I suppose she's going to college?"

"She wants to come back after she gets her degree." It was getting easier to say the words. "I'll get out of the dress while you grab a soda out of the fridge."

I ducked into the bathroom and took another look in the bathroom mirror before I slipped the dress off, raising up on my tiptoes so I could see better. I was starting to see what Greta had seen. The very simplicity of the dress was what made it beautiful.

She was waiting on the porch when I came out, petting Clancy.

"Don't forget your bandana."

"He can keep it." She reached out and took the garment bag from me.

"Greta, I know what your clothes say." I couldn't resist saying the words and I saw the answering spark of curiosity in her eyes.

The eyebrow with the gold hoops through it rose slightly. "What?"

"They say, *get to know me.*"

"You're going to love this dress, Mrs. Penny."

"I know I am."

Journal Entry: Today I got an evening gown for the pageant.

chapter 27

All afternoon, the words love and duty flashed in my mind like the pink neon sign in the window of Sally's Café. I wasn't quite sure how a sixteen-year-old girl had dug straight through to the heart of Proverbs 31 and I had totally missed it. All I had done was stand next to that saintly do-gooder and had been left feeling like a plate of spiritual leftovers. I hadn't considered what motivated her until Greta had properly introduced us. The Proverbs 31 woman would have known the verse that Annie had paraphrased only days before when we were talking about choosing God's path. "Love the Lord your God with all your heart and with all your soul and with all your mind."

That woman, the one who seemed so lofty and unapproachable, was just the opposite. She touched everything—the vineyard, the spindle, a lamp—and everyone—her husband, her children, the poor—with love, the love that grew out of her love for God. Fresh growth. Healthy extensions. I knew all about that. I'd just never thought about it in terms of my life before.

It was scary. I could almost feel the knot of bitterness inside that had somehow taken root in my life. I wasn't sure of its source, but it had slowly crept its way in and distorted my perspective. All these years, I'd sensed that people thought I was a failure because I hadn't gone out and done what I'd said I was going to do. I'd practically shouted from the rooftop that I was too good for Prichett, that I had bigger plans for my life. When I'd married Sam, I could hear their silent laughter. See their smug looks. *You're one of us now, Elise.*

I wondered how I could let so many years go by without realizing what was happening to me. It had even affected my relationship with God. I had been afraid to get too close—hiding my heart, when all the while, He could see it anyway.

I could feel God working on that knot, plowing my heart just like Sam plowed our fields in the spring. Working the soil, exposing the rocks lodged in it. Maybe that was what my cranky flashes and restlessness were all about—bringing everything to the surface so God could plant something new. The thought was both frightening and exciting at the same time.

The phone rang while I was making supper and even though she was whispering, I recognized Bernice's voice.

"I want to keep her."

I laughed. "Bern…"

"I'm serious, El. She has to leave at the end of the week and I don't want her to go."

That didn't surprise me a bit. "I take it the two of you are getting along well?"

"We have so much in common it's scary," Bernice admitted. "Especially because we've never been around each other to pick up each other's little quirks. We made spaghetti last night and she eats it the same way I do."

"No." That was hard to believe. No one eats spaghetti like Bernice. She prepares the sauce and the pasta separately, twirls the spaghetti onto her fork and then dunks it in the sauce.

"I'm not kidding you," Bernice said. "Exactly the same way. But what's really weird is that sometimes she reminds me of Alex. She laughs just like him."

I heard something wistful in the memory. "Does she know?"

"No. I can't tell her about him yet. She still hasn't asked, but I can tell she wants to. I'm afraid she'll be mad at me. I left *him,* you know."

"I think that Heather has a big heart and she'll understand."

"I don't know. I know it's too late for her to think I'm perfect, but I want her to…like me."

"So, when are you two coming back out to the farm?"

"Tomorrow night after work, if that's okay. But do I have to wear my old clothes?" Bernice joked.

"You never know. Sam may need you to fix the tractor." I heard a funny sound. "Bernice? Are you crying?"

"Yes."

"Why?"

"Because I feel...loved."

"Bernice, you are."

"But I wasn't sure before. Annie called this morning and read a verse out of the Bible that she said spoke to her and she wanted to share it with me. Do you want me to read it?"

"Sure, go ahead." Annie was on assignment again!

"'He stood me up on a wide-open field; I stood there saved—surprised to be loved.'"

Now I was crying. A wide-open field. Of newly plowed ground. Ready for planting.

"That's exactly how I feel. Not that everything is going to be perfect, but from now on, everything is going to be *right*." Bernice paused and her voice lightened. "But I suppose the Proverbs 31 woman knows all this stuff."

This Proverbs 31 woman has a lot to learn. That's what I was thinking.

Sam stopped in just as I was pulling the roast out of the oven. Gordon had an emergency and needed his help. Of course he did.

"I'll be home later." Sam kissed the frown that had settled between my eyebrows, attempting to inject it with his infinite patience for all things Gordon-related. "Love you."

"I love you, too." I sighed the words.

When Bree came in, she showered and then we ate together on the porch. I was starting to wish for fall, when the days would be sunny but crisp.

"Do you think we can start on the files tonight, Mom?" Bree asked.

"Dad won't be home until later."

"Exactly."

"You are quite the little plotter, aren't you?"

"I know Dad keeps everything," she said. "Maybe we can just start by weeding out some reams of paper."

"I suppose we should start sometime. You only have a few weeks to help me get this going before you leave for Madison."

Bree, the sassy child, made a face at me.

Armed with M&M's and a garbage bag, we attacked. Sam did keep everything. I pulled a box of receipts out of a drawer and gave it to Bree, then started looking through a shoebox marked Important. Keep.

"Doesn't Dad realize that the government only wants you to keep things for seven years, not twenty?" Bree complained after an hour had gone by and we were still sitting cross-legged on the floor, sorting.

"Your dad is careful. He got that from Grandma Mary."

"Wow. Who was your fairy godmother?" Bree suddenly whistled.

"What?"

"There's a receipt here for twenty-five thousand dollars," Bree said.

"Twenty-five…" I held out my hand and Bree gave me the receipt. It was old, I could tell because the paper was discolored. I looked at the date and mentally counted back the years. Bree would have been about four years old. The strange thing was, it was from a bank in Chicago, not Prichett.

"What was it for?"

"I'm not sure."

"You're not sure?" Bree laughed. "You can't remember getting twenty-five thousand dollars in cash?"

I couldn't. I caught my bottom lip in my teeth and tried to piece together what would have been happening in our life at the time the receipt was dated.

The hail storm. How could I have forgotten? It had happened just a few years after we were married, right in the middle of August, close to harvest time. We'd lost almost everything. The corn. The tomatoes. The pumpkins. Even the carrots hadn't been protected underground. The tops had been damaged so badly that we lost three-quarters of those, too. The old-timers said that there hadn't been a storm like that for over fifty years. The fields looked as if they were covered in snow the next morning.

We took such a financial loss that we weren't even sure we could afford to buy seed for the following spring. The bank had refused to give Sam a loan. We weren't the only farm who had been hit by the storm and to make matters worse, the farm was in Sam's name now instead of his father's and the bank didn't consider him a good risk yet.

I didn't pay much attention to the finances and only knew that Sam had somehow gotten the money he needed to get us through the winter and to buy next year's seed. I hadn't even thought to ask how it had happened, assuming that, in the end, the loan officer had changed his mind.

If the money had come from Will and Mary, Sam would have said something. I tried to think of who our mysterious benefactor could have been and why Sam hadn't told me about it.

First National Bank of Chicago.

My mother's bank.

"Mom, are you okay?" Bree leaned over and put her hand on mine. "You're shaking."

"I…" I staggered to my feet. "I need to go for a walk."

"Mom!"

"I can't explain…I just need to clear my head for a few minutes. I'm fine." I walked outside and headed blindly down the steps.

My mother had been gone for several years when the storm hit. I had no idea she'd left money for us. The house she and I had lived in had been rented. All Mom owned was our furniture and a car. She'd never mentioned having twenty-five thousand dollars saved…and neither had Sam.

My mind tried to come up with different ways Sam could

have gotten the money to keep the farm afloat, but everything returned to one possibility—Mom had left us a sizeable amount of money that I'd never known about.

The sun was setting and I looked around wildly for an escape route. One that would take me from turbulence to peace. There was a light on in the barn and I walked toward it.

Sam's corduroy jacket was hanging on a hook by the door, waiting for the change of seasons. The collar was frayed and the pocket ripped. He'd definitely need a new one. I reached out and ran my fingers down the sleeve, loosening the sweet scent of hay and Sam's cologne.

I climbed the ladder to the hay loft and sat down on one of the bales, tucking my arms around my legs. That's how Sam found me two hours later.

He didn't even call my name, just climbed the ladder and sat down beside me. He didn't even try to touch me.

"When your mom knew she wasn't going to beat the cancer, she told me about the savings account she'd made in our name," Sam finally said. "She told me some of the money was to pay for our wedding. The rest, she wanted me to have in case of an emergency."

The significance of that conversation, which had taken place without my knowledge, was so painful that my lungs hurt when I took a careful breath. "That was money she'd saved for my future, wasn't it?"

In the soft glow of the light, I saw Sam nod.

"Then why didn't she tell me?" Even as I asked the question, I already knew what the answer was. She'd been afraid that I would leave Prichett. Leave Sam.

"Money can be a burden. She didn't want it to drive a wedge between us, she said. I told her I didn't like the idea of keeping it from you, but she made me promise. She said she trusted me to do the right thing with it. I didn't want it, Elise. I left it in the bank in Chicago and ignored it. I knew someday I would break my promise to her and tell you about it and you'd be happy, knowing that your Mom had given us a gift like that. To use for Bree's education, or to take a trip somewhere…"

The thought suddenly struck me that maybe Sam hadn't been so certain of my love, either. After all, I was only eighteen years old and determined that my name would someday become a household word.

"Until the hail storm."

"Until the storm." Now Sam reached out and found my hand in the darkness. He wove his fingers through mine.

For two hours, I'd wrestled with God before Sam found me in the loft. And He brought to mind that night when I'd felt Sam's body shaking with tears when he'd thought we would lose the farm. And I remembered praying that God would somehow provide a way for us to keep the farm. God had answered my prayer. I'd relived the past nineteen years, trying to imagine Sam being something other than a farmer. Trying to imagine Bree growing up in the city, without

Buckshot and her animals. Trying to imagine tending a garden in a container on my patio instead of the wildly beautiful drops of color that my flowers created around the house. And I couldn't. Somehow, my dream had changed and I hadn't even realized it.

"You cried when you thought you were going to lose the farm," I said. "When you thought I was sleeping."

"No." Sam shook his head. "I was crying because I felt like somehow I was stealing *your* future."

"Sam, you idiot," I whispered. "You did the right thing. *You* were my future."

chapter **28**

Sam brought me coffee in bed the next morning. We'd stayed in the loft for another hour but we hadn't said a word. Any words that we would have spoken were transformed into kisses and wrapped in a long embrace. When we finally made our way to the house, Bree was already asleep.

"I'll come in for lunch," Sam told me. "Will you be here?"

"I'm not planning to do anything special. Bernice and Heather are coming over this evening." I let him take a sip from my coffee cup.

He hesitated beside the bed.

"Don't you have chores to do, farmer?" I teased.

Sam sat down and I was shocked to see tears in his eyes. "You are…Elise, I love you so much. And I know you love me, but all these years I've wondered if you had regrets. When you reacted so strongly about Bree not going to college, I started to think that I made a mistake…I wished your mother had never given us that money, then you could have had the life you wanted."

"I've been seeing things differently," I said and reached out to trace his jawline. "And we aren't going to talk about this again. Promise?"

Bernice wasn't the only one who could celebrate a new beginning.

"Now that I think about it, I might have a few free hours to sit on the tractor with you," I added.

Sam leaned over and said something in my ear that made me blush. Then, as he reached the door, he blew me a kiss.

"A down payment."

As soon as I walked outside, Clancy joined me and I knelt down to attack the weeds that tried to disguise themselves as zinnias.

God, You sure have a way of getting people's attention, don't You? Not that I'm complaining.

I really wasn't. I was in awe. In the loft, God had shown me where that root of bitterness had started and why. It had been after the storm, when I'd carried the secret hope that we would be forced to sell the farm. While my husband had surveyed his damaged crops and gone to every bank in the county, I was silently packing our possessions and moving back to Chicago. When it hadn't happened, when somehow our finances had been righted, I had to accept the fact that I'd be in Prichett forever, but my stubborn heart told me I didn't have to like it. What I hadn't remembered was the prayer that I'd prayed that Sam's dream wouldn't die. Until last night. And I asked God to do some surgery and cut out the bitterness, and to forgive me for letting it grow all these years. And that's where Sam had found me—transplanted into grace and pruned for growth.

The sound of a truck rattling up the driveway drew my attention. I recognized Lester Lee's pickup and it was pulling a trailer behind it. I figured he had to see Sam about something, so I went to meet him.

Lester had lived in Prichett all his life. He was a dairy farmer who wore his Carhartts like a uniform and never, at least while I was in earshot, spoke more than a sentence or two. He tapped out his thoughts in some kind of secret code by striking his soiled cap against his leg. The taps were then picked up by his wife, Carolee (yes, Carolee Lee), and relayed to whomever Lester was talking to. I'm pretty certain that's why he married Carolee—so he wouldn't have to talk. She took his simple sentences, consisting of a noun and a verb, and embellished them with adjectives and adverbs and colorful prepositional phrases so Lester sounded quite articulate. People got so used to Carolee being Lester's translator that they end up ignoring him completely. I had a hunch that suited Lester just fine.

But this morning, Lester was alone. With no Carolee at his side, he looked like a puzzle with a missing piece.

"Hello, Lester!"

His cap struck his thigh once. I figured that meant hello. "Are you looking for Sam?"

"No."

I waited for a second and heard a pitiful bawl come from the trailer. "What can I do for you?" I was beginning to admire Carolee's patience.

Sweat began to bead on Lester's head like moisture in a terrarium. "The calendar."

The hat tapped out the rest of this obscure message but I couldn't quite catch it. I had no idea…oh, yes I did. The calendar. Every year the farmers had their own calendar printed and it followed a common theme. One year, every month had been a photo of a different tractor wheel, last year it was hay bales (a replica of the Pentagon being the most creative). I highly doubted the calendars ever crossed the county line, but everyone around Prichett bought one because the proceeds went into a scholarship fund for a high-school senior who was going into the agriculture program at Madison.

"I'll buy a calendar from you. Are they still ten dollars?" Lester stared at me.

"You don't want me to buy one? Where is Carolee this morning, by the way?"

"I want you to be in it. You're in that beauty pageant, right?"

"Yesss." I wondered if this year's theme had something to do with people in the community who'd made it onto Sally's Pride and Joy Wall. "Who else is going to be featured in it?"

"Junebug."

"Junebug."

"My cow."

My gaze darted back to the trailer. "Lester, what is the theme this year?" I asked suspiciously.

A grin bisected Lester's face. "Beautiful bovines. That was my idea." Tap, tap, tap. "I'll go get her."

"You want to take the picture now?" I squeaked. I needed time to wriggle out of this questionable honor.

"I got the cow. Got my camera." Lester was already striding away. He paused and looked back at me. "Ah, Junebug had a bath this mornin'. She looks real pretty."

His hat tapped out a silent message that I didn't need Carolee to translate. *You might want to step up to the plate and look pretty, too.*

I looked down at my grubby blue jeans and faded chambray shirt and dutifully headed toward the house.

"Nice dress!"

Lester yelled the words but I wasn't sure who he was talking to—me or Junebug.

I washed the dirt off my face and hands, re-braided my hair and thumbed through the dresses in my closet. There was a floral print sundress...or my more formal blue linen suit. I caught myself and giggled.

Every wacky, unpredictable moment in the past month was somehow connected to the pageant. I was beginning to wonder if this was my penance—that my teenage dreams of fame and fortune were now being played out like an off-Broadway comedy in which Prichett was not only the producer, costumer and set designer but also my audience.

I decided on the blue linen. When I went back outside, Lester was holding Junebug by the rope he'd tied around her neck. As far as cows go, she *was* pretty, a Holstein with jet-black spots against a milky-white background.

Lester gave me the end of the rope. His hat was on his head now, leaving me to wonder whether he was going to speak to me at all. A frown of concentration had plowed a furrow between his bushy eyebrows.

Junebug swung her enormous head around and sized me up immediately as her competition. I knew the look. Then she tried to take a bite out of my sleeve. I stepped away.

"Does she bite?"

"Never bit me." Lester was studying the camera. Junebug started to walk toward my hydrangea bush while I jostled along behind her, yanking on the rope.

"Lester!"

"No film. Don't let her eat grass, Elise, or she'll get stains on her face. Don't let her roll, either." He jogged back toward his truck.

I dug in my heels but my one hundred and fifteen pounds was no match for Junebug's one thousand. I bounced in her wake like a barefoot water-skier.

"Junebug, no!"

The hydrangea was now within reach and Junebug let out

a victory moo. Suddenly, a sharp whistle pierced the air and Junebug stopped so abruptly that I ended up pasted against her massive side.

Lester hurried up to us. He swatted her on the rump with his cap and Junebug actually hung her beautiful bovine head in repentance.

"I'll take her." Lester took the rope from my amateur hands and Junebug followed him, docile as a puppy. But she rolled a look in my direction that clearly communicated the battle for the hydrangea bush wasn't over yet.

"I have to find the best place to take the picture." Lester surveyed the yard.

"How about that tree over there?" I pointed to the willow.

Lester shook his head. The cap tapped his leg in agreement.

"The barn?"

"No. Where're those flowers everyone talks about?"

"We cut most of them." A picture of John Crandall wearing the boutonniere flashed in my mind. I smiled.

Twenty minutes later, I was wilting in the heat while Junebug still glowed like moonlight. It was obvious that Lester took the calendar *very* seriously. Normally, I would have felt a cranky flash starting by now but instead I found myself writing a journal entry for the pageant that would *never* make it onto paper.

"Here." Lester stopped by the bale of hay that Bree used as a mounting block. I successfully resisted the urge to mention that we'd walked past it four times already.

Lester untied the rope from Junebug's neck and set her free. I filled my lungs with air, just in case I needed to scream for Sam if we had a runaway cow on our hands.

"Down, Junebug."

To my amazement, like a bovine supermodel, Junebug's legs buckled and she lay down, arranging herself artfully next to the hay bale. She even tilted her head.

"Elise, you get right behind her."

I slid around Junebug's back and stood behind her.

"Put your cheek against her face."

"Lester…"

"Go on. She won't hold a pose like this very long," he told me, his eyes bright.

Well, all right then.

"Prima donna," I whispered in her ear.

"This is gonna be perfect," Lester said gleefully. "No one is gonna have someone as pretty as you in their month."

I smiled. "Thank you, Lester."

"Oh, I was talking to Junebug," he said. "But you look real nice, too, Elise."

Journal Entry: Today I had my picture taken for a local calendar.

Everyone laughed when I retold the story at supper that evening and Heather wanted to know all about the pageant.

She was the first person I knew who'd actually heard about the Proverbs 31 Pageant.

"I think you need a pit crew, Elise," she said. "What do you think?" She turned to Bernice.

Bernice had been quieter than usual and I knew why. She was shoring up her heart for Saturday, when Heather had to leave. "Not a bad idea."

"I volunteer," Heather said. "And maybe Bree can come with us."

"And Annie," Bernice said. "I like the way she prays."

I glanced at Sam, who was depositing the maraschino cherry from the top of his hot fudge sundae onto mine. The pageant was in the middle of September. It wasn't harvest time, but Sam was still busy enough. I wasn't even sure he was planning to go with me. We'd never discussed it.

"We'll do your hair and makeup." Heather studied me and I could see her restyling my hair in her mind.

"I can sew on a button if you lose one," Bree chimed in.

"You can?" Sam teased her. "I know you can repair a bridle, but I had no idea you could sew on a button."

"It's not that different, Daddy." Bree tossed her head.

"You would really come with me?" I asked. "That's a three-day commitment and I wouldn't get to spend much time with you."

"Girl time," Bernice said. She was excited now, too, but I knew a big part of the reason was because she'd be with Heather again.

"That leaves me out," Sam said with a heavy sigh.

"I wasn't sure if you were going with me or not. We haven't really talked much about it," I said.

"If you want me to, I will. Gordon can take over for a few days." Sam grinned. "He owes me."

Thursday to Saturday. No matter how agreeable he appeared, I knew what a sacrifice it would be. Sam would have to pay someone to come and do all the work.

"I think I'll be in good hands," I told him. "You just hold down the fort while I'm gone."

"What do you think, Bernice?" Heather had her hands in my hair, swirling it up in the back. "A French twist?"

"Either that or a chignon," Bernice said.

"You need to shop for a dress, don't you, Mom?" Bree asked.

"Um, as a matter-of-fact, someone's making one for me." I'd completely forgotten to tell them about Greta.

Bernice's eyes widened. "Not that girl in black?"

"She's the one," I said and patted Bernice's knee when she gasped. "It's fine. I've tried on the dress. I don't know if I can do it justice, but it's actually quite beautiful."

"You'd look good in a potato sack," Sam murmured.

I caught Bree looking at me with a strange expression on her face. "What?"

"Greta Lewis is making your dress?"

"Mmm-hmm. Is something wrong with that?"

"No." Bree shook her head so quickly that her ponytail began to spin. "It's just that most people think she's weird and don't give her a chance, that's all."

"Prichett needs people like her," I said. "To loosen its seams."

Bree leaned over and dropped her cherry—the part she always saved for last—into my dish of ice cream. Then I saw the flash of warmth in her eyes. Another gift, blooming out of the difficult weeks we'd had recently and one I wouldn't forget.

chapter **29**

After Heather and Bernice left, Bree waited until we were alone, and then she sidled up next to me at the sink where I was rinsing out the ice cream bowls.

"Mom? Is everything okay between you and Dad?" she whispered.

"Everything is fine."

She didn't look convinced. "Last night, when he came home, I showed him the receipt we'd found," she said. "Mom, I've never seen Dad look like that. He asked me where you went and he looked...*scared*...when I told him you'd left."

"I just needed some time to think." I wondered how much to tell her. How much would she need to know to put her mind at ease? "When you were four, there was a hail storm. It wiped out everything. Your grandma, my mother, had set aside some money for us before she died—for emergencies. If Dad hadn't used it, we would have had to sell."

"And you didn't know about it?"

Leave it to Bree to cut right to the heart of the matter. "I didn't know about it."

Bree picked up a dish towel and absently began to wipe the bowls as she processed the information I had just given her.

"Are you mad at Grandma?"

It wasn't the question I'd been expecting and for a brief moment, my heart stumbled over it. During those two hours in the loft with God, anger was one of the things that I'd had to wrestle. "At first I was mad, but then I prayed about it and I realized it didn't matter. I was committed to your Dad—I loved him. The money wouldn't have made a difference. Maybe I'm a little hurt that Mom didn't have more faith in me, but I guess up until that point, I hadn't given her much reason to." It was still a painful thought.

"It was a blessing that she saved that much money. I mean, maybe that's what it was meant for all along," Bree said.

God's sense of humor again. This time, I laughed along with Him.

The day Heather left, Bernice showed up on the porch. I couldn't offer her much comfort. Bree and I had spent the afternoon sorting through her closet, packing her clothes.

She was leaving home. No more damp bath towels draped over the banister. No more muddy boot prints in the front hall. No more impromptu M&M's parties.

"I don't like this," Bernice announced. She plopped down on the swing and set it swaying in an irregular motion, probably similar to my heartbeat. "I think I liked guilt and denial better."

I could see her point but I knew that I had to set her straight. "New beginnings, remember? She's part of your life now. Nothing is going to change that."

"I called Phoebe, an old friend. Alex is filming a movie in Australia."

"You're going to tell him about Heather?" I still couldn't get over the fact that Bernice had been in love with Alexander Scott. I'd just seen his face on TV within the past week because his newest film was about to be released.

"I don't know what I'm going to tell him exactly." Bernice groaned. "But I just talked to Phoebe a few days ago. She's Alex's publicist but she was a friend of mine, too. I made her promise not to tell him I'd called. But I think I need to tell him why I left and that I'm sorry. It's a start."

"It sounds like a good place to start."

Bree came out of the house just then, saw Bernice and without a word wrapped her in a hug. When they separated, both of them were teary-eyed.

"She'll be back," Bree said. "She loves it here. She loves *you*."

"Did she tell you that?" Bernice demanded.

"No." Bree shook her head.

Bernice's face crumpled and I gave Bree *the look*. She ignored me. "But when she was over the other night she said, 'don't forget to hug *my mom* for me when I'm gone.'"

"My mom?" Bernice's body slumped against the porch swing like an underbaked cake. "She said *that* word? *Mom?*"

"That exact word."

"I was wrong." Bernice looked at me. "Guilt and denial are *not* better."

The three of us sat on the swing together and Bree's foot against the floor kept us gliding smoothly back and forth. She was wearing her red cowboy boots. I wondered if any of the other girls in her dorm would be wearing red cowboy boots.

"Look!" Bree pointed to the sky. "There's a huge Christmas tree."

It was a game Bree had played for years. The cloud game, she called it. When she was little, I would weed the flower beds while she lay on her back in the grass, telling me all the things she saw in the clouds.

"Wow." Bernice leaned forward. "It does look like a Christmas tree."

Bree chuckled. "Haven't you ever played the cloud game, Bernice?" she teased.

"If I did, it was so long ago that I can't remember it," Bernice said in her own defense.

"Oh, now it's a clipper ship." Bree hopped to her feet and watched the cloud. The wind had smoothed the sharp edges of the tree away in seconds and created a billowing sail.

"It's going to hit that other cloud." Now Bernice stood up. "And make a…"

They waited. I couldn't stand the suspense anymore. I stood up, too, just as it merged with another cloud.

"A castle!" Bernice and Bree shouted together, jumping up and down.

My gaze dropped from the sky to the summer kitchen, a cozy little package nestled in the field, tied with a ribbon of daylilies. I couldn't imagine not having Bree here every day but suddenly I could imagine her coming home. And I could imagine curtains billowing in the breeze in the windows of the summer kitchen.

The next few days went by too quickly. I wanted to slow them down and savor them but there was too much to do. As Bree filled up boxes, Sam would carry them down and line them up in the hallway. I checked off the list of things she needed to take. Her bedroom looked bare. Never one for ruffles and knickknacks to begin with, her room was almost skeletal now. I wanted her to tell me she was excited about going away to school, but I had a feeling she was confiding most of her feelings to Buckshot. She saddled him up every evening after supper and didn't come back until almost dark.

I brought a laundry basket filled with clean towels and sheets down and lined it up with the rest of Bree's things in the hall. That was the last of it....

"She's leaving tomorrow," Sam said, coming up beside me as I stood on the porch with a cup of tea. It was supposed to be Comforting Chamomile, but it didn't feel very comforting at the moment.

"I thought I'd be happy that she decided to go to college but all I can think of is how empty the house is going to feel now."

Sam and I hadn't shared much of ourselves in the past few days either. He was right in the middle of harvest now and I barely saw him. At night, he collapsed in bed beside me, dropped a sleepy misplaced kiss somewhere on my face and promptly fell asleep.

"It will be different," Sam said, a slight catch in his voice. "A different season."

"Spoken like a true farmer." I nudged him with my elbow. But I knew he was right. The season of two.

I could see Buckshot flying across the field in a canter, an ink-black silhouette against a coral-tinted sky. There were two riders on his back.

The next morning Sam loaded up the truck and we got an early start. Freshman orientation started at nine and we were planning to attend the parents' meetings all morning while Bree went to a special one for incoming freshmen.

As the day progressed, I could tell Bree's cheerful confidence was being tested. I felt helpless to do anything about it. Several times I saw her eyes glisten. She had a folder stuffed with information and had met her roommate—a rail-thin girl who'd glanced at Bree's red cowboy boots and smirked. I helped her make up her bed and unpack her suitcases while her roommate stretched out on the narrow bunk above us and chatted into her cell phone. What I wanted to do was pull Bree into the truck and drive home with her.

We took her out for supper but ate in silence. Bree had insisted that we only take one day away from the farm to settle her in. Now I was wishing we hadn't given in to her request. On the way back to the dorm, Sam drove under the speed limit. I knew why.

Bree's smile had faded at some point during the day and had yet to resurface. Sam parked the car in a temporary parking spot. As if on automatic pilot, we all got out of the car but none of us moved. At least, not on the outside. Inside, I was being torn into small pieces.

"Bree, I think we should pray," I said. Other than small prayers at bedtime and before meals, I couldn't remember ever saying those words before.

"That's a good idea," Sam said. He looked at me a little strangely. What did he expect? New seasons called for new changes.

I took Bree's hand. I don't know what I prayed for. All I know is that the words flowed out of every hole in my heart that the day had torn open and sealed the gaps closed as soon as they left my mouth.

"Thanks, Mom." Bree hugged me hard. "I'll be fine. Don't worry about me."

I was more worried about *me*. And Sam.

"Here." He fished around in his pocket and sprinkled something on her head.

"Daddy!" Her smile came back and she leaned against him with her eyes closed while he rocked her in his arms. Then, she broke away and walked toward the dorm, with just a hint of her long-legged, cowgirl swagger.

"So you can fly," I heard Sam say softly.

I wondered what her roommate would think when Bree walked in, red cowboy boots on her feet and sawdust in her hair. I smiled. That girl obviously needed someone to loosen *her* seams a little.

Sam's arm eased around my waist. "Ready to go?"

"No."

We walked to the truck together. And cried most of the way home.

My pageant notebook was open on the nightstand when I leaned over to turn out the light that night. I hadn't written in it lately. I'd made the last entry on the day Lester Lee had brought Junebug to the farm for our photo shoot.

I chewed on the end of my pen.

"Well, Lord," I murmured. "Let's hope they're good at reading between the lines."

Journal Entry: Today we took our daughter to college.

The next evening I happened to glance out the window and was surprised to see a truck parked in the orchard. It looked suspiciously like Riley Cabott's.

"What's Riley doing out there?" I called to Sam.

Sam peered out the window. "It looks like he's working on the summer kitchen." His shoulder lifted in an innocent shrug.

"Do you know how long *that's* going to take?"

"I'd guess about four years."

chapter **30**

I saw the billboard when I was heading into town to take some of my homemade salsa to the farmers' market. The last time I'd looked, the billboard had sported an advertisement for a mud-spattered truck that was a favorite of the local teenage boys. Now, it was an enormous picture of me...and Junebug the cow.

My foot hit the brake and I pulled over to the shoulder, closed my eyes and prayed, then opened my eyes again. I was still there, my smiling face resting against Junebug's. Lester Lee, in his quest either to a) show up the other farmers or b) launch Junebug's modeling career, must have paid to rent the billboard.

Congratulations Junebug and Elise Penny, Proverbs 31 Pageant Contestant. See This Photo and Others in the Beautiful Bovines Calendar, Available This October.

Of course Junebug got top billing.

I had two choices. I could go to the farmers' market, where I was bound to see half the population of the county or I could hide out at the farm for the rest of my life. I sat in the car for ten minutes, trying to decide. When I heard another car on the highway, I slouched down in my seat so they couldn't compare faces.

Finally, I drove into town.

I'd been canning salsa for four straight days in a row and it had turned out to be a blessing in disguise—it had kept my hands busy and had helped—only slightly—to ease the ache of missing Bree. Bernice and Annie even came over one evening to help me and as we chopped onions and diced tomatoes, we talked about our children. We planned out Annie's nursery right down to the curtains. While the salsa simmered in its water bath, we kicked off our shoes, sat on the porch swing and sipped iced tea.

The farmers' market in Prichett is held three days a week in the park during harvest season and *everyone* is there. From past experience, I knew there was more gossip doled out than produce. Another thing I was sure of was that every truck, camper and car that rumbled into town had gone right past that billboard.

I parked my car, abandoned my salsa and ducked into the Cut and Curl. One look at Bernice's face and I knew she'd seen *it*.

"Dye job? Dark sunglasses?"

"Please."

"She's very photogenic." Bernice grinned.

The woman under the dryer peeked out from behind her magazine. Mindy Lewis. "Hi, Elise! Saw the billboard. I'll bet the calendars will really sell this year!"

They would, because at that moment I made a silent vow to buy every single one of them.

"I saw the dress Greta is making for you," Mindy went on. "It's beautiful. She's so excited."

"She's very talented…"

"Mindy, one side of your head is going to look like you've been hit by lightning. Back under the dryer!" Bernice pointed her finger and Mindy shot her a sulky look but obeyed.

"Since you're still in a state of shock from the billboard, Elise, you might as well hear the rest. I heard something through the grapevine."

I slid a pointed look at Mindy and Bernice walked over to the dryer. "Mindy, I'm going to turn the dryer up a little now."

"What?"

"Turning the dryer up!" Bernice pressed a button and shouted over the noise.

Mindy looked a little put out and I could tell she was going to put her lip-reading capabilities to work. I moved closer to Bernice.

"Candy, our beloved mayor, came in here this morning.

She was pretty excited about the billboard. They want to have a launch for you before you leave for the pageant."

"A launch? What am I, the *Titanic!*"

"She asked me to help coordinate it." Bernice looked guilty.

"And you said *no,* right?" It was written all over her face. Bernice Strum was going soft on me.

"It's sweet, El. Sally is planning to cater an old-fashioned ice cream social in the park. There's going to be a little parade—"

"A parade!"

I shouldn't have been surprised. Candy the Mayor loved parades. Every Fourth of July, she personally guilts all the local businesses into entering floats and supervises their construction, even buying extra rolls of crepe paper if she thinks they're being skimpy.

"You get to ride in the convertible."

The convertible. It belonged to, of all people, Mr. Bender from Bender's Hardware. It was as red and glossy as a ripe McIntosh and only rolled out of the garage for special occasions. I refused to be tempted by the convertible.

"Is there any way I can get out of this?" I sighed.

"Nope. Just give in gracefully." As far as I was concerned, she looked way too excited about the whole idea.

"I'd better get going, you traitor. I have to sell some salsa."

"I hope you saved some for me."

"Not anymore."

Bernice laughed. "For someone who once dreamed of this kind of stuff, you're really dragging your heels."

"I might have dreamed about it once upon a time," I said. "But I don't remember Prichett being in any of those dreams."

"Funny how that happens, isn't it?" Bernice teased me. "Oh, here are the pictures from Esther and John's wedding. I made doubles, so you can have these."

I tucked the pictures in my purse and went out to the car to get the box of salsa. When I crossed the street, I hadn't taken ten steps when I heard my name.

"Elise. Elise Penny! Over here!"

Then it began. As I passed every produce stand, someone called to me, telling me they'd seen the billboard.

At one stand, a hollow-cheeked farmer pulled me aside.

"You're lucky you have all your fingers," he said in a low voice. "That Junebug is the meanest cow I've ever met." He waved his bandaged hand under my nose.

I didn't want to know if Lester's beautiful bovine had been the culprit.

On a positive note, my salsa sold in less than an hour, allowing me to pack up early and slink home.

"Excuse me, isn't that your picture on the billboard outside of town?"

I glanced up. A woman about ten years older than me was standing a few feet away. Her clothes told me she wasn't a local but she didn't quite look like a tourist, either. She wore a sleeveless denim dress with a bright yellow sweater knotted casually around her shoulders. On her feet were a pair of old-fashioned espadrilles. I remembered my mother had had a pair.

"The one without the spots, yes."

The woman smiled. "So what's that all about—the Proverbs 31 woman?"

I wasn't quite sure how to answer the question. "Well, Proverbs 31 is the last chapter of the book of Proverbs in the Bible. It's a mother telling her son what to look for in a wife."

"Really?" She looked fascinated. "So you're it, then?"

"Not hardly!" I choked out the words. "My daughter entered me in the pageant. To be honest, I never saw myself like *her* at all."

"So what's she like? Perfect, I suppose?"

I didn't know if I should give her my original version of the Proverbs 31 woman or the new-and-improved updated version that Greta had introduced me to.

"Not perfect." I couldn't let her go away thinking that. "She loves God and her family. Everything else sort of flows out of that."

The woman stared at me for a moment. "So she doesn't have to be beautiful? I thought this was a beauty pageant."

"No." I shook my head. "It's about inward beauty."

"Everyone says that but I don't think they believe it."

I really looked at her, then. She was pretty enough that

she could have been a model herself. Dark-brown eyes with an exotic tilt at the corners. Barely discernable wrinkles near her eyes. A nose that was probably a model in a plastic surgeon's coffee-table book somewhere. Glossy dark hair shot with silver. I wondered if she'd been told how pretty she was from the time she was a child, too. If all she thought she had of value was the top layer of her skin.

"It's the truth, no matter if people believe it or not," I said. "And I don't think I'm beautiful on the inside, by the way. But with God working in there, I'll get there someday."

It's hard to explain, the moment of connection between us. It should have been awkward. I couldn't believe I was talking like this to a complete stranger. I blamed Annie.

"It's been nice to talk with you, Elise."

"Here, have a jar of homemade salsa. And if you wander down Main Street, I guarantee you'll end up with either a piece of pie or a bag of bird seed."

chapter 31

"Hold still, Elise. Honestly, if you keep wiggling like this, I'm going to make you sit in the elephant chair."

Across the room, Annie giggled. She was sitting sideways on one of the plastic chairs, with her bare feet dangling over the one next to it and her hand pressed against the slight bulge above her waist. Every so often, she'd give us a report as to what was happening on Main Street.

"I'm not wiggling." I felt the need to protest.

Technically, I was *shifting*. A perfectly acceptable thing to do when you'd been sitting in a chair for almost an hour. And it was only because Bernice wouldn't let me see myself in the mirror as she fixed my hair. She had a tray full of bobby pins at her disposal and a mysterious tool that looked like a cross between a comb and a switchblade. I winced every time she picked it up.

Across the street, I could see the top of a huge canvas tent where the ice cream social was going to be. After the parade.

Isn't it funny how some childhood memories never completely fade away? One of mine takes place at the beginning of the school year, when the teacher handed out a syllabus for the semester and the words Oral Book Report were printed on it. It seemed light-years away from the moment. I had all the time in the world to read a book and scribble out the details on a three-by-five card. Then, suddenly, without warning, that date on the syllabus was staring me in the face and I was frantically skimming the last few pages of the book the night before my report was due.

That memory was my life over the past month. I was leaving for the pageant in the morning. Bernice, Annie and I would drive to Madison, where we'd meet up with Heather and Bree. My pageant pit crew. I didn't know what I'd do without them.

The dress Greta had created was hanging in my closet, dry-cleaned and pressed. She had torn the sleeves completely off and reconstructed the neckline "to flatter the shape of my face." The sixteen-year-old wonder had even found an antique necklace at a garage sale, gold and bulky and crusted with amethysts that to my untrained eye looked real. On the hanger beside the dress, swathed in plastic, was a satin wrap in a pale cotton-candy pink. We went shoe-shopping together one afternoon and I noticed the curious looks we got from people. One woman was actually bold enough to ask me if Greta was my daughter. It gave me the opportunity to wrap my arm around Greta's shoulders and say that no, she wasn't, but I'd adopt her in a minute.

My suitcase was packed. My journal had arrived safely in the capable hands of Shelby Hannah a week ago. Sam had a list of phone numbers in case there was an emergency.

The night before, Bernice and Annie had surprised me with a visit, bearing gifts. Bernice presented me with a cute pair of pajamas decorated with eggs, strips of bacon and waffles with wings. Annie gave me a slim leather New Testament and slippers that looked like cows, which stirred up so much laughter that Sam had peeked in the room to check on us.

Now all I had to do was survive the parade and ice cream social. The day had started out overcast with an ominous prediction of "light showers" by evening. I asked Sam to check out his knee for a more accurate version. So far, the air was warm and the sky dotted with innocent-looking clouds.

A knot had formed in my stomach sometime during the night and I couldn't get anything to dissolve it. Not peppermint tea. Not chocolate. Not the glimpse I'd had of the apple-red convertible parked outside Bender's Hardware. Maybe my nervousness had something to do with the fact that by noon lawn chairs had begun to sprout along Main Street like dandelions. I couldn't believe the parade was attracting so much attention. Not that there was much to compete with it on a Wednesday night in September.

Mr. Bender shuffled into the salon, his face pleated with worry. "Elise, I can't get the convertible started. I've got the guys from the garage looking at it, but one of them thinks it's the transmission."

Chance of showers. No convertible. The ice cream was probably melting, too.

"Isn't there another vehicle we can use?" Bernice asked.

"Lester mentioned that his flatbed is clean, but he says if Elise uses it he wants his fool cow to ride on it with her."

There was no way I was sharing a float with Junebug. She still hadn't gotten her revenge for the hydrangea bush.

"The flatbed might be clean but it's a rust bucket," Bernice said in disgust. "Someone in this town has to have a decent car. We'll just have to put our heads together."

"You have an hour," Mr. Bender said, shuffling backwards toward the door. I don't think Bernice realized she was waving her curling iron while she spoke.

"I'll call Pastor Charles." Annie slid off the chair and headed to the telephone on Bernice's counter. "He knows everyone in the area."

"Here. This should cheer you up." Bernice swung the chair around so I was facing the mirror. Finally.

I still looked like me…but not. There was no question about it, Bernice had a gift. She'd laced my hair into tiny braids on either side of my face and then drawn them up into a crown on the top of my head. What was left spilled to my shoulders in soft curls.

"Pastor Charles knows someone with a yellow Firebird," Annie said, the phone tucked against her chest. "Wow. Elise, you are *bee-utiful*. All the way through."

I rolled my eyes but grinned. "You don't think it's too much, do you? I mean, especially if I'm sharing a rusty flat-bed with Junebug?"

"This town is expecting a beauty queen." Bernice tucked a bobby pin between her teeth. "We're going to give them one. Besides, it's good practice for me for the evening gown competition."

"Oh, really?" Annie had the phone against her ear again. "Well, keep trying, okay?" She hung up and shrugged helplessly. "The guy sold it."

A lawn chair bounced past the window suddenly, carried by the gentle breeze that I'd noticed earlier. The gentle breeze that now had teeth. A puffy little cloud had paused over Prichett, too, but it was black not white. I could see the sun behind it, trying to shoulder its way through. Raindrops began to pelt the sidewalk.

"Don't worry." Bernice picked up a can of industrial-strength hairspray. "Nothing is going to touch your hair after I put this on it."

Outside, I could see people scurrying for cover.

"Do you think God is giving me a reprieve from the parade?" I asked hopefully.

"I'm praying it stops," Annie informed me.

"Uh-oh. Put your umbrellas away, girls." Bernice leaned over and bussed Annie's cheek. Over the past month, our friendship had sent out runners and now included a certain perky youth pastor's wife. Our duet had become a trio.

Candy pushed her way inside, her hair plastered against her head. "Just a shower," she said through chattering teeth. "That cloud is already passing over. Ready?"

I balked. "Do I have to?"

"Is there a flatbed truck out there with a cow on it?" Annie asked, covering her eyes.

"No, more like a knight in shining armor with your coach, Cinderella." After a quick glance out the window, Candy grabbed my wrist and pulled me toward the door. "Look."

Coming down the street was a black, horse-drawn carriage. The horse that was pulling it was Belle, our Belgian. The rain had turned her coat to a gleaming cherrywood color. Sam was driving.

"Your ride is here." Bernice smiled widely.

"Wait." Annie hurried up to me, carrying a box. A familiar box. *The Box*.

"Annie, you didn't. I'm not wearing that silly tiara."

"You don't want to disappoint your loyal subjects, do you?" Candy slapped me on the back, moving me two feet closer to the door.

Annie carefully put the crown on my head. "You can wear a different crown for the next parade."

"This is too cheesy for words." *God, You control the heavens. Please rain on my parade!*

I ducked outside and Sam swung down from the seat to help me up. Candy had been right. I only felt a sprinkle of rain now.

"Where did you get this?" I asked, arranging my skirt around my knees.

"Gordon. He owes me one. Or two."

"Or a thousand," I said under my breath.

"I'm sorry I'm still in my work clothes," Sam whispered. "I had to make a choice between changing or catching Belle and hooking her up to the buggy."

"You made the right choice." I dared to kiss him. Right there on Main Street.

As far as parades go, this one had to be the shortest in history. Candy was in the police car—borrowed from the sheriff's department because Prichett didn't have its own full-time police force—and a dozen members of the high-school marching band. I'm not sure who had bribed them with what. Behind the buggy was Lester, who had bowed to pressure and left his truck parked by the hardware store. He was leading Junebug, who bawled occasionally at her fans. At the end of the procession was Irv, the postmaster, who had slyly slipped in behind us in his little blue car with the flashing light, waving like an honored guest and tossing Tootsie Rolls to the children. I should have thought of that.

"Smile," Sam said with his lopsided Sam grin. "You look like you're scheduled for surgery."

Dutifully, I smiled. And waved. The entire population of Prichett was waving back. As the carriage turned into the park, everyone, Pied-Piper-ish, followed us.

A platform had been hastily constructed by the playground. A particle-board stage with a concrete block to step on. Someone had tried to decorate it, but the rain had melted the crepe paper and now it looked like overcooked pasta.

Sam squeezed my hand. "Here you go."

I didn't move. Candy jumped up onto the platform without the help of the concrete block. Someone had loaned her a hat to cover up her wet hair. She motioned to me. There were three men standing at the side of the buggy, all with their hands extended to help me down.

I saw Bernice, Annie and Stephen clustered together under an oak tree with Esther and John. Tears burned my eyes. I didn't think I would feel anything but pure relief when this evening was over but here I was, fighting back tears. I paused by John's wheelchair.

"How are my favorite newlyweds?"

Esther blushed that adorable shade of pink. "Oh, Elise!"

"You look beautiful," John said sincerely.

"John, I hate to point this out, but you're blind."

"I can hear it in your voice."

"Remember what I said about roses, Elise," Esther reminded me. "Even when you can't see them, you know them by their fragrance."

I hugged her and moved to the platform, where Candy was patiently waiting for me.

"Ladies and gentlemen…our own Elise Penny!"

If Prichett had staked a claim on me *before*—before this summer, before Annie, before Bernice and Heather, before Sam and the receipt, before God had dug out that root of bitterness and transplanted me into His garden—I'm pretty sure I would have bolted from the park and never looked back.

Now, I stood on that rickety platform, surprised to be loved, and by a whole town.

chapter **32**

"Elise, it's after eleven. You should get some sleep." Sam rolled over in bed and watched me fussing over my suitcase.

"I don't think I'm going to be able to sleep." I pushed the cow slippers into a separate bag and the bells around their necks jingled lightly.

Sam sat up and opened his arms, leaving a space for me against his heart, which I burrowed into. "All right. I'll come to bed."

I didn't think I'd fallen asleep, but I must have because when the phone rang, it was two in the morning. Sam answered it, his voice low and husky.

"Oh no."

When I heard him say those two words, a chill rippled through me. Was it his parents? Bree?

"We'll be right there."

He hung up the phone and turned to me. "Annie's at the hospital. She's…Pastor Charles said she might be having a miscarriage."

Numbly, I got dressed and hurried out to the car with Sam. The half-hour ride to the hospital seemed to take forever.

God, you know how much this baby means to her. To Stephen. Please don't let anything happen!

I said it silently over and over as the car sped down the highway. When we got to the lobby, Pastor Charles and Jeanne were waiting for us.

"She's on the fifth floor," Jeanne said, linking her arm with mine. "She wants to see you."

I nodded mutely. I didn't know what to say to Annie. What words would give her comfort?

A nurse was just slipping out of the room when I came in. Annie had her face turned away from me and I wondered if she was sleeping.

"Annie?" I whispered her name, almost hoping she was asleep so I would have more time. More time to prepare words I didn't have.

"Hi." She rolled over, an expression of sorrow on her face so terrible that I rushed over and sat down beside her. Her hands were ice-cold when I reached for them. "They're scheduling some tests," she murmured. "But there was blood and—"

"I'm sorry." I didn't know what else to say and yet the words sounded so small. "I'll stay here until you know."

"Silly. You have to go to the pageant."

"No." I'd already decided that. "I'm not going. It's not important." Not as important as you. Not even close.

"I really wanted to be part of the pit crew."

"Annie, didn't you hear me? I'm not going."

"Yes, you are. For Bernice. For Greta. For Bree. For *me*."

"We'll talk about this later."

A shadow of pain skimmed her face and she closed her eyes. "A bad cramp," she gasped.

I held her hand until her expression relaxed again.

"Stephen is talking to the doctor and filling out paperwork. It all happened so fast. I was fine when we went to bed and then…" Her voice hitched. "I just don't know what to do, Elise. I mean, do you ever feel like you've reached the point of no return? I *know* that God loves me, that He's good…I've watched Him work and He takes my breath away. I can't *not* love Him back, no matter what happens. But right now I want to pound on His chest and ask Him *why*."

"Go ahead and pound," I said. "He won't love you less for it. I'd say right now the best place to be is in His arms."

It was because of Annie that I could say it. That I *believed* it. I guess I had reached the point of no return, too.

"'Though He slay me, yet I trust Him,'" Annie said, closing her eyes again as another cramp rolled through her body and crested. "I just love you, Elise. Do you know that? You're a great mentor."

"I'm going to tell you something, Annie, and I don't want

you to forget it. You've been *my* mentor. All these years, I've just been going through the motions, pretending, and I didn't even know it. I was the farthest thing from a Proverbs 31 woman that you could find. I didn't even know how to love God until I met you." My voice began to wobble but I had to make her understand. "And here you go again, teaching me to trust."

A faint smile tipped the corner of Annie's mouth. "Then as your mentor I'm going to ask you to do something."

"Annie, no—"

"Go to the pageant." She must have seen the expression on my face because she put her hand up before I could argue. "For me."

When I left the next morning with Bernice, I'd had less than four hours of sleep. Annie had been wheeled away for an ultrasound and blood work. Sam was staying at the hospital with Stephen and promised he'd call as soon as they knew anything.

Bernice and I shared a silent car ride to Madison and had to share the news with Heather and Bree when we met them for lunch. Bernice hadn't seen Heather for a month, although they talked frequently on the phone. Bree hadn't come home yet, either, but our entire reunion was bittersweet.

"I can't do this," I said as we turned down a winding road lined with ancient oaks. The pageant was being held at a restored mansion outside Madison that had been turned into a conference retreat.

"You can," Bernice said.

"It just seems so…" I struggled to find the right word. Smiling, answering questions, pretending someone I loved wasn't in pain…it seemed *light. Frivolous.* But Annie told me someone needed to hear the words I was going to say at the pageant. I held on tightly to that thought.

"Elise Penny!" A woman waved cheerfully to me when we walked into the marble-tiled foyer. She was tiny, like a hummingbird, with bright-red hair and oversized glasses. If her nametag hadn't said Shelby Hannah, I never would have guessed it was her. She was taller on the phone.

"It's nice to meet you." I was going through the motions. Polite greetings. Polite introductions.

"You're in the Rose Cottage by the lake. Sharing with Frances King and Stacey Reeder." Shelby glanced at the Palm Pilot in her hand. At least I'd been right about that. "Dinner at five, a short presentation at six and interviews begin at seven. You're first!"

Bree pressed something into my hand. M&M's.

"Are you staying on the grounds?" Shelby looked curiously at Heather, Bree and Bernice. Maybe no one else had shown up with reinforcements.

"No, we have a room downtown," Bernice said. "We're the pit crew."

"Lovely." Shelby smiled and handed me a thick purple folder. "I'll see you at five, Elise."

She glided away to greet the next person.

By five, Sam still hadn't called.

"They should know something by now," I fretted as Bernice fixed my hair for the interview. "Why hasn't he called? I even left a message for him."

"I don't know. But I've been bothering God all day with this." Bernice put down the curling iron. "What do you think?"

I glanced at my reflection in the mirror. It was much more subdued than the hairstyle she'd given me for the parade, for which I was grateful. She'd just twisted it into a casual knot at the back of my neck and secured it with several gold pins.

"It's perfect."

"You better get down to dinner. I won't see you until tomorrow morning, but call us at the hotel and let us know how the interview went, okay?"

"And you call if you hear anything. I mean it. No matter what time, no matter what I'm doing."

Bernice promised.

I was on my own. I'd met Frances and Stacey earlier, but then they'd disappeared and I hadn't seen them since. I did see Frances's notes for her speech lined up in neat, color-coded cards on the table. And I saw Stacey's dress. It wasn't purple.

Somehow, I made it through dinner and the welcome, listened to the schedule for the weekend and then heard my name being called for my interview.

God, still no word about Annie. Take care of her.

The judges were in the Blue Room and there was a fire

in the fireplace, a table with fresh flowers and a chair that I was supposed to be comfortable in.

"Hi, Elise."

Sitting at the table was the woman who had talked to me at the farmers' market. The woman in the yellow sweater who hadn't told me her name. A Proverbs 31 spy.

"I'm Jennifer Seaton." She half-rose and shook my hand. "Last year's Proverbs 31 woman."

I didn't feel betrayed. I found myself wanting to smile for the first time all day. There were two more judges, another woman who reminded me of a kindergarten teacher and a man wearing a stuffy suit and tie.

"Ah, yes, Mrs. Penny, your journal entries were rather, what's the word...sparse." The man coughed lightly.

I couldn't argue with him on that. "To tell you the truth, I'm just not a writer. And sometimes, it was too hard to describe what happened during the course of a day."

Junebug came to mind.

"And you only sent us two photos and we can't quite understand them," Mrs. Kindergarten Teacher said delicately.

I noticed they had my journal and the photos in front of them on the table.

"That one," I leaned forward and pointed to a picture of John in his wheelchair, "is on my friends' wedding day. The rose on his lapel is one that I grew."

"Oh." Jennifer smiled approvingly.

"And that one," I touched the corner of the photo I'd

taken of the summer kitchen, the daylilies and Greta, "was taken by the orchard on our farm. That girl designed my dress for the evening-gown competition."

The man coughed again. "Very good." He slid the pictures into a folder.

"Tell us about yourself, Elise," Jennifer said.

I took a deep breath and told them what I thought they wanted to hear. About Sam. Bree. What I liked to do. My gaze wandered to the clock. Why hadn't anyone called me?

"I know for a fact she makes excellent salsa," Jennifer said after I mentioned that I had a big garden.

"Did you grow up on the farm?" Mr. Stuffy Suit wanted to know.

"I would have to say yes to that." I chuckled.

They didn't understand the humor.

"You also put *Undecided* for your platform speech."

"You *are* scheduled to be first in the morning to speak."

I looked at them and saw a flash of sympathy on Jennifer's face.

"I'm still not sure what I'm going to say."

Another cough. "Yes, well, thank you, Mrs. Penny."

Jennifer walked with me to the door. "You did great," she whispered reassuringly.

"My friend is in the hospital," I whispered back. "Her name is Annie. Be sure to pray."

Jennifer studied me for a second, then she nodded.

"I will."

★ ★ ★

The outfit Greta had picked out for me to wear for the speech part of the pageant was a black chintz dress and a tiny sweater, embroidered with flowers, to go over it. She'd found it at an antique store. I knew she'd sneak black in somewhere. At least my dress matched the circles under my eyes. I used the concealer Bernice had given me and watched them disappear like magic.

Still no call from Sam. And no answer at our house. I did manage to talk to a nurse at the hospital when I called, but she had just come on duty and couldn't tell me anything.

Now *I* was pounding on God's chest.

The speech segment of the pageant was being held in the Garden Room, a huge atrium made of glass. The room was set up with round tables, white linen and elegant taper candles. Even the ceiling was glass. I saw the podium and the microphone set up in front and felt the Danish I'd just eaten jump around in my stomach.

God, Annie said someone needed to hear what I had to say, but how can that be, because I still have no idea what to say?

That's when I saw it. Right above my head. A cloud that looked exactly like a staircase. For a moment. Then it split apart and became two white swans.

Shelby Hannah was the emcee for the morning program and she hurried up to the microphone while I watched the birds migrate out of sight.

"Our first contestant is Mrs. Elise Penny from Prichett,

Wisconsin, a small farming community. And Elise will be speaking about…" Her eyes scanned her notes frantically.

I stood up. "I don't have a title."

The microphone hummed as I moved closer to it. "I don't have a title because I don't have a speech prepared."

I could see the astonished faces of the women sitting at tables not far away. I didn't dare look at the judges.

"I always dreamed of something like this happening to me from the time I was this high," I said, touching my knee. "But Shelby is right, I live on a farm, which I *never* dreamed of doing. But the funny thing is, that dreams can change shape over time, like clouds. That's what God's been showing me this summer. If you go His way, you've dreamed the right dreams. I think that's why the woman in Proverbs 31 smiles at the future. Not because she knows what's coming, but because she trusts the One who planned it out for her…"

Bernice slipped into the room. She held up two fingers and I thought she was giving me the peace sign. Did that mean everything was okay with Annie?

Then she held up her two index fingers and mouthed a word.

Twins.

I did something that the judges had probably never seen before in the history of the Proverbs 31 Pageant. I walked off the stage during the middle of my platform speech. Bernice and I fell together, laughing. Surprise.

Twins! Annie was having two babies in a few months.

I couldn't wait to see Annie when I got back. But it turned out I didn't have to wait that long. She was there with Stephen on Saturday night for the evening-gown competition and the final vote. So was Sam. Not only did I have my own pageant pit crew, but I also had my own fan club. They were a noisy group. If I didn't love them so much, it would have been embarrassing.

Frances and I stood side by side, Frances in light green satin and me in vibrant purple. Bernice had done my makeup, though, so I didn't look so pale. She told me that she heard Mr. Stuffy Suit telling someone that the evening gown each contestant chose to wear would say a lot about us. I wondered what the judges thought about purple.

When they called my name as the winner, I was planning Annie and Stephen's nursery decor. I didn't move until Frances gave me a gentle nudge.

"You just won," she whispered in my ear.

The little crowd at the back table whooped and howled. Jennifer put the tiara on my head and kissed my cheek.

"It was the billboard, wasn't it?" I asked in a low voice.

"Actually, it was the purple dress." Jennifer winked.

Sam gave me a bouquet of wild daisies that I'd seen growing by the silo and slipped his jacket around my shoulders. Then he asked if I could possibly smuggle him into my cottage later.

"Cottage?" I snuggled against him. "Take me home."

epilogue

I tucked my coat underneath me and sat down on the bench of the merry-go-round. Fat, silver snowflakes had begun to fall like confetti. Early for the end of October. Two of them got stuck in my eyelashes and I blinked them away. Annie, Bernice and I were planning to have lunch together, but when I got out of the car, I'd been drawn to the park.

I sat on the merry-go-round and pushed off with my feet, collecting different angles of Main Street as it spun in a slow circle. The bright awning of the Cut and Curl. The sign for Sally's Café that jutted over the sidewalk. The spot under the tree where the platform had been built that I'd stood on before the pageant.

The pageant. It seemed like it had happened ages ago. I didn't even want to contemplate having to go on to the national finals, but Greta was already planning my wardrobe. And every time I caught Bernice staring at me, honestly, I just knew she was plotting a new hairstyle. I'd just decided to smile at the future, knowing God would somehow use the next pageant, just like Annie had said He would do with the first one. A picture of me being crowned the Proverbs 31 woman was hanging on Prichett's Pride and Joy Wall.

Annie had been right about something else, too. There *had* been someone who needed to hear my speech at the pageant that day. *Me.* After I'd figured out what God was trying to show me, there'd been so much new growth sprouting from my life that sometimes I just had to stand back in wonder and admire it. Suddenly, even life in Prichett seemed like an adventure. Maybe because I'd tucked myself under the wings of a God who loves surprises. And new beginnings.

"Hey!"

They'd found me.

Annie trudged toward the merry-go-round, her coat a bright splash of scarlet, with Bernice beside her.

"What are you doing?" Bernice panted as they got closer.

"Imagining."

They plunked down on the seat beside me.

"Imagining what?" Annie lifted her face to the sky and let the snowflakes melt on her cheeks.

"New playground equipment."

"Ah." Bernice nodded. "That makes sense."

It did. I'd already signed over my pageant check to Candy.

The minute I'd received the check, I knew exactly what I was going to do with it.

Annie folded her hands over the twins and I could tell she was imagining, too. Children in the park, playing tag between the swings and sliding down a new, splinter-free slide. The horses would stay. Some things just had to. Contentment was a new feeling but it was one I knew I could get used to.

Bernice closed her eyes. That's why she didn't see it.

But I did.

A black limousine glided down Main Street and pulled up right in front of the Cut and Curl. I had a feeling the marquee was about to change. And maybe the billboard, too, if I was lucky.

"Um, Bernice…"

"Hmm?"

"Your ride is here."

★ ★ ★ ★ ★

Bernice's world is about to be turned upside down. Look for her story next year, only from Kathryn Springer and Steeple Hill Café. And look for Kathryn's Love Inspired book, HER CHRISTMAS WISH, the fifth book in the TINY BLESSINGS series.

DISCUSSION QUESTIONS

1   When you were a child or teenager, what did you want to be when you grew up? What does your life look like now compared to the way you imagined it when you were younger?

2   What do you think Elise's real struggle was when it came to Bree's relationship with Riley Cabott?

3   Annie asked Elise to be her mentor. Do you have any cross-generational friendships in your life? How have they impacted you? Why is it important for women to seek out relationships with other women who are younger (like Annie and Greta) and older (like Esther) than they are?

4   Have you had to "let go" of someone? Who was it? What were the circumstances?

5   In her Sunday school class, Annie draws a spiritual parallel between life and the buttons on a remote control. Which "button" do you find yourself pressing the most—the rewind button (looking back, regrets, what-ifs) or the fast forward button (always looking toward the future)? What is your definition of contentment and how can these "buttons" affect it?

6   Whom do you most identify with in this book? Why?

7   How did Elise and Bernice's friendship change after Bernice told her about Heather?

8   Elise had a faulty perspective about the people
     of Prichett because she had allowed bitterness to
     creep into her heart over the years. What areas of
     her life did this affect? What areas of your life have
     been under divine "construction"? What did you
     learn from the experience?

9   Do you think Elise had a right to be angry with Sam
     when she found out about the money he'd kept a
     secret from her? If Elise had discovered it earlier,
     do you think she would have reacted differently?
     What does this say about God's timing?

10   What is your perception of the Proverbs 31
     woman? Has it changed? How or why?

SUSPENSE
RIVETING INSPIRATIONAL ROMANCE